Thank ,

Hard and Deep

A Football Romance

By

KRISTA LAKES

Krista Lakes

HARD AND DEEP

About This Book

I'm Oliver Lance. Yes, the Oliver Lance. The one that all men want to be and all women want to be with.

Every Sunday a million fans watch me throw a ball down a field, win games, and sign huge endorsement deals.

Everything was going perfectly, until a car accident tore it all away from me. I want it back, and only *she* can help me.

At first, I think about 'Doc' Elsie the same way I think of every other woman. Just another possible conquest, another notch on my bedpost.

Only Elsie is different. She's not starstruck by me. She's not interested in my money. She's the most real woman I've ever met, and those tempting curves are making it hard to stay focused on my recovery.

Now, I'll do anything to keep her by my side. I'll defy my manager, my coach, even lay down my career as quarterback to stay with her.

It's third and long, and I'm gonna make my play *Hard and Deep*.

Chapter One

Ollie

My life could never get better than this.

Oliver Lance thought quietly to himself as he glanced around the VIP section of the club. He had a voluptuous blonde girl under one arm and a petite brunette under the other. He didn't really know either of them, since he had met them just five minutes before at the bar. But that really didn't bother him. Because in addition to the two beauties, he was surrounded by friends and fans, drinking expensive champagne and smoking expensive cigars. He felt like a god; powerful and loved by all.

"This is what it's all about," he said out loud, though wasn't speaking directly to anyone.

"Hey, Ollie, how about another shot?"

His buddy, Joseph, shouted from the other side of the VIP section. He poured two shots of expensive tequila into glasses and handed one to Oliver.

"Sure, why not?" Oliver said, gladly accepting the glass.

"Cheers, bro," Joseph said. "Here's to a career full of winning seasons."

"Cheers," Oliver echoed the sentiment and then drank down the clear liquor. "To winning everything professional football could throw at us this season!"

This was his night and he was living it up, sparing no expense. The tab was likely over two grand already, but he hadn't really been keeping much track. He didn't care. There was no need to. Between endorsements and his salary, he was making more money just sitting there than he could possibly spend. And it felt amazing.

The girls on either side of Oliver couldn't get their hands off of him. The blonde clamored over his lap and wrapped her arms over his shoulders. It made the brunette jealous and he heard as she whispered "bitch" underneath her breath. It only made him smile. He loved getting fought over by two beautiful women. He figured that it could never get old.

"Ladies, be nice," he said, with a smirk. "There's plenty of me to go around."

"It's not often we get to meet the star quarterback, though," Blondie said. "An offensive lineman or a kicker, sure. But not the star quarterback. This is a very special night."

"Yeah, well, I'd like to order another bottle of champagne," Oliver said, carefully lifting the blonde off of his lap and setting her to the side. "And you just insulted my team by saying that."

She bit her lip and looked down at the floor.

"I'm just giving you a hard time," Oliver said. "Ease up. You'll learn that I like to joke around a lot."

Her smile returned and Oliver poured the two girls a glass of champagne each. Then he called for the waitress, who approached quickly.

"Three more bottles of Dom," he said, as he pulled a wad of hundreds out of his front pocket. "And another bottle of Patron."

Oliver handed her a handful of the bills, without even bothering to count.

"Keep the change," was all he said.

A stray fan pushed past security. He was wearing a blue and white jersey with Oliver's number on it. He clamored over the velvet rope that separated the VIP section from the rest of the club. He knocked a few drinks over as he made his way toward Oliver.

What in the hell is this guy doing? Oliver asked himself.

"Lance," the guy said, clearly inebriated. "Oliver Lance. You're my hero. Please sign my jersey. Please."

Three security guys approached the man and grabbed his arms. They began to pull him away.

"Hold up," Oliver said. "He just wants an autograph."

Oliver stood up and quickly signed the back of the man's jersey, before motioning for security to finish what they had started.

"Thank you so much, Ollie," the stranger said, as security pulled him back into the crowded club. "You just made my entire week!"

Oliver chuckled to himself, shaking his head. It happened every time he went anywhere. It didn't matter if he was at the grocery store, in line at the bank or just trying to walk his dog around the park. Inevitably, there would be a point when someone would come out of nowhere and run toward him, begging for his attention.

Typically, they'd want something as simple as an autograph. But he'd get other offers, too. It wasn't uncommon for a pretty girl to approach him and offer her bed up, which he was known to accept on occasion. He was living the kind of life most guys would only ever dream of and there was nothing in this world that was going to put an end to that. At least, not if Oliver had any say in it.

The booze was really kicking in now. He didn't know how many bottles of champagne they'd gone through, but it was a lot. His best friends were all drunk, at least from what he could tell. But they all seemed to be having a great time, which is what really mattered most to him. He'd spend a million dollars tonight if it meant that he and his team would have memories for a lifetime.

"Hey, Sean, why do you not have a drink in your hand?" Oliver looked toward his best receiver, who hadn't dropped the football once in three full seasons. He was Oliver's good friend and colleague, and the high respect he held for him was completely mutual.

"I'm not drinking tonight, Ollie, I told you that," Sean said, with a shrug. "Last time we went out I drank way too much and it took me two days to feel normal again."

"When was that?" Oliver asked.

"Last week," Sean said, as he clenched his jaw and placed his hand on his belly. "My stomach still doesn't feel right. I can't keep up with you, man. I need rest. I'm old."

Oliver let out a deep belly laugh. "You're a year older than me, Sean. You're thirty-three, man. It's not like you're eighty."

"If I keep going out with you on a regular basis, I'm going to look like I'm eighty soon," Sean said, with a smile.

"We'll see about that."

The waitress came back with the new bottles of champagne and opened them in front of everyone. Oliver watched as she poured the drinks and she saw him staring. As soon as she was done, she batted her eyes at him and licked her lips.

Maybe I should take that girl home tonight, he thought. *Big breasts, black hair, blue eyes and a tight ass. That might be the one.*

Oliver smiled back at the waitress.

"Come over here," he said, motioning her to sit by him.

He scooted over, opening a space between him and Blondie.

"You're an ass," Blondie said, rolling her eyes.

"I love you, too," Oliver responded, without taking his eyes off of the waitress.

"What can I get you now, Oliver?" the waitress asked, taking a seat between him and Blondie.

"Your phone number would be a good start," he said. "Or maybe you could just come back to my place, since I think we both know where this relationship is headed."

"Relationship?" she asked, while raising an eyebrow.

"Come on, there's no point in beating around the bush here," he said, wrapping an arm around her.

She chuckled and pushed her hair over her ear. He had her and he knew it. He could feel it. Some would have called it over-confidence, but Oliver just *knew* when a girl was into him. This waitress was no exception.

"I don't get off for another couple of hours," she said, looking at him with sultry eyes. "But if you're still here, we can talk."

"Sounds like a plan," Oliver said. "Not sure if I'll still be here, but find me if I am."

Then he pulled her close and kissed her, which she didn't resist at all. Their lips touched for a few seconds, before Oliver broke the kiss. She looked bewildered, but wore a large smile, as she got up and went back to doing her job. Her actual job. Because kissing Oliver was not what she was getting paid to be there for.

The night continued like this. Oliver drank and flirted heavily with every girl he thought was pretty. The more liquor that entered his blood stream, the more he felt like celebrating.

An hour passed, maybe two. He couldn't be sure. But at some point, the club became a spinning mess of lights and sounds. He'd lost complete track of how many drinks he had had. The conversations with fans and friends were on autopilot and he wasn't even sure what he was talking about any more.

He plopped down on the seat next to Sean. "Hey, you said you weren't drinking right? I think I need to head back. That tequila is not sitting well right now."

"You're ready to go home?" Sean asked. "But what about that waitress I saw you talking with? She's a dime. You can't let that go."

"The waitress? Yeah, she gorgeous, but it's whatever," Oliver said, his words slurring a little at the end and the taste of liquor covering his tongue with each outward breath. "There's plenty of fish in the sea. And I'm a fucking shark. I don't care about one cute little goldfish. It's more important right now for me to lay in my bed and try to get the room to stop spinning."

"Alright, man, whatever you say," Sean said, standing up from the couch. "Let's get out of here then."

Blondie and the Brunette tugged on Oliver's arms as he tried to leave the VIP.

"Wait, baby, can't we go with you?" they asked.

Oliver turned around and smiled. "Of course."

They both grabbed their purses and got up, with excitement written all across their faces.

"Really?" Blondie asked.

"No, not really," he said, shaking his head. "You two have a good night. I hear there's a defenseman for another team running around here somewhere. Maybe he'll take you home?"

The girls pouted out their lower lip, clearly saddened by Oliver's denial. Girls that wanted Oliver for his fame and money were a dime a dozen, though. It wasn't that he didn't appreciate the attention, because he did. It was just that, right now, he really needed to get home, and these women didn't matter to him.

Those girls couldn't have cared less about how hard he worked to get what he had in life. All they wanted was a piece of Oliver Lance so that they could talk about that "one crazy night in the club". He'd done it before, sure. But not tonight. Not after countless shots and glasses of champagne. His king- sized bed in his mansion was the only thing that really sounded appealing in that moment.

"You ready, Ollie?" Sean asked.

Oliver turned back around and nodded. "Yeah, let's go."

VIP security made an opening for them to exit. "Do you guys need to be escorted out? The club is a lot busier than it was when you first got here and everyone has been drinking."

"We'll be fine," Sean answered. "Thanks, though."

Oliver followed Sean through the crowd. A few girls screams in excitement and ran toward him, but Ollie shrugged them off. His focus was keeping his stomach from emptying its contents onto the floor and that was about the only thing he could think about. From the VIP section to the front door of the club felt like a million mile march. He got asked by at least five people for an autograph and had two girls lift up their shirts to expose their breasts to him. Being king was pretty nice, but Ollie wished he hadn't drank so much that he couldn't enjoy it.

He was glad when they got outside to the cold air. Late February's winter grip felt good against his skin, and helped him feel less like the world was spinning out of control under his feet. The valet ran and got Oliver's black Bentley, pulling up to the curb within minutes. Sean took the keys and got into the driver's seat, while Oliver slid into the passenger. The noise of the hollering fans faded into the distance as he closed the door.

"You aren't going to puke, are you?" Sean asked, putting the car in drive and pulling away from the curb.

"I'd never throw up in my own car," Oliver said, not even sure if he was telling the truth. "Now if we were in your car, it may be a possibility."

"Very funny." Sean punched Oliver in his upper arm.

"Hey now, that's my money arm," Oliver said, rubbing the spot that Sean had just hit. "Without that, we won't be going to nice clubs any more and getting bottles all night. You better treat it nice."

"I still can't believe you didn't want to take that waitress home," Sean said. "Man, if she were looking at me like she was at you, I'd be all over it."

"That's what you don't understand, Sean. Sometimes the fun part is just knowing that she *would* go home with me. I don't always have to act on it to get the pleasure from it. You know what I mean?"

"I actually have no fucking clue what you're talking about," he said, with a chuckle. "You've gone from throwing thousands of dollars around at a club and having women all over you, to getting all philosophical."

"Whatever, man, you'll understand when you get older," Oliver said, his eyes half closed.

"I'm older than you, Ollie. You need to learn to respect your elders," Sean said, hitting Oliver's shoulder once again with a closed fist.

As the two made their way down the main street in the center of town, they passed by a number of loud clubs. The sound of the music would increase as they got near and then fade out as they passed. It created a dizzying Doppler effect that certainly wasn't helping Oliver's nausea. He closed his eyes completely and focused on his breathing. As much as he hated to admit it, he definitely couldn't party like he used to. There would be no way he'd be going home at this hour if he were still twenty two.

The blood-curdling roar of screeching tires filled the air. He heard Sean yell something and opened his eyes, just in time to look over to his right. A car's headlights were pointed straight at them. He knew immediately that the car wasn't going to be able to stop before impacting his door. The vehicle was going too fast. The headlights got brighter as they neared their final destination. Time slowed down, enough for Oliver's life to flash in front of his eyes. He thought about his brother and his mom and his football team.

I'm going to die, he thought. *God, no. Not now. Not right when everything is going so perfectly.*

He squinted and turned away as the car t-boned the side of them. The sound of exploding glass and crumpling metal filled his eardrums as his world turned dark.

It was his last memory of that evening.

Chapter Two

Elsie

"It's a unique opportunity, and given your history with sports medicine, one I think you'd be perfect for," the woman in a power suit told Elsie. "So, are you interested?"

Nikki Roberts asked the question with the same seriousness in her tone that she'd been using for the entire interview. When Elsie had scheduled this interview for a potential new patient, she hadn't quite been counting on this. This lady meant business.

Elsie paused for a moment. What she knew so far about this "opportunity" baffled her. An unnamed patient was coming to her tiny town in Iowa for ACL reconstruction physical therapy that was to be top of the line. They wanted her, with her in-depth but underutilized sports medicine background in physical therapy. No one around here cared that she interned with the top sports physical therapists, but apparently that's why this client was coming here. The strangest part of the whole situation was that it was supposed to remain a secret. They hadn't even told her what the patient's gender was yet.

"Yes." The word spilled past Elsie's lips before she could change her mind. "I'm definitely interested."

I don't have much of a choice if I want to keep my uncle's clinic up and running, she thought. *I could use the money right now and this one client will equal about twenty of my usual patients. Not to mention the huge signing bonus.*

"Excellent." Nikki beamed, exposing the first genuine smile that Elsie had seen from her all day. "Sign this."

A contract slid across Elsie's desk in a smooth motion. Elsie read it over quickly, shaking her head as she did so. It was the strongest non-disclosure agreement she'd ever seen. There were clauses for everything regarding the client's security. Elsie knew she would never divulge patient information, but the penalty for doing so, at least according to the contract, would be a financial number high enough to cause her to lose the clinic and everything she owned.

"This is just the non-disclosure agreement," Nikki explained. "I'll give you the full contract to bring to your first appointment. If there's something you disagree with, you can have your lawyers contact me tonight."

As if I could afford a lawyer, she thought, as she scribbled her name on the bottom of the contract. *Who could this patient possibly be to require this kind of legal work?*

The amount they were offering her to take on this patient was enough for her to look past the odd level of secrecy. In fact, it was enough for Elsie to be able to pay off her school loans and keep the physical therapy clinic up and running with all of the newest gadgets. Both were goals that she had been trying to obtain for years. Because of this unique job offer, they were going to become a reality.

Elsie pushed the contract back across the desk. Nikki gave it a glance and nodded as she slipped the paper into her briefcase. Elsie turned and pulled up her schedule on the ancient laptop she'd used to get through grad school.

"For an ACL reconstruction, I have openings here at my clinic on Monday mornings, Wednesday afternoons or any time on Fridays," she continued. "Of course, since his identity is clearly a secret, I assume that he'll want the place to himself. I can always schedule him over a lunch break, that way I'll be the only one here."

"He won't be coming to the clinic," the other woman replied, matter-of-factually.

"What do you mean?" Elsie asked, cocking her head to the side. "All of my equipment is here. I can't do my job effectively without my equipment."

"His home location will be properly equipped with everything you need," Nikki replied with a wave of her hand. "I can assure you it will be suitable."

"His home is equipped with hundreds of thousands of dollars worth of physical therapy equipment?" Elsie crossed her arms as she posed the question.

"Yes, of course." The woman answered as though that were an obvious fact and that it was normal for a person to have that kind of expensive equipment at home.

There is no way that this lady knows what she's talking about, Elsie thought.

"So you have a massage table, weights, a TRX, a sled..."

"Yes, yes, yes and yes," Nikki replied, clearly annoyed that Elsie might think otherwise. "We also purchased an ice wrap machine and bath under the surgeon's recommendation."

Whoa. Those machines are expensive, Elsie thought. *What does this patient do for a living?*

"Okay, then. We'll meet at his place." Elsie opened up a new scheduling window on her computer. "When will the patient be arriving?"

"Monday," Nikki stated. She peered down at one of her perfectly manicured fingernails. "That's three days."

"You want me to clear my schedule and drop everything for a new patient in three days?" Elsie managed to keep her voice level and keep most of the shock out of her tone.

"Yes, that's what needs to happen," Nikki replied with a shrug. "You currently only have three patients, and one of them is on their last week of shoulder therapy so it shouldn't be a problem. My client has full priority."

How did she know my patient schedule? Elsie's eyes widened. *I live in a small town, so I suppose it's not rocket science to figure something like that out. But still. A little disturbing.*

"Don't look so surprised," the woman said, frowning at one of her nails. "It wasn't that tough to figure out. A little amateur investigating is all it took. Your patients were more than happy to give me that information and more when I was checking your references."

"Oh." Elsie wasn't sure quite what to say to that. She had to wonder just what else her clients had mentioned.

"You can see why no one can know my client is here." Nikki looked up from her offending nail. "If your clients found out who you were working with, it would be all over social media in five seconds. I'm afraid they aren't very trustworthy."

"Apparently," Elsie replied. "But what am I supposed to tell them? I can't just cancel on them out of the blue."

"Yes, you can. And you will. I don't care what you tell them," Nikki said with a shrug. "Maybe say that you're trying a new hobby or something. I don't know. It's up to you. I'm sure you'll think of something."

Elsie sighed. In a town as small as hers, gossip was the main food group. As soon as anybody caught wind that she was clearing her schedule, questions would be coming from every direction. They'd want to know where, when, how and why she was canceling those appointments. If she gave them a bone, they'd take it and chew it for a while, but it wouldn't stop them from digging for more.

I'll figure something out, she thought. *Just need to come up with a good excuse. Or maybe I just don't tell them anything at all as to why I'm clearing my schedule. They're going to create whatever stories they want anyway. This town loves nothing more than something to talk about.*

"Okay," Elsie said, with a polite nod. "I'll make sure that my schedule is cleared for next week then."

"Here's the address," Nikki said, handing Elsie a slip of paper from her briefcase.

The address didn't look familiar, but then all of the addresses around here had "county road" as the street. It was one of the perks of living in the middle of farming country. *I'll either look it up or ask my Uncle,* she thought to herself. *He knows this town better than anyone.*

"Do you have any questions for me?" The woman stood and picked up her briefcase as she spoke, letting it swing by her side.

"I actually do," Elsie said, slowly standing up from her seat. "Is there anything at all that you can tell me about the patient? I'd like to know what to expect when I get there. Things like activity level, time frame, injuries..."

"The time frame is as quickly as humanly possible," Nikki said, inching toward the door. "The rest you'll find out tomorrow. After I've cleared the paperwork."

"I understand that, but I'm able to offer better care if I have a little bit of background information on the patient. I need to know what kind of injury they had and the type of surgery they went through afterward. If you want me to do my job in the best possible way, then I need some basic medical information so that I can prep everything."

The tall blonde crossed her arms. "It's an ACL reconstruction."

Elsie put on her best, most polite smile and tried not to grit her teeth.

"Thank you, but I need just a little bit more. Is the patient a 90-year-old woman or a 16-year-old professional snowboarder? Both can have ACL repairs, but their care plans are going to look incredibly different. If you want the best, I need to know more."

With a sigh, Nikki said, "A thirty-two-year-old male."

"What's his fitness level?" Elsie asked.

The woman stared at her for a moment, unblinking. The way she looked at Elsie made her think she was rethinking the decision to hire her.

"He's in good shape," Nikki replied.

Elsie wanted to scream in frustration. She was used to getting patients where she would learn everything she needed to know about them before their first appointment. She felt like she was going into this thing blind. She didn't like it at all. It just wasn't how things were done.

"How did the injury occur?" Elsie asked, knowing that each question was making her interviewer's eyes narrow.

"You don't need to know that," Nikki replied, rolling her eyes. "You just need to get him back up and running. They said you could do that."

"But I do need this information," Elsie said. "I need to make a plan of care for him for our first appointment. If you want this ACL healed fast, I need to start coming up with a plan now."

"I've given you more information than you need." Nikki spoke as she took a few steps toward the door. "You only signed the basic NDA and I'm still waiting on some of your information to clear."

"My information to clear?" Elsie frowned, confused. "What do you mean?"

"You don't think we'd hire you without a through background check, do you?" Nikki scoffed. "I'm still waiting on some more information. Plus, my boss has to officially approve of you."

"What information do you need?" Elsie asked. Her life was pretty simple. She went to the state college for undergrad, then earned her physical therapy doctorate in California. She'd interned with an amazing sports rehabilitation program and had been planning on working in professional sports when her uncle suddenly gave her his physical therapy clinic in Iowa. She'd moved back home to help him and her family.

"Your college roommate, Anastasia, hasn't returned my calls," Nikki replied.

"Anastasia?" Elsie had to think of who belonged to that name. "You mean my freshman year roommate I had for three weeks? I don't think she's going to be able to tell you much. I haven't spoken to her since she moved out. And that was over seven years ago."

"That may be," Nikki replied, waving her hand dismissively. "But I'm still waiting for it. Therefore, you don't get any information yet."

"I'm not trying to pry into your client's life or get information I'm not entitled to," Nikki tried to explain. "But, if you want this ACL construction rehab done in the time-frame you quoted, I need to start working on a plan now. I need-"

"No, you don't need anything," Nikki cut her off. "With what we're paying you, and how good everyone says you are, you don't need to know anything." Nikki waved her hand dismissively. "Honestly, it's not like it's brain surgery."

It took every professional bone in Elsie's body not to throw the contents of her desk at the woman. Instead, she just took a deep breath and thought about the money that was coming her way for this. The idea that Nikki wasn't her patient was comforting. Hopefully, her client wasn't as obnoxious as she was.

"You know what? I'll just do my best when I get there," Elsie said, giving up. "We'll just add an extra appointment in or something."

Nikki eyed her critically for a moment before frowning.

"Elsie, I realize that as a medical professional, you're already very aware of the importance of patient confidentiality. But in this case, it's even more important that the patient's identity, whereabouts, and physical condition are all kept quiet," Nikki told her for what felt like the millionth time. "Top secret. You don't tell anybody, not even your closest friends or your mother."

"Of course." Elsie nodded. "I keep every single one of my patient's information under lock and key, and this one will be no exception. I follow the law strictly on this."

"I understand, but in this case, it's more than just the law." Nikki frowned despite the botox around her eyes. "We're paying you a very large sum of money to make sure that nobody even knows that my client is even in this town."

"I won't breathe a single bit of information." Elsie leaned forward, bringing her hands to rest on the top of the desk. "You have my word."

"Good," the woman replied. "You can expect a courier with the full contract in a day or two. Given that your background check clears, of course."

Elsie did her best to smile. This entire interview had been more about how well she could keep a secret than her medical abilities. Though, Nikki had definitely made sure that Elsie's extensive training in sports medicine was still current. The last time Elsie had this level of questioning had been to pass her boards for her degree.

Needless to say, it had been a long interview.

Nikki tossed her hair and turned to walk out the exit. "It was a pleasure doing business with you, Elsie."

"Likewise," Elsie replied, lying through her teeth. The interview had been anything but pleasurable. Unless, of course, one considers things like getting their teeth drilled at the dentist to be a pleasure.

As the suited woman walked briskly out of the door, Elsie plopped back down in the chair and took a breath. It felt like the first time she had been able to breathe in over an hour. She was nervous and excited about this new patient, and her mind churned with all of the possibilities as to who he was. She considered the possibility that he was a president from another country or maybe some kind of James Bond. He could be anybody, really. The suspense was killing her.

I can't wait to see what tomorrow brings, she thought. *I have a feeling this is going to be very interesting.*

Chapter Three

Elsie

Elsie double-checked the address, making sure that she was on the correct County Road. As far as she knew, there wasn't anything out this far besides huge amounts of acreage covered in corn fields. It was all coated in white with late winter snow, looking desolate and lonely.

She drove along for another five minutes until a small wooden farm house with a red thatched roof came into view at the top of the hill.

"I guess this is it," she whispered to herself, pulling her car down the snow-packed dirt road that clearly hadn't been maintained in over a decade.

In fact, the whole farm around the small house looked about as neglected as the road did. Mountains of untouched snow surrounded it and a rundown old tractor was parked out front. It was obviously not a working farm any more, just a house in the middle of nowhere. Still, though, she thought it looked charming and cozy in its own way.

The tires of her car skid to a halt in the driveway. She put the car in park and then adjusted the rear view mirror so that she could get a good look at herself. Her shoulder-length light brown hair was down, looking frazzled because of the dry winter air. She quickly pulled it back into a tight ponytail.

Her heart was pounding in the back of her throat as she turned the car off and grabbed the handle of the door. She was nervous.

Calm down, Elsie, she told herself. *You've done home visits plenty of times. There's nothing different about this one. It's just another patient who needs your help.*

But it wasn't the unknown patient that made her nervous. It was the weird circumstances that surrounded all of it. Between the odd interview and the lack of information she had obtained before coming here, she hadn't a single clue as to what to expect. Even the contract had been incredibly vague.

All she'd been able to glean was that her client had recently undergone ACL repair surgery. She was to get him back up to full use of his knee as quickly and quietly as possible.

Wearing her favorite lime-green scrubs, Elsie tromped through the snow and up to the front door. She shivered off the cold as she knocked and then rang the doorbell immediately afterward. A moment later, the woman from the interview opened the door and crossed her arms.

"You're late," she said.

Elsie's eyes widened, shocked to be greeted in such a way after driving over twenty minutes through the snow. She glanced down at her watch to see that the woman was right, but only by three whole minutes.

"I'm sorry, there was a plow on the way here," Elsie explained. "They aren't exactly easy to drive around and my car doesn't do so hot in the snow."

The woman didn't say anything, but rolled her eyes as she held the door open. Elsie stepped inside, making the decision to ignore the woman's bitchy attitude and just pretend that she wasn't actually as hostile as she appeared.

"Did you bring the contract?" Nikki asked, crossing her arms.

Elsie carefully pulled out a folder with the documents tucked neatly inside. They'd come at nearly ten o'clock PM last night. She'd been up half the night reading them, making sure she understood exactly what she was getting into. She handed them to Nikki, who quickly took them and flipped through them to double check her work.

"So, where's my patient?" Elsie asked, setting down her purse in the wooden chair next to the front door.

"He's in the training room," Nikki replied. "I want to impress upon you again the need for silence."

"I will not violate my patient confidentiality," Elsie said, for the millionth time.

The woman gave her one last hostile look and then led her through the house to the back room. Elsie gasped when she stepped inside, immediately noticing the state-of-the-art equipment that filled it wall-to-wall.

"I'll go get your patient," Nikki said. "Please wait here."

Elsie nodded, but didn't look toward her. She was too hypnotized by the equipment.

There has to be at least a million dollars worth of medical equipment here, she thought. *This is like a physical trainer's candy store. What kind of athlete could afford all of this?*

Her attention was swayed when she heard the familiar creak of crutches. She turned around to see her patient standing in the doorway, with a crutch under each of his arms.

Whoa, she thought, trying to keep her jaw from dropping completely to the floor.

During the interview the day before, Nikki had told Elsie that her patient was in "good" physical shape. That wasn't exactly an accurate description of the kind of shape he was in, though. The guy was in *amazing* physical condition. Definitely professional athlete territory. In fact, his ultra-muscular chest and torso were obvious, even through his white t-shirt.

But despite how strong his body appeared, he looked exhausted. Beaten up and tired. His bottle-blonde hair was messy and unkempt. His shoulders were slouched forward. A fading purple bruise circled his right eye, making it look like he left a boxing ring after losing a ten-round fight not too long ago.

Elsie approached him and he watched her, his blue eyes never looking away.

"I'm Elizabeth," she said, holding out a hand. "Most of my friends call me Elsie, though. Either one will do. And you must be..." She paused for a moment, feeling a bit embarrassed for not knowing her patient's name. "I'm sorry, I actually don't know much about you. Your assistant hasn't been telling me anything at all."

He looked a little surprised, but smiled. "Call me Ollie." Ollie shifted his weight on the crutches so that he could shake her hand. "It's a pleasure to meet you."

"You as well," Elsie said, glancing over his shoulder to see the woman from the interview walk out the front door without saying goodbye.

Real nice lady, that one, she thought.

"If you'll come over to the table, I'd like to test your range of motion." Elsie walked slowly toward the exam table in the center of the room, letting Ollie follow behind. "I'll also need to get some history from you. It's just basic stuff, but things that I need to know in order to treat you properly."

Ollie hobbled over to the table and Elsie took a step back to watch him. Just by seeing the way he used his crutches gave her a head start on her evaluation of the new patient.

He's got strong arms. Clearly right-handed. Seems to compensate well using his left leg, though, she thought, making notes in her mind.

Ollie heaved himself up onto the edge of the table. Elsie took her clipboard and sat on a swivel chair just a few feet away. The seated position put her at a lower elevation than Ollie and really brought into focus just how tall of a man he was. He was much larger than the average guy, and much more muscular too.

This is going to be quite a bit different than treating my usual 80-year-old ladies with hip replacements. It'll be more like when I fix the young farmers, she thought, taking a glance at Ollie. *And he's probably just as stubborn as they are, too.*

"So tell me, Ollie, how did this injury on your right leg happen?" Elsie asked, holding the clipboard in one hand and her pen in the other. "And also, what other injuries do you have, if any, that I'm not seeing here?"

"I was in a car accident a couple of weeks ago," he said, pushing his blonde hair off of his forehead.

"I'm sorry to hear that," she said. "Car wrecks can be traumatizing in more ways than just physically."

Ollie shrugged. "I'm just glad it wasn't worse. I walked away with just a black eye, a cracked rib, a torn ACL and fourteen stitches. But I'm just happy to have walked away at all, honestly."

Elsie parted her lips. She was going to ask what caused the accident, but then decided that it was fairly irrelevant. If he didn't want to share, then she wasn't going to pry. It wasn't her job. She wasn't getting paid to ask unnecessary questions, so she decided to keep her curiosity to herself.

"Are there any other injuries that I should be aware of?" she asked. "Any back issues or shoulder problems? Any family history of either of those things?"

Ollie shook his head, and rubbed the back of his neck. "Not really. I did have some whiplash from the accident. My neck was really sore for the first week, but it seems to have subsided for the most part. The doctors at the hospital weren't too worried about that, though. They said it was normal after an accident like mine. Besides all that, I'm as healthy as a horse."

Elsie scribbled on her clipboard, jotting down everything that he said so that she could refer to it later if needed. She loved that she could actually get some information from this guy, unlike the gate-keeping Nikki.

"And what do you do for your profession?" Elsie asked.

"Really?" he asked, sounding surprised. Ollie raised an eyebrow and cocked his head to the side.

"Yes, really," she said, tapping her pen against the side of the clipboard. "I need to know so I can get you back to it."

"You don't recognize me?" He seemed utterly shocked by the idea.

"I'm sorry, I don't," she replied, shaking her head. "Should I?"

Ollie leaned forward, bringing his elbows to his knees. He looked directly at her with his crystal clear blue eyes and she felt a tingling inside of her, which she tried to ignore. The man had presence.

"You're being serious?" he asked. "You're not just messing with me?"

"Look, Ollie, I'm not here to joke around," she said with a polite smile. "I'm not messing with you. I've no idea who you are."

"I'm Oliver Lance," he said, as if his name was all the information she needed. Elsie shrugged. He blinked twice before adding, "I'm the starting quarterback for the San Francisco Bandits."

Elsie raised her eyebrows, initially wondering if he was pulling her strings. The Bandits were her nephews' favorite professional football team. She didn't actually know any of the players on the team, so she couldn't be sure he was telling the truth or just trying to impress her.

"I've heard the name," she asked, twirling her pen in between her forefinger and thumb.

"So you have heard of me?" he asked, a satisfied grin crossing his face.

"No, I've heard of the *team* name, the Bandits," she said. "But only in passing. I'm not a huge football fan. I'm sorry."

Ollie's smile shifted out of cocky and into amazed as he shook his head in disbelief. "It's not often I meet someone who doesn't recognize me."

"I'm sorry to disappoint," Elsie replied, with a smile and a shrug.

"No, don't be." Ollie sat up straighter on the table. "It's kind of refreshing, actually. I'm just surprised is all."

Ollie being a professional football player certainly explained some things, including his muscular physique and his ability to afford all of the medical equipment than surrounded them.

"Can I ask you something?" Elsie asked, setting her clipboard to the side.

"Of course," Ollie said, looking completely at ease.

"Why did that woman stress so hard that you being here was a total secret?" she asked. "She reminded me of it over and over, making sure that I wouldn't tell a soul."

"Because nobody can find out that the Bandit's quarterback has been injured," he said, his face loosing the confident smirk. "The car accident stayed quiet, but if word gets out that I'm injured, it's bad news for my team. If news of this injury gets out, it changes the game. It changes how we play."

"I have to ask, does your coach know?" Elsie asked.

Ollie nodded, his blue eyes watching her. "He knows everything. This is actually his idea. I only play if I'm back to full speed. But this is my life. I need your help."

Elsie sighed. She could see the pain and desperation in Ollie's eyes. His career was everything to him and it was clear by the lengths he had gone in order to preserve it.

"Okay, well let's get going," she said, putting on a smile. "I can't promise a full recovery. No physical therapist can. But I'll do my best to get you back into tip top shape."

"Thanks, Doc."

She raised her eyebrows as she looked at him. "Please, call me Elsie. I'm a physical therapist, and 'doctor' just isn't me."

"Whatever you say, Doc." He winked at her.

Elsie shook her head and pushed on. "Now tell me, what was your level of activity before the accident? How many workouts a week were you doing and for how long? Cardio or weights?"

Ollie chuckled. "In the off-season, I worked out every single day for two to three hours. Mostly weights, but always at least thirty minutes of cardio as well. During the season, I cut all of that back since we have practices. I can't afford to be sore during games."

Elsie continued scribbling on her paper as she listened. This was going to be a unique patient, no doubt. This wasn't just someone who wanted to get back to a "normal" life of walking around the park or the mall. This was a man who was a professional athlete and who was asking her to bring him back to that level of activity.

She'd worked on similar athletes, but she knew this was going to be the biggest challenge she had faced in her career. It made her nervous, but also excited, to be presented with such a unique opportunity. The fact that Ollie happened to be easy on the eyes was just a little added bonus to the situation.

"Let me take a look at your knee," she said, standing up and approaching Ollie.

"Sure thing, Doc," he said, with a smirk.

"I'm not that kind of doctor, Ollie."

His smile faded. "Are you going to be able to fix me?" he asked, as Elsie removed the brace around his knee.

"Like I said, I'm going to do everything I can," she replied, setting the brace behind him on the examining table. "I'm confident, though. ACL repairs are not the end of the world and many athletes go back to returning to their normal level of activity."

As Elsie examined Ollie's knee, she could feel his eyes on her. It was like he was absorbing every one of her movements. It made her feel on-the-spot and admittedly a little self-conscious, but she did her best to ignore it and continued investigating his injury.

After unwrapping the bandages, she checked the incisions first. They seemed to be healing very well, considering the short amount of time since the surgery. He'd definitely had a good surgeon, which was going to make her life easier.

"I'm going to move your leg around a bit," she said, placing her hand on the underside of his ankle. "Let me know what hurts and what doesn't."

She lifted up his leg and watched his face, stopping her movement as soon as he winced in pain. His range of motion was about seventy-five degrees, which she was expecting after an injury like his.

"Your surgeon seemed to have done an excellent job," Elsie said, slowly bringing Ollie's leg back down to a resting position. "It looks like you're healing up nicely."

"I was told he was the best." Ollie looked relieved, now that Elsie wasn't pushing on his leg any more.

"It certainly looks that way," she said, wrapping some gauze loosely over his incisions. "I'm going to massage your knee a little bit. It's just to keep the blood flowing so that you heal better. Let me know if it hurts and I'll stop."

"Massage away, Doc," Ollie said.

Elsie gave him the side eye for the "Doc" comment, which Ollie responded to with a grin. Without saying anything, she began working on his knee. With her hands busy, she let her brain start coming up with a plan. She'd worked with another pro-football player with a similar injury before taking up her uncle's clinic, so she had a good idea of where to go next.

"So here's the game plan," Elsie said, watching Ollie's face to gauge his enthusiasm. "This week and next week will be pretty simple. We're going to work on getting your full range of motion back and begin the process of getting strength back in your leg. Once I feel like you're steady enough for it, we can get you out of the brace. You're probably still going to want your pain meds, but if you're able to, it would be a good time to begin weaning yourself off of them."

"I'm ready to take this thing head on," he said, with beaming confidence. "Whatever it takes to get back in the game."

He's not as ready as he thinks he is. Nobody is, she thought. She smiled at him. *But at least he's got the right attitude.*

She heard a rumbling coming from Oliver's belly and she looked up at him.

"You hungry?" Elsie asked, nodding toward the noise.

"A little, yes," he said, patting his stomach and looking a little bashful.

"How are you getting your meals out here?" Elsie continued to massage his knee as she spoke. "Nobody that I know delivers this far out."

"What, are you worried about me, Doc?" he asked, grinning wide.

She chuckled and shook her head. He wasn't giving up with the "Doc" reference. Oddly enough, she was beginning to find it to be kind of endearing, but she didn't want to fuel the fire, so she just ignored it this time.

"It's my job to worry about you, Mr. Lance," she replied, gently patting his knee.

"Ollie," he said with a soft smile. "Please, call me Ollie. And you don't need to worry too much about me. Nikki dropped off a bunch of pre-made meals that are easy to heat up."

"Nikki?" she asked. "The same one that interviewed me yesterday?"

"Yep, that's her," he said, sitting forward on the edge of the table. "She's my manager, so she wants me back on the field as much as I do."

"Are you eating the meals that she's prepared for you?" Elsie asked, pausing in her work to look up at him. "Sometimes it can be easy to forget to eat when you're on pain meds."

Ollie reached into the front pocket of his shorts and pulled out his cell phone, holding it up in front of her. "I have a timer that reminds me when to eat. And I promise that I'm sticking to it. I kind of have to anyway, because the pain meds make me nauseous if I take them on an empty stomach."

"These meals are healthy, right?" she asked. "Nutrition is an important part of the healing process, so I want you eating correctly."

Ollie leaned his head back and let out a laugh. "Yes, Mom. They're healthy. And I'm eating all of my fruits and vegetables too. Would you like to make sure that I'm washing my hands?"

"Yes, and in addition to that, I'm going to need to make sure that you're doing all your homework and making your bed." She winked as she grinned up at him.

"So, what you're saying is that you want to see my bed?" Ollie asked, with a chuckle. He grinned naughtily at her.

She had walked right into that one. Elsie felt her cheeks burn with embarrassment by his comment, which only made Ollie laugh harder.

"Hey, you said it, not me." Ollie put his hands in the air with his palms out, an expression of innocence.

She just shook her head and did her best not to make it worse. She needed to stay professional here. Even though it was innocent enough right now, she needed to maintain her position as medical provider. So she focused on the massage and tried to ignore the heat in her cheeks.

"I know that I'm not supposed to ask a ton of questions, per the contract I signed yesterday," she said, clearing her throat. "But these sessions are going to be very long and tedious if we don't have something to talk about. If I ask something and you don't feel like answering, just tell me to stop and I will."

"Sure," he said with a small shrug. "Ask me anything."

"Favorite food?" she asked, pausing for a moment to look up at him.

"That's an easy one," he replied. "Pizza. I know it's not the fanciest thing to ever grace the planet, but it's my favorite because I hardly ever get to have it. It's my kryptonite."

"If you like pizza, there's a place in town called Fo's Pizza," she said, happy to be making small talk with him. "They have a Thai chili pizza that just might be the best thing in the entire world."

"A Thai chili pizza?" Ollie asked, stating each word slowly, as though she had just suggested something so amazing he had to savor the words.

"Yes, and it's incredible." Elsie practically began to drool at just the thought of it. "Fo's does deliver, though

I'm not sure if they'll come out this far. I can always bring it to you sometime if you're concerned about privacy stuff."

"I'd love to try it out, but it's really not on my diet," he said, with a sigh. "Sounds great, though."

"Can be you move your knee for me this way?" she said, re-positioning Ollie's leg. "Thanks."

She continued to massage the other side of his knee. She was pushing hard on the tissue and Ollie didn't even flinch.

"Do you have any family nearby?" she asked, lifting her gaze momentarily to look at him. "Anyone that's going to come visit you?"

Oliver cocked his head for a moment, as if her question was something that he wasn't used to being asked.

"I have a younger brother," he said slowly. "He's in college right now, though. He's studying a lot and planning on going to medical school. He's the closest, but also the busiest. So I guess the answer to your question is 'no'. No visitors planned."

"What about Nikki?" Elsie asked, deliberately keeping her tone neutral.

"She's heading back to San Francisco," Ollie replied. "Which is good. I don't think she'd last long here."

Elsie raised her eyebrows and looked up at him. "She's not a country girl?"

Ollie barked a laugh. "Not even close. I think this trip might be the first time she's seen a cow in real life. If there isn't a fancy shoe store within three miles, she starts to develop hives."

Elsie chuckled. She was secretly glad she wasn't going to have to deal with that awful woman on a regular basis.

There was a quiet pause between them for a moment. It was the kind of fleeting pause that made her heart skip a beat. An exciting and tension filled second, which she brushed off and tried to ignore.

"Your brother's in medicine, huh?" Elsie asked, trying to keep him talking. He had a very pleasant voice. "He must be smart."

"Crazy smart," Ollie said, pride filling his voice as he smiled.

"Does he play sports like you?"

"No," he replied, shaking his head. "Sports aren't really his thing."

"So he got the brains?" she asked.

Ollie grinned. "You saying I didn't?"

"I, uh... I mean, uh..." Elsie felt the blush coming back to her cheeks.

"I'm just teasing you. But, yes, he got all the brains," Ollie said with a laugh. He groaned as Elsie pushed deep into the tissue of his knee. "What about you? Any family?"

"I have two sisters," she said, easing up the pressure of the massage a little. "They both married farmers, which is kind of the thing to do around here. Farmers are what Iowa is known for."

"And being the political starting point for elections," Ollie added.

"Who's the smart one now?" she said, with a wink.

The two of them laughed. It felt good and natural. Ollie was easy to talk to. Any nervousness that Elsie had felt about the situation walking in, was now completely gone. She was actually looking forward to the weeks ahead.

"Okay, that's the end of our session today," she said, as she re-wrapped his knee in the cloth bandage and began to put his brace back on.

"That's it?" he asked, surprised.

"Yep." She grinned at him.

"I was expecting a lot more sweat and tears, to be honest," he said, slowly stepping off of the examination table. "That wasn't bad at all."

"That's because this was your first one," she said, raising an eyebrow. "I'm always gentle at first."

"Me too, Doc," Ollie said, with an over-exaggerated wink.

Elsie rolled her eyes but chuckled. "I'll be back tomorrow. Until then, I want you to take it easy. You just had a major surgery and your body needs time to heal. I promise you, though, when your body is ready, we'll push it to the limit."

"Is that so?" he asked, winking again and making her words sound dirty.

This time, his comment made her blush.

This guy is trouble, she thought. *He is a total flirt.*

"You're going to start feeling like you can do more over the next couple of weeks," she said, picking up her clipboard and scribbling down a few notes and ignoring his comment. "But your symptoms do not necessarily reflect your ability to perform activities."

"Please, Doc, tell me what kind of activities I *can* do," he said, with a suggestive smile. How was he able to twist everything she was saying into some sort of innuendo?

Elsie shook her head and tried not to encourage him. "You may sit and watch TV. How about that? Watch recordings of football games. Sports people do that sort of thing, right?"

Ollie chuckled, obviously enjoying the game.

"You're alright, Doc," he said, as he grabbed his crutches and used them to hold himself steady. "I think my knee feels a little better already."

"Take it easy and I'll see you Wednesday," Elsie said, standing up herself.

With her clipboard in hand, she turned and left the farm house, grabbing her purse on the way out. A smile was on her face as she drove home. She felt like she already had an easy friendship with Oliver, which was always a good sign. She was surprised by how much she enjoyed his company, and got the sense that he was going to be both a compliant, and a fun, patient.

I think this is going to work out just fine, she thought. *I'm already looking forward do the next session.*

Chapter Four

Ollie

Oliver hobbled across the house, distributing his weight between his left leg and his crutches. His knee was a bit sore from the massage. He hadn't told Elsie that, though. He didn't want to look weak in front of her.

He approached the window above the kitchen sink and looked out, watching as she got into her car and backed down the long driveway. His eyes on the window, he opened an orange bottle and popped two pills into his mouth. He watched until she disappeared from view, then he made his way to the living room, where he plopped down on the overstuffed leather love seat.

"That was... interesting," he whispered to himself.

She didn't know who I was, he thought. *I can't remember the last time I met someone who didn't immediately recognize me and start asking for an autograph or something.*

It was shocking to him. Just strange. He was so used to everyone knowing all of the intimate details about his life. But Elsie didn't. She didn't know a thing. She didn't recognize his face, or know his name, and hadn't heard the tragic story of his ultra-intelligent brother in medical school. It was oddly refreshing to him. Wonderful, even.

It's so nice to be able to have a conversation with someone where they can ask me questions and they don't already have the answers, he thought, reaching forward to grab the TV remote from the coffee table.

He clicked on the television, to find that the antenna only got two stations. One was an infomercial for a blender and the other was televising a game of golf. He went with the golf one, and watched lazily while his thoughts wandered. He had a lot on his mind. He worried about the future of his career and about whether or not people would find out about the severity of his injury.

"I've got to stay tough," he said out loud. "I've got to grind hard and get through this."

It's not like physical therapy is going to be the worst thing I've ever gone through anyway, he thought. *If the rest of it is anything like today, then it'll be a piece of cake. Some massages and a few simple exercises. No problem.*

In the back of his mind, though, he knew that it wasn't going to be quite that easy. He'd seen enough players with an ACL injury to know that recovery was not all sunshine and rainbows. Most of the players that had it never came back to play the game, at least not in a starting position.

"Not me, though," he said, slowly standing up from the chair. "I'm the strongest one out there."

He hardly finished the sentence before his injured leg gave out from underneath him. A soaring pain shot through him, starting at his knee and radiating up and down his leg. He immediately collapsed back onto the love seat, letting out an agonizing groan.

"Dammit," he grunted, in frustration.

It was a reminder that he was, indeed, human. He was going to have to take the time to heal. It wasn't something he could rush, which drove him crazy. Ollie wanted nothing more than to be just be able to work hard and make himself better, but unfortunately, there was only so much he could do.

His mind whirled around the ever-looming idea that this could be the end of his career. The idea haunted him constantly and he hadn't been able to stop thinking about that possibility since the minute he had woken up in the emergency room the night of the accident.

What if I didn't have football? He thought. *What in the hell would I do?*

Oliver *needed* the game. From the time he first held a football as a kid, until now, it was the biggest thing in his life. Playing was the only thing he ever wanted to do and the only thing that he would *ever* want to do. It was also the only thing that he felt he was actually good at.

Being photogenic and good-looking was simply luck, though it had definitely served him well. Combined with his talent for playing football, it opened up some very lucrative doors for him. A few well placed sponsors, a couple of championship games, and some shrewd business purchases was enough to add up to millions in the bank. Not too bad for a kid with a single mom and a sick little brother.

But it was never really about the money. He had more money than he knew what to do with, and checks continued to roll in all the time as he got signed with new endorsements. No, Ollie didn't do it for the dollar bills. It was always for the simple love of the game. It was about the thrill of throwing the perfect ball, the adrenaline of the line up, the deafening noise of the crowd... that was his lifeblood. That was his everything. That was what made him feel alive.

If this goddamn car accident ruins everything I've worked for, I'll be devastated, he thought, feeling a tear well up in his eye.

He quickly wiped it away and shook his head.

That's why this has to be a secret, he thought.

So far, Nikki had done a good job of keeping the severity of the accident out of the press. It was known that he had been involved in a car collision, but the details had been kept under wraps. As far as anyone knew, all injuries had been minor, the culprit was in jail, and Ollie was just taking a relaxing break from a very busy season. The truth about his ACL tear hadn't been exposed.

Oliver looked over, glancing out the window next to the front door. It was snowing again, and the window sill had at least six inches on it. He thought about Elsie, hoping that she'd drive safe in the snow.

I can trust Elsie with my secret, though, he thought. *I don't know how I know, but I feel that I can really put my faith in her. She's genuine and devoted to her job. It's obvious in the way she carries herself. She wouldn't stab me in the back.*

The pain medication that Ollie had taken earlier had begun to kick in and he felt his eyelids grow heavy. The monotone voice of the golf announcer on the TV hypnotized him. He tried to stay awake, but quickly began to lose the battle to sleep. As he slowly drifted off, his mind was filled with images of Elsie in her cute, lime green scrubs.

I'm actually looking forward to the next session, he thought. *I hope that she asks me about my brother, so I can tell her how proud of him that I am. It'll be nice to share that with someone who doesn't already know everything about my life. This could be the start of a beautiful friendship with a beautiful woman.*

With that, Ollie relaxed his head back and let himself drift into a deep sleep.

Chapter Five

Elsie

Elsie stared at her computer screen. She had a search window up and Oliver Lance's name already typed out. Her finger hesitated over the "go" button. Did she really want to find out about him?

She chewed her lip for a moment before finally giving into temptation.

Apparently, he was just as famous as he said he was. There were thousands of pictures of him and tons of websites devoted to not only his football prowess, but his life as well. She clicked on the "images" tab first. In all his pictures, his hair was a rich black that made the blue of his eyes pop. She definitely preferred it to the bleach blond hairstyle he currently wore.

She glanced through all his football pictures. Some were action shots from various games, many were of him lifting the championship trophy over his head, and then the obviously staged photos made to put on TV with his stats underneath. Mixed in with all of these were him around the city. The most prevalent were pictures of him at various clubs around his city- always with a different gorgeous girl hanging off his arm. He sure knew how to pick attractive women.

Elsie shook her head and marked him as a player in her head. He was attractive and funny, but obviously a womanizer. If he wasn't her patient, he would be the exact opposite of her type. She wanted a family and loved being at home on Friday nights cuddled up in front of the TV with a movie and popcorn. From the pictures, that was the last thing Oliver Lance would enjoy.

Elsie moved her mouse back to the results tab and clicked on the top link to his Wikipedia page and started to read. She only got through the first sentence before stopping. It felt like snooping.

"This isn't against my contract," she whispered to herself, but it didn't matter. Her eyes wouldn't go past the words "Oliver Lance was born December 28th..." She had her medical file on him, so she knew that already, but it didn't feel right to read all the details of his personal life.

Elsie chewed on her bottom lip for a moment, unsure of what to do next. There was so much information on Lance right in front of her. The headings tempted her with his football games, his money, his history... but she didn't click on any of them.

She thought of what it would feel like if there were a Wikipedia page about her that Oliver could read about. Where he could find out all about her sisters, her uncle, how she left a promising sports training career to come run her uncle's PT clinic, even her past romantic history...

"I don't want to know," she said out loud to the computer and shut the window. "I'll let him tell me what he wants."

Her heart felt lighter after closing the window. It felt like she was doing the right thing. She was excited to have him tell her all the information instead of the emotionless website page. She would ask him if he preferred her to look at it, but she suspected he didn't. Besides, she liked the way his eyes widened and the shocked look on his face when she told him she didn't know who he was. It was rather fun to surprise him with that.

Elsie smiled and closed her laptop. She'd had a busy day and should be heading to bed and not messing around on her computer anyway. With a deep breath, she stood up from her office desk, turned off the lights and went home.

***

"Okay, Ollie. That's it for today. You did a good job." Elsie finished massaging his knee like she did after all their sessions. She wanted to get as much blood flow to the injury as possible. In addition to the massage, she'd spent the last hour putting Ollie through simple, yet important, leg exercises.

Oliver wiped his brow and sagged back onto the treatment table. Sweat soaked through his shirt and he seemed very relieved that the punishment was over. "You sure, Doc? I think I can handle some more torture."

"You're done for the day. We don't want to push you too far, or you'll just re-injure yourself. It's a delicate line we need to walk, between challenging you and letting you heal." Elsie patted his shoulder. "Plus, your check hasn't cleared yet, so I need to keep you liking me for at least a few more hours."

She watched as Oliver cocked his head to the side and froze. It was like she had said something wrong.

"I'm only teasing you," she said, with a smirk. "Your check is just fine."

Ollie released his breath and relaxed once again. Elsie grabbed a bottled water from the mini fridge in the corner of the room and handed it to him.

"You need to stay hydrated now," she said. "The more water, the better."

Oliver nodded as he took down a big gulp. When he finished, he set the bottle next to him. "I've been working out for most of my life and I think this might have been one of the hardest workouts I've gone through. I'm not joking either. Even the drills that coach made me do as a rookie didn't kick my butt like you just did."

"The worst isn't over." Elsie took a step back from the table to make room for Ollie to get up. "Just wait until I make you stand up again."

Oliver groaned and wiped his face. "Don't remind me. Do you think there's any way you can just let me lay here the rest of the day?"

"Would you like me to throw the ball for you at your next game too?" she teased, glancing down at his knee. He gave her a good-natured glare as he wiped sweat from his brow again.

The swelling had gone down significantly and the incisions were nearly healed. Still, though, they had a whole lot of work to do before Ollie could consider himself recovered.

"I feel like I should be all better by now," he said, gently touching his knee. "It still freaking hurts, though. But, it's been a whole week!"

"Ollie, you had three men attack you with knives and dig around in your knee for several hours." Elsie gave him a reassuring squeeze on his shoulder. "They were just nice enough to sedate you first."

Ollie frowned at her.

"Your body doesn't know that it was actually surgeons and not masked murderers that did this to you," she explained. "You have to be patient. Give yourself a little time. You're going to get better and better as the weeks go on. I promise."

Oliver was silent for a moment. Contemplative. "I'm just not used to feeling like this. I've always been able to push through. I've never spent one day on the injured list. This just isn't like me."

"You're doing great, Ollie," she said, feeling an urge to pull him in for a hug. She didn't, but she wanted to. "You're doing far better than any patient I've ever had. Honestly. You'll be up and running before you know it."

Oliver lifted his gaze to meet hers. His clear blue eyes caused her feet to melt to the floor. She felt magnetized toward him, a pull which she forced herself to ignore. He was her patient. She picked up her clipboard and pretended to write something just to break the connection.

"If you say so, Doc," he finally said with a sigh.

Elsie looked up and smiled and Ollie slowly returned the gesture. He was so obviously down about the whole thing. He put on a brave face, but she knew how scary an injury like this could be for an athlete. This jeopardized his whole world, and he was doing his best to smile through it. It broke her heart.

"I *do* say so," she said, patting his knee gently. "I'd tell you if you were sucking. That's actually an important part of my job. I won't sugar coat anything. You can count on that."

"You sound like Coach," Ollie said, taking another swig of water.

Elsie chuckled. "I like your coach already." She jotted a few notes down on her clipboard about the day's session. "Sounds like he and I think the same way."

"Yeah, but he'd say it with an angry sneer," he said, with a chuckle.

Elsie twisted her mouth and narrowed her eyes, looking up from her clipboard. With her voice lowered as much as possible, she growled, "You're doing a great job. Now hit the showers, kid!"

For the first time that day, Ollie let out a genuine laugh. He cracked up for a full minute, which put a smile on Elsie's face. Hearing him laugh was the best part of her day.

"If I didn't know better, I'd say you do a better Coach than Coach does." Ollie said, wiping tears of laughter from his cheek.

"You know, I *do* help coach little league in the fall for the local elementary school," she said, beaming with pride. "That's probably where I picked it up."

"What sport do you coach?" he asked, eyes widening and ears perking.

"Football, actually," she replied, with a laugh. "I love it. There's nothing more satisfying, or hilarious, than watching 6-year-olds run around in those pads."

"That's awesome. You probably know more about football than you've let on." Ollie's eyes were still locked with Elsie's. "Who roped you into coaching kid's football, anyway?"

"My oldest sister," Elsie admitted. "Her son is on the team and they needed a coach. It worked out great, though, because it gave me a chance to hang out with my little nephew."

"So let me get this straight," Ollie said, scooting to the edge of the table. "You coach football, yet you had never heard of me before we met last week?"

Elsie shrugged. "I like football a lot, I just don't have any time to watch it. I haven't been able to be a real fan since I took over the physical therapy clinic from my uncle. There's just too much work for me to do and not enough time to watch the games."

"When was the last game you watched?" he asked. "Any from last season?"

"I wish," she said, shaking her head. "You're going to laugh, but I haven't watched a professional game in three years. No, wait... four years."

"You're kidding," he said, eyes wide with surprise. "You haven't been to a game in four years?"

"*Been?* I've actually *never* been to a professional game," she said, pushing her hair over her ear and biting her lower lip. "We don't have a professional football team in Iowa and I couldn't afford a ticket in grad school."

"That would make it more difficult to go to a game," Ollie admitted.

"I used to watch all the games on TV while I was growing up, and I loved going to college games," Elsie explained. She leaned against the massage table across from Ollie and shrugged. "But once I graduated, I just couldn't find the time."

"You've missed out on a lot of good games." Ollie looked up at the ceiling, as though recalling great memories from his past. "I wish you had been able to keep up on the sport. It's come a long ways."

"I hope to get back into sometime. I used to love my Sunday afternoons cheering at the screen. Maybe things will slow down for me one day," she said. "But I promise, I'll watch a game once you're playing again."

"I'd love for that to happen." Ollie looked down at the ground, an expression of sadness written all over his face as he remembered what he was facing. "Let's hope I'm playing again and you can watch me next year."

"Hey, we'll get you there, Ollie," she said, sounding sure of herself. "The two of us are a team now and we'll work together. I've got your back."

His eyes lit up and he reached forward, placing his hand over hers. His touch sent a pleasurable chill through her. She liked it, a lot more than she cared to admit.

No, Elsie. No, she thought. *Sure, he's cute and he's got a great story, but he's your patient. That's all.*

Slowly, she pulled her hand away and picked up her pen. Then she pretended to jot some notes down on her paper.

"I appreciate all that you're doing for me," he said, after a few moments of pause. "Truly, it feels good knowing you're on my side. I was hopeless when I woke up in that hospital. But you've really made me feel like there's a chance I can pull through this thing."

Warmth spread through her chest and she couldn't stop the smile on her face.

"Thank you. Just don't get down about it," she said, placing a hand onto his shoulder. "Stay positive and keep the same 'work hard' attitude that brought you into your career in the first place."

"That's some very sound advice," he replied. "You sure you're not related to Coach?"

She chuckled.

"I hope you take it to heart," she said, her lips curling up into a wide smile. "Anyway, that's it for today. Keep yourself comfortable tonight and don't be afraid to put ice on that knee. You know the drill."

"I do." Ollie nodded.

Elsie grabbed her clipboard and purse, but then paused. The session was over, but she didn't really want to leave. She was having a nice time. There was a great connection between them and it made for smooth and relaxing conversation. It had been a while since she had been able to enjoy that with someone. Still, though, she feared if she stayed much longer than she would wear out her welcome.

"You have my phone number if you need anything," she said, turning toward the door and mentally telling herself it was time to go.

"That I do." Oliver grabbed his crutches and eased himself back down to the floor. "And you have mine. Which is good, that way if I do call you, you won't think it's some crazy spam caller or something."

She grinned at his comment, but couldn't think of anything else to add. The session was over and it was time for her to leave, even though she was having a nice time.

"Okay, I'll see you Friday," she finally said, and started walking toward the front door.

Just as she touched the doorknob, she heard Ollie call out, "I'm looking forward to it."

Elsie grinned and stepped outside into the icy air.

It almost feels like a date, she thought.

She liked the idea of that, but also feared the implications. Combining her professional world with her personal was never a good idea. They'd gone over that plenty of times in school and she'd seen coworkers get in trouble with patients.

But she couldn't get rid of that feeling of attraction toward Ollie. It wasn't about his good looks or money, either. It was something different. Maybe it was his playful personality or how he made her feel important. Whatever it was, she couldn't get him off of her mind. And Friday couldn't come soon enough.

Chapter Six

Ollie

Oliver was laying on his back, looking up at the ceiling. He was on the floor of the makeshift gym in his temporary home and Elsie was standing nearby, counting out his movements. He was in pain and beyond exhausted. A part of him felt like passing out would be a better alternative than staying conscious, but there was no way that Elsie would let him quit. He loved that about her.

"How is this so hard?" he asked, through gritted teeth. "I'm hardly doing anything. This shouldn't be so difficult."

"Just keep going until I tell you to stop," Elsie said.

She was wearing her lime-green scrubs again and Ollie couldn't help but to take a peek at her backside every chance he got. She looked really good and the weeks of therapy with her had created feelings toward her. He knew there was a deeper connection than just the doctor/patient one. There was something there that was undeniable and he wondered if she'd noticed it too.

"Come on, Ollie," she said, crouching down next to him on the floor. Her brown eyes were warm and encouraging. "Just thirty more seconds and you can take a break."

He pressed the back of his head into the padded floor mat and clenched his jaw. Then he focused on the movement, which was very basic. All he had to do was straighten out his right leg and then slowly lift it up to a vertical position. Then, after holding it there for three seconds, he was to bring it back down and start all over. He'd been doing it for a while, though, and combined with the bicycling and weights they'd already done, he was beat.

"How many more seconds now?" he asked.

She gave him a half smile and looked at her watch. "Twenty-five."

I've done much harder workouts than this, he thought. *Coach has put us through drills that would make a normal man puke. How is it that I've survived that, but somehow this physical therapy is killing me? I'm sweating like I've been running stairs while wearing a weight belt at altitude.*

Oliver wasn't one to quit, though, so he pushed through until Elsie finally told him to stop. He drew in a breath of relief and relaxed his entire body. His knee was throbbing and his sweat-soaked skin felt cool as the fan across the room blew air toward him.

"This is harder than it should be," he said, not looking at Elsie and just staring at the ceiling. He hated this feeling. "I feel so weak right now. It's frustrating."

"It's hard because you're healing," she replied, jotting some things down on her clipboard. "Be kind to yourself, Ollie. You're doing great."

"Sure, Doc," he said, shaking his head. "Whatever you say."

In the matter of a few weeks, Oliver had gone from being at the top of his game to the very bottom. He'd gone from throwing touchdown passes in a championship game to writhing on the floor in agony and unable to walk without the help of crutches. It made him feel like a cripple.

How in the hell am I going to take my team to a single victory next season if I can hardly even move my damn leg? he thought, as he pushed himself up to a seated position on the floor and leaned against the wall.

Deep frustration bubbled up in his stomach. And below that, despair tried to creep in, but he was too frustrated to let it make its appearance. Despair would have its chance to rear its ugly head when he was alone later that night.

Yeah, that's when I can fully feel bad for myself, he thought, still wincing in pain. *When I'm hungry and it hurts too much to make it to the microwave, so I just drink protein shakes instead. That'll be a great time for self-loathing. The same damn thing I've been doing every night for two weeks now.*

Elsie was looking at him and her stare caught his attention. Her dark, caring eyes locked with his and for a fleeting moment, he felt a tiny bit better. Just having her in front of him made him feel that all was not lost and that there was still a chance that good could come from this whole thing.

"I can tell you're upset," she said, taking a seat next to him against the wall. She stretched out her long legs in front of her. "But I'm not lying when I tell you that you're doing a great job. It's only been two weeks since your surgery. You shouldn't expect to be in peak condition quite yet."

Oliver harrumphed.

"When I was in my residency, I helped treat a professional football player who had an ACL tear just like yours," she told him. "He injured himself in January and we had him back on the starting lineup in September. His team won the championship game that year."

Oliver looked over and their eyes met. She had the most beautiful, caring eyes he'd ever seen.

"Why are you just now telling me this?" he asked. Nikki had said something about Elsie's credentials so the story sounded familiar, but he hadn't paid much attention at the time.

"Because when we first starting working together, I wasn't sure how quickly you'd progress," she explained. "I didn't want you to think we could have you up and running in just a couple of months, just in case it wasn't feasible."

"Does it seem feasible now?" Oliver turned to face her, sitting in a weird semi-cross-legged position, which felt better on his knee.

"Let's just say that you're doing better than that particular patient was at this point," she said, patting his hand and smiling. "Keep it up. You're doing great."

"That's good to hear," he said, slowly massaging the tender tissue around his knee. "Believe it or not, I think actually know the guy you're talking about. He was one of my favorite players before I went professional. Addison Lamone, played for Denver, right? The guy is a legend."

"I cannot confirm or deny that he's the patient I was talking about," she said, putting on a serious face. "I'm not allowed to divulge any information about previous or current patients."

"I have to respect that," he replied, liking that she smiled at him.

She re-positioned herself against the wall, crossing her legs at the ankle. The soft scent of her shampoo hit him. She smelled amazing. Like roses. He tried not to think about it. She was off limits.

"Ollie, you mentioned you have a brother," Elsie said, staring through him. Her dark eyes looked evaluating and concerned. "Tell me about him."

Ollie raised an eyebrow and cocked his head to the side. He still wasn't used to interacting with someone who didn't already know every detail about his life. "What would you like to know?"

"Only what you want to share with me," she said, turning to face him and tucking her legs underneath her. "I can tell that you're feeling down right now. You sounded really proud of your brother the other day, so I thought it might lift your spirits to talk about him. It'll give you something to focus on that's positive, rather than how difficult your recovery is and how you feel like you're never going to walk again, let alone run, jump and play."

Oliver's face softened.

This girl can read me like a book, he thought. *That's the perfect subject to distract me from my current situation.*

"His name is Michael," he said, feeling his lips curl up into a smile. "He's finishing his senior year at college and has already been accepted into Harvard's medical school. He's going to be a doctor."

Pride washed over Oliver. He knew that he was grinning like an idiot, but he couldn't help it. He was so proud of his little brother. In fact, he was more proud of Michael's success than he was of his own.

"That's wonderful, Ollie," Elsie said, her response so genuine that it caused goose bumps to pop up on Oliver's skin. "It takes a lot of hard work and a special kind of person to be a doctor. And Harvard... wow!"

"He's going to be amazing," Ollie said. "He's really passionate about it and has a knack for making people feel better."

"That's fantastic," she replied, slowly standing up from the floor. "Keep talking while I help you stand. We're going to go to the leg extension machine and do some reps to keep the blood flowing to your injury."

"I was really hoping that we were done for the day." Oliver flashed a hopeful smile as he took Elsie's hands and she helped him up.

"Not quite," she said, wrapping an arm around his waist to help steady him. "Soon, though. One more exercise to get through."

Oliver had his arm over Elsie's shoulder, letting her help carry some of his weight. They made it to the leg extension machine and he took a seat, putting his leg in the position to use the weights. She'd put him through this exercise before and it was even less fun than the one he had just finished.

"I'm going to set it at a low weight," she said. He had a feeling it would still feel like a million pounds.

"Now, keep telling me about your brother," she continued, making sure to smile at him. She had a great smile. "Does he play any sports? Is he an athlete like you?"

"No," Oliver said, abruptly. There was a hint of anger in his voice that surprised him, even after all this time.

"No?" Elsie said, looking up to meet his gaze. Her delicate dark brows were raised.

"No, but he should have," he said, trying to concentrate on the motion of his leg as his mind went to the past. "He was a better runner than I ever was. Kid had speed. And, if a sport had a ball, he could play it and be the best at it. A natural athlete in every way."

"What happened?" she asked, with a concerned expression.

The memory washed over Oliver, filling his mind and body with emotion. He could still see it like it was yesterday down to the way the grass was cut.

"It was my rookie year playing for the Bandits," Ollie said. "It was game four. My mom and brother attended all of my home games, but couldn't they make this one because Michael had a doctor's appointment. He'd been feeling sick for a while, and the doctors wanted to run some tests. My mom wasn't sure what was wrong with him, but she was worried. Even I knew something wasn't right."

He paused for a moment, remembering it like it in real time. The way the bench felt, the sound of the crowd behind him, the feel of his phone hidden in his pocket as he waited for updates.

"I should have gone to the doctor's with them," he said, shaking his head. "It still eats me up that I wasn't there. I spent the entire game on the bench, not even playing, while my little brother was at the doctor."

"What happened?" Elsie asked, worry creasing her brow. A strand of hair fell in her eyes, but she didn't notice it. He thought about reaching out and moving it for her, but he stayed still.

"Cancer," he stated, the word causing him to wince at the pain of the memory. "He was only twelve. He wanted to be the next Jordan or Babe Ruth, but that all came to a crashing halt when he got sick. He could have done it, too. He could have been a pro. He was better than me."

"I'm so sorry, Ollie," she said, touching the top of his hand. Oliver looked up at her touch, drawing him out of the memory. Her hand was warm and comforting against his.

She meant her words. He could see it in her eyes. It was genuine, just like every other part of her. She continued to prove to Oliver that she was actually a real person, unlike most of the people he was forced to interact with because of his career. She was the real deal and this felt like actual human interaction. He'd forgotten how good it felt.

"How's your brother now?" she asked after a moment. Her voice was soft. "How did things turn out?"

"He's cancer-free." Ollie smiled at her. "The doctor says that he's basically cured. We caught it early and he's one of the lucky ones."

"That's so good to hear," she replied, relief in her voice.

A smile lit up her face and it caused Oliver's heart to skip a beat. Her lips were so beautiful, the thought of kissing her jumped into his head. He quickly shook it off. She was an ineligible receiver and he shouldn't even think of what her kiss might taste like.

"Yeah, I'm really proud of him," he said, after a moment of pause. "He fought so hard. In fact, he became my inspiration for when things got rough. I dedicated every one of my games to him while he was in the hospital with chemo and radiation."

"Wow," she said. That part always impressed the ladies. She smiled at him and adjusted the knob on the machine again. "I'm sure that was a tough time."

"It was hard," Ollie admitted, shaking his head. "Michael was so sick. There were complications with everything. The chemo made his hair fall out and the radiation made him puke. He was almost sicker because of the treatments than he was with the cancer."

He paused. This part of the story was hard.

"It was the beginning of the end for Michael's chance at a career in sports. The chemo affected his bones. I don't remember exactly how the doctor explained it, but something in the medicine had made his bones weak." Oliver shrugged, trying to move the weight that settled on his shoulders whenever he thought about what his brother had gone through. "He had to stop playing contact sports altogether. His athletic dreams were killed."

"I'm sorry," Elsie replied, her words soft and soothing. She squeezed his shoulder with her hand, and somehow it helped. "It sounds like you have a strong little brother, though, to survive all of that. It also sounds like you two are very, very close. It's great you have someone like that."

"I really think Michael had something to do with me becoming famous," Ollie said, grunting as he focused back on working his knee. "The game after I found out about his diagnosis was the first game that I got a chance to play. The starting quarterback was injured and so I was put in the game."

"As a rookie?" she asked, adjusting a knob on the weight machine.

Ollie nodded. "Nobody expected us to be able to win that one. We were fourteen points behind and I hadn't ever played a professional game before. But I said a little prayer, and asked for the same strength that Michael had to go through with his treatments. I went out there that day and played as though I was my brother. I told you he was the better athlete."

"How'd it work out?" she asked, finally brushing the hair from her face. He loved that she didn't know the story already. It was refreshing to be able to tell it for the first time.

"We won the game." He still felt the exultation of winning from that game just thinking about it. "And we won the one after that, and the one after that. In fact, we won every game the rest of the season. That's how I became the starting quarterback."

The story was falling out of him now. He hadn't ever told anybody all these details and it wasn't something anybody could look up on the internet. This was his version of what happened and it was the absolute truth. It felt incredible to be able to share it with someone who actually cared and wasn't going to immediately put it up on social media or sell it for a profit.

Elsie listened intently, her eyes locked with his. He felt so drawn to her, but in such a different way than with other women. Sure, he was physically attracted to her. Who wouldn't be? She had a beautiful body, nice butt and perky breasts. But what he loved about her most is that she was just so real. And "real" was not something that most people were, at least in Ollie's world.

Oliver pumped his leg, pushing himself to the limits of his strength. He hissed as a lightning bolt of pain shot through his knee, forcing him to slow down with his exercise.

"Tell me more about your brother," Elsie told him, lowering the weight on the machine.

"My dad died when Mike was six. I was seventeen at the time, so I ended up taking on the father role. I felt the need to protect him from everything." Ollie paused, his voice about to crack with emotion. "I didn't want him to ever feel another ounce of pain in his life, since he had already felt so much at such a young age."

I can't believe I'm actually telling her all of this, he thought. *But she's the first person I've ever wanted to open up to. I don't know why, but I trust her so much.*

Elsie touched Ollie's knee. "Okay, take a rest on this leg and do the same thing with the other one so you're even."

Ollie did as she asked, relieved to be using his good leg once again. It made him feel like he still had strength left in his body.

"That's really nice of you to look out for your brother," she said, leaning against the machine while facing Oliver. "It's admirable."

"Not really," Ollie said, with a sigh. "He's my brother. That's what family does for each other. I'd have given him my right arm if it would have made him better."

"I feel that same way about my sisters," Elsie agreed. "Family is everything."

The way she said it made him look over at her. She smiled and shrugged.

"Has your brother picked a specialty to study in medical school yet?" she asked, bringing the conversation back to his brother.

Ollie nodded. "Oncology, as expected. He wants to help kids that are sick like he once was."

Elsie held her hand up, motioning for Ollie to stop the exercise. "If Michael is anything like his older brother, then cancer is in for a nasty surprise."

Oliver chuckled and then looked away. He found his throat to be a little tight. He wasn't used to talking about his brother like this.

I've done hundreds of interviews, but this feels different, he thought. *This is like telling it for the first time. It's making the memory feel more real than ever.*

In an effort to change the subject to keep himself from tearing up, Ollie said, "So you said you have sisters?"

"Yep," she replied, still leaning against the weight machine. "Two of them. I'm the baby of the family."

"And they have kids?" Ollie asked.

"My oldest sister has two boys and the middle sister just had a baby girl last year," Elsie said, with a smile that showed her pride.

"And one of those boys is who you coach football for, right?" Ollie said, slowly turning to put his feet down on the floor once again.

Elsie smiled, seeming pleased that he remembered that she coached little league. "Yeah, Ryan is six and has big dreams of being a professional football player. But he has a backup. He said that if football doesn't work out then he's going to be a garbage truck man."

"Both good options," Ollie said, with a playful smirk.

Elsie laughed at the comment, which made Oliver smile even more. He loved the sound of her laugh.

"They're great kids," she said. "I'm glad that I've been able to grow so close to them. I pretty much spend any free time I have chasing them around in order to give their mom a break. They're my world."

"It's great you can be around them," he commented, wiping sweat from his brow. He was glad the workout part of the session was over, but he found himself sad that it meant their time together for the day was almost done.

"I'm so glad I get to be in their lives," she agreed. "My uncle is my favorite person in the world. He's actually the person that got me into physical therapy medicine and helped make me who I am today. If I can be half as cool an aunt to my nephews and nieces as he was to me, I'd consider myself a success."

As Ollie listened, he couldn't stop thinking about the fact that Elsie might just be the perfect woman.

She likes football, she's great with kids, he thought. *She's smart, funny, sweet, beautiful. She's a unicorn, that's for sure.*

Ollie knew that he was too much of a player to ever marry. He loved the playboy lifestyle and all the women that came with it. He wasn't ready to give all that up to settle down with just one woman. At least, that's what he told himself.

Besides, a girl like her wouldn't want anything to do with the football lifestyle. Plus, I would hate to drag her away from her home, which is where her clinic and her family are.

"Okay, exercise is done for the day," Elsie said, stepping close to Ollie to help him up. "Time for stretching."

"Oh goodie," he said, sounding anything but enthusiastic. "My favorite, Doc."

Oliver chuckled a bit as Elsie's eyes narrowed at the "Doc" comment. He knew that she hated it, but he loved riling her up. It helped to take away from of the professionalism and reveal her human side underneath. That was the side of her like he was finding he liked the most.

"Stretching is good for you," she said, making her way back to the cushioned mat on the center of the floor.

Ollie followed her and took a seat on the mat. "Yeah, yeah. You just want to torture me some more. Can't we be done for the day? Or maybe do the massage part? I like that part."

Elsie crouched down on the mat in front of him. "Hey, Ollie, do you know what the difference between a physical therapist and a terrorist is?"

He shook his head.

"You can reason with a terrorist," she replied, with a smirk.

"Hardy, har, har," Ollie said, though he did find the joke to be a little bit funny.

"I'm hilarious, I know," she said, with a laugh. "But I probably shouldn't quit my day job."

The way she grinned at him made it impossible for Oliver not to smile back. Her good attitude was infectious and he truly wished that she'd stay longer than for just these sessions. She was a bright light and he was enjoying the hell out of working with her.

Right as Oliver was about to begin his leg stretches, his cell phone rang in his pocket. He grabbed the phone and then looked toward her, as if asking permission to answer it.

"Saved by the bell," she said. "Go ahead and answer it. We'll take a five minute break. I'll go to the bathroom and give you some privacy."

"Thank you," Oliver said, as he answered the call. He tried his best not to watch Elsie as she walked away, but her pants hugged her ass to perfection.

"Hey, it's Nikki," the woman's voice said on the other end of the line, before Oliver could utter a sound.

"Hey, Nikki, what's going on?" Oliver held the phone against his ear with his shoulder as he found a comfortable position for his injured knee.

"Just wanted to check in and see how the therapist was working out," she said.

"It's working out really well," Ollie said, watching as Elsie stepped out of the room. "She's amazing."

"Is she keeping her mouth shut?" Nikki asked. "Is she prying into your business too much? The last thing we need is for her blabbing about her newest patient to her friends."

"We talk enough to hold a conversation," Ollie replied, rolling his eyes at Nikki's negativity.

"She really isn't supposed to ask anything about your personal life. That was the reason why I chose her, because she'd never heard of you before," she said, with a sigh.

"What are we supposed to do, Nikki?" Ollie asked. "You want us to just work in silence and have her call out drills until I'm better?"

"I knew I should have gone with the other guy," she replied, sounding frustrated. "I *knew* it."

"No, she's great, Nikki," he said, slowly laying back on the mat and looking at the ceiling. "There aren't any problems and I trust her. She isn't going to tell anybody that I'm here. I promise."

"Good. But remember, Oliver, don't get attached," Nikki said, in that condescending tone of hers. "As soon as she clears you to once-a-week sessions, you're out of that hell hole. We're losing millions in advertising promotions right now, so we need to get you back home as soon as possible."

Ollie stared blankly at the ceiling, listening to the same old spiel from Nikki that he had heard a hundred times since the accident. It was always about the money for her. Nothing else mattered. Not happiness, or passion, or joy. It was all about dollar bills for that woman.

But despite her urgency to get him back in the limelight, he was finding that he didn't care so much about that. He was rather enjoying his time in this so-called "hell hole" and was in no hurry to stop his training with Elsie.

Right then, an idea hit him upside the head. It was one that hadn't crossed his mind before now.

"Nikki, speaking of heading home, will you ask Bob if there's a PT opening with the team?" he asked, suddenly feeling energized by his new idea.

"For back country girl?" Nikki asked, and Ollie visualized her putting a hand on her hip and cocking her body to the side as she spoke. "Are you serious?"

"Be nice, Nikki," he said, abruptly. "And yes, I'm very serious. I'm ahead of where Addison Lamone was at this stage and it's all because of what Elsie has done for me."

"Elsie? I thought her name was Elizabeth."

"It is, but she also goes by Elsie," he replied.

"Sounds like you guys have become pretty chummy," she said, with a jealous sigh. He could practically see the pout through the phone.

"Hey, either you ask Bob if there's a PT opening or I do," he said. "It's your choice."

Nikki let out another sigh. "Fine, I'll do it. Bob likes me better anyway."

"Thank you, Nikki."

"You owe me," she said, and Oliver was willing to agree. According to Nikki, he always owed her. But this was one of the few times that he actually agreed that he did.

"Anything else?" he asked.

"That's all. Just keep getting better," she replied. There was a few seconds of pause before she spoke again. "I miss you."

Her comment took him off guard. He was surprised to hear that from her. In fact, he hadn't heard anything like that since before they had broken up, over a year before.

"Um, okay," he said, unable to think of a proper response.

"I'm buying a ticket to come out and see you," she said, giggling with excitement.

"You really don't have to do that, Nikki," he said, sitting up a little straighter.

"But I do," she insisted. "I don't like you being out there all by yourself."

"I'm not by myself, though," he said. "I've got Elsie here."

"Right, right," she said, her tone dropping. "That's just what I want to hear, Oliver. You're not alone because you have a woman there with you. Great. Just great."

"Are you feeling okay?" Ollie asked. "You sound a little jealous or something. You remember that we broke up, right? We aren't together any more."

"Of course I remember. I'm not stupid, Oliver." She spoke with a combination of anger, jealousy and insecurity. "I have to go. Keeping healing."

She hung up the phone before Ollie could say goodbye. He tossed his cell to the side and stared at the ceiling for a minute.

I pray that Nikki doesn't want to get back together with me, he thought. *If so, then I'd have to fire her and she is the best at what she does. I can't have our past personal relationship affecting our business one.*

Right then, Elsie popped her head back into the doorway. "Am I safe to come in? I don't want to overhear anything I'm not supposed to."

Ollie sat up and smiled at her concern. "Yeah, you're safe. I'm all done. Thanks."

"Don't thank me yet," she said, walking toward where he was seated. "We're aren't done with the session yet. You're probably going to want to curse me in a few minutes."

I highly doubt that, he thought, smiling to himself.

Chapter Seven

Elsie

"**G**ood news, Ollie," Elsie said, as soon as he had finished his stretches for the day. "We're going to finish this session off with an upper body massage."

Ollie smiled with relief and let out an appreciate groan. "That sounds incredible. I didn't know that was part of the treatment, but I'm not going to argue."

"Why do you think all of my patients love me so much?" she replied, taking Ollie's arm and helping him walk toward the massage table that was in the far corner of the room. He was getting stronger every day. Soon, he wouldn't need her help. "Also, massage helps you to relax which is good for promoting healing. The human body is an interconnected machine. Right now, you're compensating for your knee with every other muscle in your body. So we're going to give all of those muscles a little love so that they can keep up the good work."

"Again, you aren't going to get any argument from me, Doc."

They approached the massage table and Elsie turned to face Oliver. "Go ahead and take off your shirt and lay down face first on the table."

Oliver didn't hesitate. He grabbed the bottom of his t-shirt and peeled it up over his head. Elsie's eyes widened as soon as she saw his muscular torso. She looked away quickly, though. She didn't want to stare, or else she might get caught drooling.

Oh my God, she thought, as Oliver crawled onto the table. She caught another glance of him before he laid down. *This man is physically flawless,* she thought, swallowing down her deepest urges.

He was muscular, tan, and his skin was shiny with sweat. He was sex on legs. She'd known he was in good shape, but never imagined he looked *this* good. In an effort to distract herself, she began digging through her bag to get her massage oil.

You're a professional, Elsie, she thought to herself. *It's work. Don't enjoy this too much.*

"Comfy?" she asked, drawing in a breath to try to calm herself down a bit.

Oliver grunted an affirmative sound. Elsie approached him and dribbled a bit of the massage oil onto his back, then slowly rubbed it in. It only took a few moments to realize how tense his shoulders were, so she started her massage there.

It was hard for her not to enjoy the firmness of his muscles underneath her fingers. There was a reason he had all those sponsorships and ad campaigns selling things to women. He was incredibly sexy. Once again, she had to remind herself that he was a patient and that she couldn't allow herself to feel attracted to him.

But can I really help it? She thought. *He's an attractive man. I'm allowed to think so, right? As long as I don't act on it, I can appreciate it, just as long as I stay professional.*

Oliver lifted his head and turned to face her, his eyes squinting as the light hit them. "What did you say, Elsie?"

She froze, feeling her heart skip a beat.

Did I say that out loud? She asked herself. *Oh God, please tell me that I didn't.*

"Nothing," she said, stuttering as she found her voice. "You're just really tense. Take a deep breath in and try to relax your muscles."

Ollie put his face back down and let out a long breath. Elsie felt the difference in his muscles immediately. It seemed that he knew his body really well.

He must really know how to handle himself, she thought, but then stopped herself from going any further with that thought.

Her mind was heading in an unprofessional direction again, so she looked around for something that would pull her back into the right state of mind. She noticed Oliver's hair and for the first time saw that his roots were coming in. She remembered his beautiful dark hair from the search pictures.

"What are you planning on doing with your hair?" she asked.

His muscles tensed instantly. "Why do you ask?"

"Because your roots are coming in," she said gently. "Why did you dye it?"

"So I won't be recognized as easily." Oliver lifted a hand to touch his hair, as if his fingers could see the color shift. "I'll have to tell Nikki to fix it. She's back in California, so it'll be a little while before I can get it dyed again."

Without even thinking about it, Elsie said, "I can help you fix it if you want."

Crap, talk about being unprofessional, she thought, as soon as the words came out of her mouth.

Oliver lifted his head from the table and looked up at her. "Really?"

Elsie shrugged. "My mom was a hair dresser. I've picked up a few techniques over the years."

Ollie brought his face back down once more and relaxed. "You know, that would be great, actually. Nikki really shouldn't have to worry about my hair anyway."

Elsie found a big knot in Oliver's right shoulder. She focused the pressure there, applying her weight to try to work it out. As she did, she hoped that he'd keep on talking because it seemed to help distract her from his amazing body. For some reason, though, she didn't really want him to keep talking about Nikki and she wasn't sure exactly why.

"So, what does your mom do?" Elsie asked. "You've told me a lot about your brother, but nothing about your mom."

Ollie chuckled and Elsie could feel it vibrate through her hands. "She's supposed to be retired, but she's one of those people who refuses to take it easy. So she spends most of her time volunteering with a cancer foundation near where she lives."

Elsie nodded. She wasn't too surprised, given the story of his brother. If anything like that had ever happened to one of her sister's kids, she would have volunteered at a cancer foundation too.

"What did your mom do while you were growing up?" she asked.

"Everything," Ollie stated, with no hesitation. "She did everything. She was a single mom with two sons. It wasn't uncommon for her to work three jobs, just to keep my brother and me fed and our health insurance paid up."

"Wow, she sounds like a strong woman," Elsie said, easing her weight a little harder onto the knot in Ollie's shoulder.

"She's the strongest woman I've ever know," Ollie replied. He paused for a moment. "I think she'd like you."

Her hands stalled for a moment. The compliment made her heart flutter and her stomach go bubbly. "Really?"

"You listen the same way that she does," he said. "Even though she was working all the time while we were growing up, she always made us kids feel like we were the center of her world. You do that too."

Elsie felt her face heat. She knew she was blushing, and felt grateful that Ollie couldn't see it. He had given her a high compliment, though. One that she wasn't expecting.

"Thank you," she finally said.

Oliver's phone rang. The ringtone was one of her favorite country songs, which made Elsie smile. He slowly raised his head and reached into his pocket to the pull out the phone. "I need to take this call. It's Coach. Can we finish this massage up later?"

"Of course," she said, taking a step back to grab a towel from her bag. "I was almost done anyway."

She wiped the oil from her hands with the towel, as Oliver sat up on the massage table. Despite her will power, she was unable to maintain focus on his face. Her eyes drifted downward. His abs called out to her. And his muscular pecs and the firm ridges of his shoulders.

Good lord, I can see the jagged edge of his serratus anterior as perfectly as if I was looking at a text book right now, she thought, as a warm tingling sensation filled her.

"My eyes are up here," Ollie joked.

Once again, Elsie felt as hot blood rushed to her cheeks from embarrassment.

"I, um, well," she stuttered. "Sorry."

Oliver just chuckled. Elsie spun around and put the oil back in her bag. By the time she turned back, Oliver had put a shirt on and she was grateful for it. He still looked like sex on a stick, but at least she could pretend to maintain some level of professional decorum.

"I'll see you soon, okay?" he said, as he lifted his phone to answer it.

"Sounds great," she replied, picking up her bag and clipboard. "Should I bring some hair dye for next time? Maybe some bleach to match your current shade?"

Oliver pondered for a moment. "That's probably best. I guess I'll stick with the blond for a little longer."

Elsie nodded, and Ollie's phone continued to ring. She didn't want to keep his coach waiting any longer.

"See you soon," she said, spinning around toward the door.

She left the house quickly, overwhelmed with embarrassment. He'd caught her checking him out and she'd never felt more flustered in her life because of it. Luckily, the air outside was frigid. It was good, because her face felt like it was practically on fire.

This is not how I'm supposed to feel about a patient, she thought, starting her car. *What is it about him that has me feeling this way?*

Elsie didn't understand. She'd seen hundreds of ripped, muscular men. She'd done thousands of massages and never once had anything like this happened to her. Never before had she found one of them so attractive, or had the desire to run her hands over them just to feel their strength underneath.

Makes me wonder what it would feel like to have him run his hands down me, she thought, as the naughty side of her mind chimed in.

"What am I thinking?" she whispered, backing down the driveway. "This is insane."

I'm a professional. I shouldn't even have an inkling of anything other than medical effectiveness while touching him, she thought to herself.

"Maybe it's nothing," she said. "Yeah, it's probably nothing."

Elsie did her best to justify her feelings. She told herself that Ollie was a good looking man and it was only natural for her to feel some kind of attraction toward him. Just because she was a medical professional, didn't mean that she had to be a robot.

She stepped on the gas as soon as she pulled onto the County Road, pointing her car in the direction of home. She decided to shake it off and let the feelings go for the time being.

It's just one day, she thought. *One event. Besides, it's not like he feels the same way about me. He's rich and famous and can have any girl he wants. I'd be kidding myself if I thought a guy like him would be interested in a small town farm girl like me. Especially one who is supposed to be a professional.*

She continued her drive home, hoping that these sexual feelings toward Oliver were just a phase that would soon pass.

I'll get past this, she thought. *I'm sure by the time the next session comes around, I'll have forgotten all about the way he made me feel when he was shirtless.*

She stepped a little harder on the gas as she remembered the way he'd felt under her fingers.

God, I hope so anyway.

Chapter Eight

Ollie

Outside, the wind was howling with a spring blizzard. The single-pane glass windows in the old farmhouse were showing their age, rattling to the cadence of the blizzard and sending icy air into the room. Oliver laid under the covers of his bed, wrapping himself like a burrito to stay warm. The furnace was on, but hardly did anything to take the edge off of the cold. The wind just sucked any heat right out of the house. It wasn't just the wind, though, that made the house feel cold.

This place is just too empty, he thought. *It needs some plants or pictures on the wall or something to make it feel like an actual home.*

The place felt more like a doctor's office than a house to Oliver. Especially at night. The medical equipment that was everywhere only added to this. Looming in every corner was at least one item that reminded him of why he was there in the first place. It actually felt kind of creepy being there all alone. It was like something out of a bad dream.

His stomach rumbled, loud enough so that he could actually hear it over the whistling wind outside.

"And of course now I'm hungry," he said, rubbing his belly and pouting.

He hadn't eaten much for lunch and now it was dinner time. But his knee was throbbing with the storm, and the pain medication hadn't kicked in yet. The last thing he felt like doing was getting up and trying to figure out something to cook in the kitchen. But he had to eat. Elsie had made that clear to him and he took her advice very seriously.

Elsie, he thought. *Maybe I should call her up and see if she'd come over. She mentioned that Thai Chili Pizza. And just today, she talked about helping me bleach my hair.*

Just the idea of seeing her again made him feel a little better. He was admittedly lonely and Elsie's company would have put his mind at ease. He reached over to the nightstand and grabbed his cell phone. He hesitated for a moment, wondering if he should really be calling her for anything that wasn't medical related.

My mental health has to be taken care of too, right? He thought. *I think I can spin this as medically related. At least enough so that it fits into her contract.*

With that, he opened up his contact list on his phone. He was about to hit Elsie's number, when Nikki called. The phone rang loudly and startled him, causing him to nearly drop it.

"Jesus," he whispered, feeling his heart beat in his chest. "Scared the crap out of me."

It reminded him of when he and Nikki were dating. She'd always manage to call at the worst times. It was like a gift of hers, an innate ability to interrupt things. The phone continued to ring in his hand and he looked at the screen, wondering if he should even answer.

It's late, so I doubt she's calling for business reasons, he thought. *She's going crazy, I think. I don't know if she fully understands that we aren't together any more. If she wasn't the best in the business, I'd let her go, but I can't. I guess I should answer.*

"Screw it," he whispered, before answering the call. "Hello?"

"Hey, Ollie," Nikki said, sounding more chipper than the last time they spoke.

"Hi," he said, sinking into the pillows. "What's up?"

"You doing okay?" she asked.

"I'm fine," he replied. "Just relaxing. What about you? You don't usually call this late."

"I was just sitting here thinking about you," she replied. "Remember when we took that trip to Paris?"

"Yes, of course I remember," he said, unsure why she was bringing it up. "What made you think about that?"

"I started going through old pictures. I found a few of you and I. They were the ones that were taken in front of the Eiffel Tower," she said.

Oliver recalled the trip, which they had taken about a year before. He had surprised her with it, back when Nikki was his world and he'd do anything in his power to make her happy. He figured a trip to Paris would do the trick, and it did. For the most part anyway. He spent an insane amount of money on her, bought her expensive dresses and purses, and even paid for a private tour of the Eiffel Tower.

I guess we really had chemistry back then, he thought. *Too much chemistry, really.*

Nikki and Oliver had the volatile kind of chemistry. The kind that blows up and leaves the earth scorched. It had made for a passionate love life, but nothing comes without a price. And that price was usually paid in emotionally charged arguments. It hadn't been long before they mutually decided to end it and just maintain a business relationship.

"That was a pretty fun trip," Ollie admitted. He frowned as he remembered the end of the trip. "Everything except the part where you threw a glass at my head on the way home. You remember that? You thought I was going to propose to you and I didn't. I still don't think that justified having a wine glass shattered against my skull."

"We were in Paris, Oliver," she said, her voice harsh. "You'd taken me to the City of Love as a surprise. What was I supposed to think?"

"That we'd only been dating for two months," he said, shaking his head. "It was a little too soon for marriage."

Looking back, Ollie realized that those two months had been some of the longest months in his entire life.

Being with Nikki had been exhausting. It was just too much effort to be her boyfriend. When they weren't talking business or making love, they were fighting. It was so much different than his interactions with Elsie. The complete opposite, really.

At least my conversations with Elsie are relaxing and fun, he thought. *I'm actually sad when she leaves to go home. With Nikki, it had always been a relief. I wish I was talking to Elsie right now instead.*

"I guess you're right, Ollie," Nikki said, her tone going sweet and soft. "You're always right. Two months of dating might have been a little soon to expect a proposal. I don't know what I was thinking when I hoped that the man I loved would want to be with me forever."

He cringed, as Nikki attempted to lay a guilt trip on him. There was nothing he hated more than the passive aggressive guilt that she used to manipulate him. The thing he hated most about it was that it actually sometimes worked. He felt like banging his head against the wall and he might have, if he'd been able to walk that far. For a moment, he considered hanging up on her but knew that it wouldn't do any good. She'd just call back again.

"Nikki, is this why you called? To try to make me feel bad?" Ollie asked. "I don't need this right now. I was just about to watch some TV and try to relax. I had a long day of physical therapy and I'm exhausted. If I can't help you with anything that's business related right now, then I need to go."

"Oh, we're only doing business now, huh?" she asked, her words filled with sarcasm. "And here I was, thinking we were friends."

Anger and annoyance bubbled up into Oliver's gut. She was pushing his buttons, just like she used to. She wanted a response from him. She wanted to get him mad. But he didn't give her that. Instead, he bit his tongue.

"What do you want Nikki?" he asked as gently as possible. "I'm not feeling very well right now."

"I was talking with Coach," Nikki said, forced to change the subject when her guilt trip didn't pan out as expected. "He thinks that once you reach the twelve week mark, and once a week physical therapy sessions, then you should definitely come back home. I've already lined up several functions. Your team will be waiting for you."

Oliver rolled his eyes. Just the thought of attending those functions and getting bombarded with crazed fans made him exhausted. But if she'd already booked them, then there really wasn't too much that he could do about it.

"Anything else, Nikki?" he asked, his eyes half closed.

"Yes, actually," she said. "I want you to change your physical therapist. I've already done the research and found a great one. His name is James Weaver. According to his website, he was able to get a professional football player back up to playing speed in just nine months. And that player had an injury that was worse than yours. I'm sure that with a little financial incentive, I can get him to go out to Iowa and work with you. You wouldn't even have to move from where you are now."

Oliver sat up in the bed, leaning against the headboard. "Wait a damn minute, Nikki. You want me to fire my current therapist, who is doing a really great job, on the hope that this James Weaver would want to fly to Iowa for a PT job?"

"Yes," she said, bold through every word. "I guess that is what I'm proposing."

"Why?" Ollie asked, trying to keep his anger in check.

"To be honest, I like that he's a man," she replied. "You should have men around you, not women. I'm sure this Elsie is a fine therapist, but I question if she's capable of giving you the treatment that you need. I just wonder if she's really up to the task."

"You're the one that picked her out," Ollie said, bringing his hand to his forehead in frustration. "You're the one that thought she would be perfect for this. She's a physical therapist with sports medicine training, who has experience working with patients who have undergone an ACL repair. She also didn't know who I was and was far enough out of the public eye for me to be able to handle this recovery effectively. Elsie checked all of those boxes perfectly and now you're changing your mind?"

"I just..." Nikki began.

Oliver heard a sob come from the other end of the line. Nikki was crying, clearly upset about the connection that was growing between Ollie and his PT.

"You just *what*, Nikki?" he asked.

"I'm just worried that she could be using you. That's all," she said between sniffles. "You talk about her all the time now. Something about the situation just gives me a bad feeling. I guess I don't trust her as much as I did when she interviewed."

Oliver squeezed the bridge of his nose with his fingers, in an attempt to stop the oncoming headache. "Nikki, I talk about her all the time because physical therapy is my life right now. She's the only person I see. My whole world has become this stupid knee and she's helping me fix it. So in that way, yes, she has basically become my whole world."

"You're sleeping with her, aren't you?" Nikki asked, her tone even more accusatory than usual.

"Good grief. No. I'm not sleeping with her," he explained. "When I say she's my whole world, it's just an expression. She's currently a major part of my life and the majority of my time is with her. That's all I meant. Anyway, I'm tired and my knee is killing me. I need to take some more pain medication and try to figure out something to eat. Can we do this another time?"

"You *are* sleeping with her," she said, her voice lowering. "Oh, my God. I can't believe this."

Ollie sighed. "I swear to you that my relationship with Elsie is completely professional."

"What? Like ours was?" Nikki asked.

Oliver took a deep breath. He was getting legitimately angry now and was sick and tired of Nikki pushing his buttons. "Even if I *was* sleeping with her, which I'm *not*, it really wouldn't be any of your business. Regardless, I really want to get off the phone now."

He heard Nikki sniffle on the other end of the line.

"Okay, I should let you go," she said, her voice quavering with crocodile tears. "I'm sorry, Ollie. I've had a couple of glasses of wine tonight and I guess my jealousy got the best of me. You know that I really care about you, though, right? I'm just looking out for you."

"I know, Nikki," Oliver said, his heart softening a little. "And I appreciate it."

Despite their past, Nikki was still his friend and he did care about her feelings. He just didn't want to feel controlled by her any more.

"I'm really kind of embarrassed, now that I've said all of this," Nikki said, between sniffles. "Again, I'm sorry. I hope you don't mind if I just hang up right now. Can we just pretend this phone call never happened?"

"Sure, of course," he replied. "Water under the bridge."

"Thank you, Ollie. You're the best," Nikki said, with a sigh. "I'm sorry to put all this on you while you're trying to heal."

"It's fine," he said, suddenly extremely tired. "Seriously, Nikki. It's not a big deal. Go to bed. You'll feel better in the morning."

"Okay. Goodnight, Ollie."

"Goodnight, Nikki."

Oliver stared blankly at the phone after hanging up. He thought he had been exhausted before that phone call, but the conversation with Nikki had sapped any energy reserves he had left. Even though he was still hungry, the only thing he felt like doing was curling up in his bed and watching TV. He didn't even want Elsie to pay him a visit any more, since he was in such a crummy mood now.

Maybe I'll call her tomorrow and she can come over to do my hair, he thought. It was a nice thought.

With the wind still howling outside, Oliver pulled the blankets over his head. He knew that sleep wasn't going to come visit him any time soon, but decided he might as well try to get some rest.

Chapter Nine

Elsie

The second snow storm that week was coming in fast as Elsie drove down the county road, away from Oliver's house. The lights of her small town hovered in the distance, but were barely visible through the weather.

Warm weather can't come soon enough, she thought. *I'm tired of storm after storm. I'd hoped the one last week was the end, but they just keep coming.*

It was the end of March but there still hadn't been any real signs of spring yet. The days were getting longer, but even so, it was already almost dark out and only dinner time. She couldn't wait until summer, when the sun didn't go down until nine o'clock and she could sleep with her bedroom window open.

But the thought of the changing seasons was a double-edged sword for Elsie. Because despite all of the things she loved about spring and summer, the passing of winter also meant that her time with Oliver was quickly running out. It wouldn't be long before he'd be recovered and moving back to California. She was really enjoying the physical therapy sessions with him and wasn't looking forward to their end. She didn't want to go back to the same old patients and non-sports related injuries. She wanted to work with Ollie forever.

When she got to the end of the county road, she slid to a halt at the stop sign. Then she turned right, pointing her car down the main street that ran through the center of town. It only took a few minutes of driving before she pulled up to a small building, which sat lonely at the end of the block. It's dark cedar siding looked white, as drifts of snow piled up all around it. Elsie parked the car in the back and then made her way inside.

The building, which Elsie considered both her home and office, was owned by her uncle. On the bottom floor was the physical therapy clinic that she ran. The upper floor had a small apartment, which her uncle allowed her to live in rent-free. It was a decent place, but very small. In fact, it was smaller than the apartment that she'd lived in during college. But it was a place to stay and it was nice being so close to her clinic. The commute time of thirty seconds was something that never got old.

Grumbling about the cold and dark, Elsie made her way upstairs and into her apartment. She threw her keys into a bowl by the front door, before hanging up her coat. Even though her place was small, she'd made a distinct effort to make it a space where she enjoyed spending time. She'd repainted the kitchen from plain white to a cheery yellow and the living room to a soothing beige. She'd even updated the tile in the bathroom, changing it from the 1940's pink into a more respectable classy gray. All in all, she was happy with the place, but did look forward to a time when she could afford a full-sized house of her own.

She let out a yawn as she kicked off her shoes and made her way into the living room. As soon as she approached the couch, she plopped down on it, letting the overstuffed cushions pull her in.

I'm beat, she thought. *I could fall asleep right here if I'm not careful.*

Even though Ollie was her only real patient for the moment, she still had a lot on her plate. She still had to run the clinic, and keep her regular patients taken care off. It definitely meant extra hours and some odd work days, but it was working out okay. Still, she felt like she was juggling a lot and hardly had any time to just relax. Now that she was seated in a comfortable position, relaxing suddenly felt like it was going to happen whether she liked it or not.

As she kicked her feet up on the coffee table, she thought about everything that had brought her to that point in life. From the time she was young, it was like her future had been written. Her Uncle Frank had been a physical therapist for his entire career. All throughout high school, Elsie had spent all of her afternoons at his office, just watching him treat the locals.

She loved everything about it. It seemed like magic to her. A patient would walk in holding their lower back in pain and then after a few sessions with Frank, it was like they were a different person. They were no longer in pain and could walk upright without any problem. He was a magician and she wanted to be just like him.

So when high school was over and college came around, the choice of which direction to go was simple. She decided to become a physical therapist just like her uncle. She went to a school about a hundred miles away from home, where she earned her degree in sports medicine before getting accepted into grad school for physical therapy. She'd worked her butt off in DPT school, but loved every minute of it.

After graduation, she'd been accepted into an amazing sports therapy residency. Two years flew by as she absorbed everything like a sponge. She got to work with professional and collegiate level athletes, some with very acute injuries. Elsie had landed her dream job.

But that all changed a few months later when Elsie's Aunt June passed away. Her aunt, Frank's wife, had been both the receptionist and assistant for his PT practice in Iowa. With June gone, Frank just couldn't run the place like he used to. Plus, he became deeply depressed about the loss of his wife. He didn't seem to care as much about doing physical therapy any more.

It was at his wife's funeral where he basically gave the practice to Elsie. He told her that he didn't want it any more, that it was something he and June had built together. There were too many memories there and it hurt him to be in the office. He said he wanted Elsie to have it, because he thought that she'd be able to take care of it the way June would want.

The offer had put Elsie at a crossroads. She was working the job of her dreams, but the clinic was where she grew up and it belonged to her family. In the end, she decided to move back home and take over Frank's practice. It seemed like the right move, especially since it helped her family. Her family meant more to her than any job. Plus, there were some big perks about moving back home. Her new patients were all her friends and she got the chance to help the community that she'd grown up with. Nobody stepped into her clinic whose first name she didn't already know. It made her feel like she was really part of something important.

However, working with aging farmers and the elderly was quite a bit different than working with the high-end athletes that she was used to. It took a lot more patience and a much gentler touch. It wasn't necessarily better or worse, just a different kind of work.

When she started working with Ollie, she was quickly reminded of the kind of physical therapy that she was truly passionate about. The need to get him up to peak physical condition inspired and motivated her. Working with Oliver made her feel almost like she'd landed her dream job once again.

"Oh, Oliver," she whispered, clicking on the TV. "What am I going to do about you?"

Just thinking about him put a smile on her face. It always did. She got excited on every one of her drives over to the farm house, knowing that she was going to get to spend a couple of hours with him. And each session just seemed to be even better than the one before. They could talk about anything it seemed. She loved chatting with him about his brother and mom and she enjoyed telling him all about her niece and nephews.

She chuckled at one of the stories he'd shared with her that day. He'd said that his favorite memory as a kid was going to the fair with his little brother. His mom had given them enough money to buy the ride pass, which gave them unlimited access to every single ride in the park for the entire day. Apparently, Oliver and Michael had made it their mission to get the most value for their money. They rode every ride at least four times and only stopped when they both puked.

The TV in front of her was showing some game show. She wasn't really watching it, but it was good background noise. When the show ended and the news came on, she decided it was a good time to muster up some motivation and make some food. She hadn't eaten much all day and was starving. The first thing that came to mind was a frozen pot pie that was in the back of her freezer. It was easy, quick and would satisfy the craving for something that at least gave the illusion of "healthy".

She peeled herself off of the couch and went to the kitchen, ready to indulge. But for some reason, as soon as she picked up the pot pie, she thought of Ollie.

Ollie wouldn't eat something like this, she thought. *No way. He's always talking about sticking to his diet. I know he's serious about it, too. His perfect physique doesn't lie.*

"Screw it," she said, opening the box and tossing the pot pie into the microwave. She was hungry.

Elsie realized that she should be more careful about what she ate. She always lectured her patients about eating healthy and here she was, about to stuff her face with what might as well have been a bowl full of sodium. She really didn't want to be a hypocrite, but also really didn't want to cook anything more complicated than a five-minute microwave nuke. So frozen pot pie it was.

Oliver would probably give me a hard time if he knew what I was about to eat, she thought, with a smirk. *He'd probably make the frowny face that he makes whenever I tell him to do ten more reps.*

The frowny face of Oliver's was different than his concentration face. And was also different than his happy face, which was the one that Elsie liked best. That was the one he expressed whenever he talked about his younger brother.

Before the microwave had even counted down a full minute, her cell phone rang in the other room. She walked over and picked it up off of the coffee table. Her mom's picture filled the screen and Elsie's eyes lit up when she saw it. She was always happy to have a chat with her mother, especially since it didn't happen as often as it used to.

"What's up, Mom? How are you?" Elsie said, walking back to the kitchen to see how the meal was coming along in the microwave.

"Hey, Elsie. I didn't expect you to pick up," her mom said, sniffling. "I was kind of hoping I'd get your voicemail."

It was clear that her mother had been crying. A burst of anxiety barreled into Elsie's gut.

"What do you mean, Mom?" Elsie asked. "What's going on?"

Her mother paused for a second and Elsie listened as she let out a slow breath. "It's your uncle."

"Uncle Frank?" Elsie said. Immediately, her heart began to thud quickly in her chest and her stomach turned to lead. "What happened?"

"You know how he's been tired lately?" her Mom asked.

"I guess so," Elsie replied, her hands nervously trembling as she held the phone. "But I thought he was just fighting some sort of virus or something. That was just the last week or so, though."

"Apparently, he hasn't been feeling well for quite some time," her mother replied. "In fact, for the last couple of months he's been dizzy and dealing with chronic headaches."

Elsie's brain was already going through every medical possibility she could think of and none of them were good.

"Mom, what happened? Just tell me what's going on with him," Elsie said, desperately.

"Uncle Frank had a fall today," she said, choosing her words carefully. "He was taking a walk around the park and got dizzy. He tried walking to the park bench to sit down, but he didn't make it. He collapsed and hit his head on the concrete."

"Oh my God," Elsie whispered. "Is he okay?"

"It knocked him out. He's fine now," her mom replied quickly. "Just a little out of it."

"What did the doctor's say?" Elsie asked, knowing that the fall wasn't the end of the story. Healthy men didn't just fall for no reason. "Do they know why he fell?"

Her mom sobbed and Elsie's heart sank. She knew that there was bad news coming her direction, but had no clue how to brace herself for it. Frank had been a constant and steady presence in her life. As far back as her memories went, he was there. In fact, to Elsie, he was a second father. He never had his own children, so Elsie was the closest thing he had.

"They did an MRI," her mom said, speaking the words through choked tears. "They found a brain tumor, Elsie. It doesn't look good."

Elsie heard the words, but it didn't feel real. It was almost as if she'd just heard it on TV or the radio. It was like her brain wouldn't let her absorb the reality completely. Her world went gray. She didn't remember sitting down, but the next thing she knew, she was seated on the kitchen floor with her back against the wall. Her cell phone was held limply in her hand. It now weighed a million pounds and took all her strength to hold it.

Memories flashed through her mind; images of her youth and time spent with her uncle. Countless hours of playing with him and learning all about life through his experience. She thought about his miraculous ability to heal patients. She remembered all of the family picnics and the way Frank would make everyone laugh until they cried. The Christmases, the birthdays. It came rushing back in one giant wave. Flickering images flashed across her vision, each one sending another burst of emotion inside of her, causing her heart to ache.

"Elsie, are you still there?" her mom spoke into the phone. But her words were distant. It sounded like when she was under the water at a swimming pool, but still hearing the kids laughing and playing on the surface.

"Yeah, Mom, I'm here," Elsie finally responded, wiping tears away from her eyes with the back of her hand. "Sorry. I'm just trying to process this. So what are the doctors saying now? What do they think should be the next move for Uncle Frank?"

"They haven't said anything yet. They're still looking at scans and need to run more tests before any decisions can be made," she said, taking a steadying breath. "I'm guessing they'll consider surgery, along with chemo and radiation. But you know how Frank would feel about all of that. I doubt he'd want any part of it."

Elsie stood up from the floor and walked toward the door, grabbing her purse on the way. "I'm coming to the hospital."

"No, Elsie, please don't. Frank doesn't even know that I've called you. In fact, he had asked me not to. He didn't want to worry you." The sadness in her mother's voice mimicked what Elsie felt in her heart. "I wasn't going to call, but you deserve to know what's going on. You're like a daughter to Frank. You and I are all the family that he has left."

"Mom, I need to do *something*," Elsie said. "I can't just sit around and pace my apartment. I want to be there. I want to help."

"I know, darling," her mom said as Elsie leaned against the wall next to her front door. "But there's no need to come here right now. Frank is sleeping right now anyway, so you wouldn't even get to talk to him. All you'll do here is drink bad coffee, read outdated magazines and pace the halls. I'm at the hospital now and I'm not going anywhere, so you don't have to worry. Frank won't be alone."

"What about you, Mom? I don't want you there all by yourself."

"Your father is here," her mom replied. "I'm not by myself."

"Mom..." Elsie sighed. She closed her eyes, feeling tears push out and down her cheeks.

"I'm serious, Elsie. Just stay home."

"Why did you call me if you didn't want me to come?" Elsie asked, anger starting to choke her with the tears.

"I'm actually not really sure. I think I just needed to tell someone." Her mother let out a long, unhappy sigh. "It feels more like a nightmare than reality. I'm sorry, Elsie. I didn't mean to burden you with all of this, but I couldn't keep it inside."

"It's okay, Mom. I understand," Elsie said, slowly walking back to her living room. The anger was giving way to bleakness. "It's a lot to process."

They were both silent for a moment. Elsie could hear the background noise of the hospital coming from her mother's end of the line. The familiar beeps of machines masked by the chatter of nurses and doctors. She wished she could be there, but didn't want to defy her mother or uncle's wishes.

"Can I come by the hospital tomorrow?" Elsie asked, plopping down onto her couch. "Please? I know that Uncle Frank didn't want me to know about all this, but I'm positive he'd like to see me. And I want to see him. He needs my support."

"Yes, tomorrow would be fine," Mom said. "That will give Frank a chance to get some rest. And you're right, I think he'd like to see you. I'd like it, too. Just not tonight."

"Everything is going to be okay," Elsie said automatically, though in her gut she didn't know if she even believed that herself. "Uncle Frank is one of the strongest people I know. If anybody can beat this, it's him."

"See, I knew there was a reason I called you," her mom said, a small smile coming into her voice. "I'm going to go downstairs to the cafeteria and get your father and I some food now. But I'll see you tomorrow, okay?"

"Okay. I love you, Mom."

"Love you, too, sweetie."

Elsie hung up and dropped the phone beside her on the couch cushion. All at once, every ounce of emotion that she'd been holding back while talking to her mom poured out of her. Tears streamed down her face. She sobbed harder than she'd remembered ever sobbing in her life. It was an ugly cry. A gut-wrenching, unable to breathe, whole-body bawling type of cry.

She wasn't sure how long it went on, but after a while, no more tears came out. She felt wrung out like a sponge. Her eyes were puffy and her stomach ached. She felt like curling up into a ball on the floor and going to sleep, but her Uncle's smile continued to pop up in her mind.

This just doesn't make sense. This isn't fair, she thought. *Frank has always been so strong. Larger than life strong. Superman.*

The idea that her Uncle Frank was sick with something that was potentially terminal just didn't add up in Elsie's mind. It was like saying that the sky was made out of blueberries or that grass grew on hiccups. It didn't make any sense.

The microwave beeped in the kitchen, reminding Elsie that her meal was ready. She had no idea how long the damn thing had been beeping at her to come and take her food out. She got up and went to the kitchen. The food inside the microwave was now lukewarm and shriveled. What had once sounded like an appetizing choice, now looked beyond disgusting.

"I'm not eating this crap," she said, angrily throwing the pot pie into the trash. She didn't even care that it was her dinner that she'd just tossed out.

However, her hatred toward the pot pie didn't stop her stomach from rumbling. She had to eat, but what she needed was real food. Something that would not only ease her hunger, but also ease the pain in her heart. What she needed was comfort food.

Pizza, she thought. *I'm getting pizza.*

Elsie went back to the living room to pick up her phone when an idea hit her out of nowhere. She knew that hanging out by herself all night would have been depressing beyond belief. She would have spent the entire evening just thinking about her Uncle and worrying herself sick. She needed more than just comfort food to get her through the night. She also needed companionship. And there was one person who she enjoyed talking to more than anyone else.

Ollie likes pizza, she thought, as the corner of her lip managed to force itself into a small smile. *Maybe I should get that Thai chili pizza and surprise him with it.*

Before she could even complete the thought, she had stepped into her shoes and slipped her jacket back on.

Yes, that's what's happening, she thought. *Some good pizza with a good friend. That will help ease my worries. Or at least distract me from them for a little while.*

***

The bell on the front door of the pizza shop rang out as Elsie stepped inside. In just the short walk between her car and the door, she'd managed to gather a layer of snow on her jacket and hair, so when she stepped into the warmth of the building, it was a very welcoming invitation.

"An extra large Thai chili pizza, please," she said to the teenage boy working behind the counter. She knew exactly what she wanted before coming in, so she didn't have to even glance at the menu.

With a nod, the pizza kid went to work. Meanwhile, Elsie took a seat near the back of the store to wait. It then occurred to her that she hadn't even checked with Ollie as to whether or not he was hungry, or if he even wanted her to come over at all.

Darn it. I should have asked him, she criticized herself. *What if he doesn't want pizza, or what if he has already eaten?*

She felt like a total idiot, but couldn't be too hard on herself. Given her emotional state after hearing the news about her Uncle's diagnosis, it was amazing she'd managed to remember how to drive her car.

Elsie glanced over, watching as the kid finished putting the toppings on the pizza before throwing it in the oven. It was too late to cancel the order now. One way or another, she was going to walk out of there with an extra large pizza and there was no way that she could eat that all by herself.

Well, I guess I could. But I really shouldn't, she thought. *No need to add a heart attack and a stomach ache onto my already horrible evening.*

She pulled out her phone to text Ollie. She suddenly felt a little nervous, almost giddy, about texting him. In all of their interactions over the previous few weeks, this would be the first meet up that had nothing to do with his physical treatment. Elsie was about to step over that line between patient and friend. There was a moment of hesitation. In the back of her mind, she knew that there would be no going back once that line was crossed.

Elsie wrote out a short text to Ollie three times before finally hitting send. The message simply read: "Want some pizza?" She bit her lip as she pressed send.

Hopefully he's hungry, she thought. *I really don't want to have to bring this monstrosity of a pizza home with me. I won't have room in my fridge. I really hope he says yes. And not just because I need help eating the pizza. I also want to see him. I need someone to talk to.*

The pizza shop kid pulled the massive pizza out of the oven and boxed it up, before calling Elsie's name. She walked up and paid, then balanced the box with both hands, using her backside to push the exit door open.

"This thing is heavy," she whispered, tromping through the snow to her car.

But God, it smells amazing, she thought.

Steam rose out of the pizza box as she got into the driver's seat and started up the engine. She hadn't even had a chance to put the car in reverse before her phone chimed. It was a text response from Ollie that said, "Pizza sounds great".

Elsie read the message and relief flooded through her. Not only did she have someone to help her finish the pizza now, but she also didn't have to spend the evening by herself.

"Be there in fifteen minutes." Elsie replied in text.

Without even realizing it, the start of a smile began to show on her face. She pulled out of the parking lot and pointed her car into the direction of Ollie's farmhouse. For a fleeting moment, her worries fizzled out of her mind and her heart ached just a little less. She wasn't even with him yet, but Oliver was making her feel better already.

Chapter Ten

Ollie

With a newfound energy, Oliver pushed the comforter off of him and swung his legs over the side of the bed. His knee was throbbing, but his excitement of seeing Elsie helped the pain to fade. The text that he had just received from his physical trainer was completely unexpected, but very welcomed. Not only was he hungry and unable to sleep, but he was also admittedly lonely. A visit with her was the thing he needed most and it was as though she had read his mind with her offer.

I probably shouldn't be eating pizza, but really, who cares? He thought. *I can cheat one meal, especially if it means I get to see Elsie.*

No longer having to use his crutches, Oliver hobbled out to the living room and unlocked the front door. Then he took a seat on the couch to wait for Elsie. Elevating his leg on the coffee table seemed to help the pain, but only slightly. He didn't care, though. He knew that Elsie would make him feel better. Maybe he could talk her into giving him one of those amazing knee massages to help ease the pain.

While Ollie waited, he couldn't get the conversation he had had with Nikki the other night out of his mind. He was still riled up over it. He couldn't believe that she wanted to fire Elsie and for no other reason than that she happened to be female. The idea that Nikki was letting her jealousy infiltrate his business was where he had to draw the line.

Nikki needs to be worried about the business, and only the business, he thought. *Otherwise, I'm going to have to figure out a way to let her go. I can't risk everything I've worked for, just because of an old fling. And if she thinks I'm ever going to get back together with her, she's wrong. That will never happen. Never.*

His thoughts were interrupted when his doorbell rang. Slowly, he pushed himself back to a standing position and hobbled to the door. He could have just called Elsie in, but wanted to show her how much better he was getting physically. When he opened the door, he was greeted by a blast of icy air and a warm smile from the most beautiful woman he knew.

"Pizza delivery!" Elsie said, balancing the giant box in her hands.

It smelled amazing and Ollie's mouth watered just thinking about how good it was going to taste.

"Come in, come in," he said. "It's freezing out there."

The cold air fought him as he closed the door behind her. The storm was getting worse and the snow was quickly piling up on the deck.

"Here, let me get that," Ollie said, taking the pizza out of Elsie's hands.

"Just hold it for a second while I take my jacket off," she said.

He watched her remove her coat and his eyes drifted downward. She was wearing a soft white sweater with dark jeans and looked incredible. It was different than seeing her in scrubs. It was real, not medical.

Whoa, he thought. *She looks great. I could definitely get used to seeing her like this.*

"You look really good," he said, flashing a smile. "I was starting to wonder if you only had scrubs in your closet."

She laughed, taking the pizza back. "Yeah, it's not often I get to wear something normal. So I take the opportunity whenever it presents itself."

"How do you feel about eating here in the living room?" he asked. "I'd like to be able to elevate my foot on the coffee table. It makes my knee feel a little better."

"Yeah, of course," she replied, as she set the pizza on the end table next to the couch. "We can definitely eat out here. We aren't trying to be fancy. We're eating pizza, after all."

"Okay, great," he said, taking a few limping steps toward the kitchen. "Let me just grab some plates. I'll be right back."

"No, no, no," Elsie replied, leading Ollie to the couch. "You sit down. I can get the plates if you tell me where they are."

He plopped down on the couch, relived to have the weight off of his knee. "The plates are in the upper cabinet to the right of the sink."

She nodded and then disappeared into the kitchen. When she returned, she had two cans of ginger ale and two plates with her. She set everything down onto the coffee table and took a seat next to Oliver.

"Thanks for agreeing to meet up," she said, pausing to bite her lower lip. "I realize that it was kind of short notice."

"I appreciate the company." Oliver turned to face her as he spoke. "I'll admit, though, that I was surprised to hear from you. This will be the first time we've ever gotten together and not done something that involved my injury. In fact, I'm pretty sure this is the only time we've ever spent in the living room. All of your other visits consist of us being in the gym while you torture me for hours."

"I figured a break from the torture would be a nice change," she said, pushing her dark hair over her ear. "Are you hungry?"

"Starving," he said.

Elsie put a slice of the pizza on each plate and handed one to Oliver. The smell was incredible and reminded him of his favorite Thai restaurant in California.

"This looks amazing." He was practically drooling and his stomach rumbled louder than ever. "I didn't have the energy to make dinner tonight, so this couldn't be more perfect."

"I didn't feel like making dinner either," she said. "It was kind of a weird night for me."

She paused, the pizza hovering uneaten in front of her.

"Are you okay?" Oliver asked, halting the pizza just in front of his mouth.

Elsie fidgeted for a second. "I wasn't sure you'd want me to come over and I wasn't even sure I wanted to ask. I was afraid that I'd be intruding."

"Intruding?" Oliver asked, shaking his head. "Are you kidding me? I love your company. If you hadn't come over, I'd still be tossing and turning in bed."

He took a bite of the pizza and moaned approvingly. It was seriously the best pizza he had ever tasted.

"This is so good," he said. "You weren't kidding about this."

"Told you," she replied, finally taking a bite of her own slice.

Oliver gobbled up his piece and then had seconds. Elsie did the same thing. They ate in silence, both of them too hungry to think about anything else but the food. Once they were done, they set the plates to the side and relaxed on the couch.

"You said that you had a weird night," Oliver said, bringing his leg on top of the coffee table. "Is everything okay?"

Elsie sighed and looked down at the ground. "A lot going on. I thought I'd feel like talking about it, but I think I'd rather just hang out."

"That's pretty vague," he told her, giving her a pointed look. "That makes me assume the worst possible scenario."

"I can tell you what happened, but I don't think I want to spend the whole night on the subject. It'll only make me sad," she said, with a depressed sigh.

"You don't need to share anything with me that you don't want to." Oliver could see the pain in her eyes and it made him stomach clench.

Elsie took a deep breath in. She tucked her hands up inside the sleeves of her sweater, balling the cuffs into into her palms. Her eyes focused on the floor. It took everything he had not to wrap his arms around her.

"My mom called me after I got home from our session earlier. She called with some pretty bad news," she replied. Her breath in faltered. "They found a tumor in my uncle's brain."

"Oh, my God, Elsie. I'm so sorry." Oliver sat up straighter, twisting his body to face her. "I know how close you are with him. You talk about him a lot."

She nodded. "Yeah, it's devastating for sure. But the doctors still have tests to run, so we don't know what the prognosis is yet. My fingers are crossed that it all works out okay."

It broke Oliver's heart to see the sadness in her face. She'd talked often about her uncle, making it clear just how important he was in Elsie's life. And a tumor meant cancer was a possibility. He knew all too much about cancer and the pain that it brought, not only to the patient but to their family.

"I'm so sorry," he repeated, bringing an arm around her shoulder and pulling her toward him.

She didn't resist at all, and instead, pressed her body against his. He could smell her hair and her rose shampoo as he held her close. It felt good to have her next to him and even better that she'd chosen him to confide in. He tried not to feel guilty at enjoying having a reason to hold her.

"He's the strongest person I know," she said, clearly trying to keep herself from crying. "I want to believe that he can get through this, but I just can't be sure. He's not young any more, you know?"

"If he's anything like how you've presented him in your stories, then I'm confident he'll fight it with everything he's got," Oliver assured her. "Plus, your uncle has one very important factor on his side that most people don't. It practically guarantees that he'll be okay."

Elsie pulled away and looked Oliver in the eyes. There were wet streaks down her cheeks. "What factor is that?"

"He's got you," Ollie said. "You're a damn miracle worker. I never thought I'd walk again and now I can, or at least almost can. And that's further along than I ever thought I'd be. Your uncle is blessed to have you as a niece."

She smiled, warming his heart. "That might be the sweetest thing anybody has ever said to me," she said, wiping a tear away from her cheek.

Oliver suddenly felt more drawn to her than ever before. She had dropped her walls, allowing the two of them to move past the whole patient/provider definitions, at least for a moment. He was seeing a side of her now that was raw and vulnerable. It made her even more beautiful in his eyes because she was real.

I would love to kiss her right now, he thought, as his gazed moved down her face.

Her lips were a magnet, pulling him closer. He couldn't stop himself. A force more powerful than his own will moved him and he began to lean in. Her eyes stayed locked with his as their lips neared. They almost touched, but right before they could, Elsie slowly pulled away.

"We shouldn't," she said, shaking her head. "We really shouldn't."

Oliver was a little stunned, being that no other girl in his memory had ever turned down a kiss from him. It really only made him want her more, but he didn't say anything in response. He didn't want to make things awkward between them.

God, she probably thinks I'm a total creep now, he thought. *I shouldn't have tried to kiss her. That was stupid. Stupid, stupid, stupid.*

In an effort to change the subject, Oliver ran his fingers through his hair. "Elsie, you didn't happen to bring the hair bleach with you, did you? I'd love to get my roots dyed, before someone discovers my darkest secret: that I'm not a blond surfer dude."

"Yeah, actually I did." She laughed and Ollie watched her shoulders relax. "I came prepared. Do you want me to dye it now?"

"Sure, why not?" Ollie shrugged. "I've got nothing else going on, unless you want to watch TV. I think Jeopardy is on next."

Elsie glanced toward the flat screen on the wall across the room. "That is a huge TV."

"It's not really that big," he said. It wasn't anywhere near the one he had at home.

"That's what she said," she commented, with a chuckle. "But, seriously, I think that's the biggest TV I've ever seen in a house."

Oliver looked at the screen, realizing that it actually *was* pretty big. He'd just gotten so used to everyone he knew having the biggest and the best. He'd forgotten that regular people don't have eighty-five inch televisions.

"I guess it is a little big," he admitted.

"A *little* big?" she said, with wide eyes. "That thing is a freaking jumbo-tron. You must be able to see every blade of grass when you watch a game on that thing."

"To be honest, I haven't watched much on it." He smiled at her. "Although, I did see a golf game the other day, though, and you're right. Every blade of grass was visible."

"Golf?" she raised her eyebrows at him. "You used that TV to watch golf?"

"It was that or the news, and honestly, the male anchor needs to get a better razor," he replied.

Elsie laughed playfully as she stood up from the couch. The mood between them had shifted and it was now more relaxed. His lips still burned, though, wishing that they'd been able to share that kiss. It was so close. So close that he could taste her. He wanted that, now more than before even though he knew he shouldn't.

"Come on," she said, taking his hand and helping him to his feet. "Let's get your hair fixed up."

With a grunt, Oliver got to his feet. He grimaced as soon as the weight was on his injury and Elsie took notice immediately.

"Did you take your pain medication yet?" she asked, her gaze going clinical.

"No, I've been in bed since our session today." He shook his head. "I only got up when I knew you were coming over."

"Oliver, you need to take that medication if you're in pain," she said, her hand going to his shoulder. The touch made his body heat with desire. "There's no point in hurting all day if you don't have to."

"You're probably right, Doc." He pulled away, needing and hating to sever the connection between them. If he wanted to keep this platonic, he needed her not to touch him or his body was going to override his brain. "I'll take some. They're in the bathroom, which is probably the best place to dye my hair anyway."

"Okay, well let's go," she replied, as she walked next to him toward the bathroom. "You take your medicine before I dye your hair. Doctor's orders."

Ollie chuckled at her comment. It was the first time she'd referred to herself as "doctor" and it made him laugh. He was getting to her and he liked it.

When they got to the bathroom, he took his pills and then Elsie dyed his hair. He sat in a chair in front of the sink, with his head dipped back in it. It gave him a view of the ceiling, and of Elsie, as she stood next to him, massaging the dye onto his head with her fingers. It felt like he was at the salon, only this girl was infinitely more pretty than any stylist he'd ever had.

He had to focus on not moaning in pleasure as she rinsed his hair with warm water and used her strong fingers to relax his scalp. This was far better than the pretty-boy stylist Nikki had forced him to use the first time. With Elsie doing his hair, he suddenly saw the appeal of changing his hair color more often.

"How's it looking?" he asked after a few minutes.

Her eyes widened and her jaw dropped. "I don't know, Ollie. I think I might have screwed up. It said it was supposed to be blonde, but it looks pretty orange. Like, fluorescent orange."

"What?" Ollie sat up quickly. "You're joking."

"I didn't want to say anything, because I thought I could fix it if I just kept massaging," she said, in a panic. "I'm so sorry."

He stood up on his good leg and spun around to face himself in the mirror. His hair was not orange at all and in fact, looked like the exact color of blonde that he'd been hoping for.

"Very funny, Elsie," he said, raising an eyebrow. "You're not only a physical therapist and a hair stylist, but you're apparently also a comedian."

Elsie started laughing so hard that she had to lean against the wall of the bathroom. Her laughter was contagious and soon, Ollie followed along. He wasn't sure what he was more happy about. The fact that he was seeing her smile, or the fact that his hair wasn't actually bright orange.

"Sorry, I had to," she said, once the giggling had subsided. "I couldn't resist."

"You're a cruel, cruel lady," he said, his lips curling into a smirk. "It's a good thing I like you."

The last sentence just seemed to spill out of his mouth without him even considering the implications. There was a moment of nervous silence, as he watched her absorb what he had just said. And then he found relief when she replied. "I like you too, Ollie."

He stepped close to her, placing his hands onto her forearms. The entire world shrank down the size of the bathroom and for a moment, it was just the two of them. Nikki didn't exist and either did football. Even his injury had no place there. Nothing else was in Oliver's universe right then except for Elsie.

He could see the nervousness in her eyes and it matched how he felt as well. This wasn't just some club girl that he could kiss and toss away. She was the real deal and he suddenly felt deeply afraid that he could somehow screw everything up with her.

He watched as Elsie looked down at his lips, before bringing her gaze back up. She drew in a deep breath.

"God, I want to kiss you right now. I really do. But I can't. I'm sorry, Ollie." She took a step back. "I can't cross that line. I want to, but... I don't know. Maybe I should go. I'm sorry to interrupt your night."

With that she fled from the bathroom and practically sprinted to the living room. Ollie followed her out of the bathroom, his hair still dripping with water.

"Wait, Elsie. I didn't mean to make you feel uncomfortable."

"You didn't, Oliver," she said, picking up her purse. "You didn't make me feel uncomfortable at all. In fact, you made me a feel a hundred times better than I felt when I was at home. And that's actually part of the problem. I'm your medical provider."

"I get it," Ollie said, as he watched Elsie put her coat on. "I know you don't want to mix work and personal life. Trust me, I can understand that. But dammit, Elsie, I feel more drawn to you than any woman I've ever met. Maybe we should forget the whole working relationship thing here and focus on what actually feels real."

"I just need to stay professional," she said, grabbing the door handle. Her eyes were big and shone in the light. "Plus, your recovery is almost over, Ollie. You'll be leaving in a few weeks. Why start something now that we can't pursue? That's just asking for heartache."

She pulled the door open, sending a gust of cold air into the house. Ollie hobbled toward her, feeling deeply conflicted as well. He wanted so badly for her to stay with him that night. And not so that he could make love to her either, but just to have her there. Elsie was right, though, and he knew it. He would be leaving soon. Getting too close to her now would only end in heart break for them both.

"I'll see you tomorrow then?" he asked. "For my session."

"Yes, of course," Elsie replied, putting the hood of her coat on and stepping into the snow. She stopped after just a few steps and turned around. "Ollie?"

"Yeah?" he said, squinting against the blizzard outside.

"Thanks for hanging out tonight," she said. "Seriously. It made my evening."

"You made mine too," he agreed with a smile. "My knee feels better and you didn't even have to do anything but eat pizza with me."

She smiled and paused, looking Oliver in the eyes. The attraction was still there and as potent as ever. Oliver could feel it and he knew she could too. Both of them knew it wasn't a good idea to pursue it, though. Nothing more needed to be said.

"Goodnight," she said, then turned and walked toward her car.

"Goodnight." Ollie closed the door and hobbled back to the couch.

His emotions were in turmoil. The most amazing woman he knew was slowly stealing his heart. It was absolutely the last thing he'd expected when he moved to Iowa for his recovery. He wasn't sure how to handle it.

I want that girl, he thought. *I really, really want her. But I don't want to hurt her. God, she's something special, though. I've never met anyone like her. Nobody has ever made me feel the way she does. What am I supposed to do?*

Chapter Eleven

Elsie

Elsie had managed to get home through the blizzard, but it was scary. Her car slipped around every corner and she'd almost gotten stuck a half a dozen times. She parked and went upstairs to her apartment to slip into her pajamas and snuggle into bed. As she crawled underneath the covers, she couldn't stop thinking about how she'd almost kissed Oliver. She'd almost crossed a line that she knew she shouldn't and the idea of that scared her.

What if that had happened? She thought. *I could get in so much trouble.*

Still, though, she couldn't deny the fact that tasting those lips of his did sound nice. She wondered what kind of kisser he was, whether he was slow and sensual, or firm and aggressive.

No, Elsie, no, she told herself. *Stop thinking about that right now.*

She shook her head, trying to rid the naughty thoughts that were infiltrating it without her permission.

"I need to just go to sleep," she whispered. "But maybe I should text him and tell him thank you for getting together."

Elsie reached for her phone, then quickly changed her mind.

That's exactly the opposite of what I should do, she thought, setting the cell back onto her night stand. She was falling for him, hard and deep.

She pressed her head back into the pillow and stared at the ceiling. Outside, the wind continued to howl and she pulled her blanket tightly around her to help fight the cold drafts that haunted the old building. Then she closed her eyes, slowly drifting off to sleep.

But Elsie's slumber didn't last long. The sound of a rumbling engine on the street out front woke her up. When she opened her eyes, she glanced at the clock to find that she'd only been asleep for about an hour. The sound of the motor faded off, and immediately after, she heard a knocking coming from the front door of the clinic downstairs.

"Who the hell?" she whispered, throwing the blankets off and getting out of bed.

It was past midnight and nobody in that town would have been awake at that time and certainly not roaming the streets in the middle of a snow storm. Her adrenaline spiked as the knocking got louder and more frantic.

Elsie wiped the sleep from her eyes and slipped on her fuzzy blue robe. With no idea who could be at the door, she decided to play it safe and grab her baseball bat from the coat closet. Then she walked down the interior stairs that went straight to her office below.

Whoever is there better not be trying to rob the place, she thought, turning the corner with her bat in hand. *I'm in good shape and I'm not afraid to use this bat.*

But when she turned the corner and looked out the front glass windows of the clinic, she didn't see a stranger or a burglar. She saw Oliver, standing on the sidewalk and shivering, as snow blustered around him. He was wrapped in an orange parka with the hood pulled up over his head.

"Let me in, Elsie," he said, knocking a few more times. "It's freezing out here."

"Hold on a second, Oliver," she called out, as she dug through the drawers of the front desk to find the key to the front door.

The lights were off, which made things difficult, but she finally found the key. She quickly went and unlocked the door. When she pulled it open, an icy wind followed Oliver inside.

"Ollie, what are you doing here?" she asked. "Is everything okay?"

He nodded and closed the door. "Yeah, everything is great."

Oliver took off the parka and hung it on the coat rack. Snow slid off of it and into a pile on the floor.

"Are you sure everything is okay?" Elsie asked. "It's late. I'm surprised to see you right now. How did you even get here?"

Ollie chuckled, as he rubbed his hands together to get them warm. "I asked one of the neighbors for a ride. I hope you don't mind that I showed up here without calling. But after you left my house, I couldn't stop thinking about you."

Now that his jacket was off, Elsie got to see Oliver in a tight white t-shirt and black workout pants. He looked as hot as ever, and obviously tempting. But she couldn't let her mind go in the wrong direction. She needed to remain a professional.

"That's really sweet, Ollie," she said. "It's nice to see you, but you should have called. I came down here with a baseball bat. You scared the bejeezus out of me, you know that?"

He smiled and took her hands in his. "I'm sorry. I just thought that you'd talk me out of coming if I called. I know that you're fighting yourself over all of this. You're afraid to cross that line between patient and provider. I get it. But look, it's midnight. Your office is closed. You know what that means?"

Elsie raised an eyebrow. "What's that?"

"It means you're not working right now," he said, with a devilish smirk. "I'm not technically your patient."

Without waiting for her response, Oliver leaned in and pressed his lips to hers. She hesitated at first, pulling away in surprise. But he was like a powerful magnet and she only stayed distant for a millisecond. Then she leaned back in, letting the kiss resume.

A passionate spark ignited and Elsie parted her lips. Their tongues danced in each others mouths, delicately touching and then pulling away. In the back of her mind, she knew that she shouldn't be allowing something like this to happen. But the logical side of her brain had been trumped by her need for intimacy with Oliver. It was like she had spent weeks trying to build a wall between them and Ollie just showed up and knocked it down with that beautiful smile and perfect body.

Elsie placed her hands onto his face. Her fingertips tickled from his beard stubble as she pulled him close, turning the light kissing into an aggressive make-out session. The wall that she'd built between them continued to crumble and the sexual energy poured through like a flash flood.

Maybe this is wrong, but whatever, she thought, trying to justify it to herself. *It's clear that we both want this. Maybe it's destined to happen no matter how badly I try to fight it.*

Oliver undid the front of Elsie's robe and pulled it open, slipping his hands to her sides. She let out a soft groan as he stepped forward, pressing her back against the wall near the patient check-in desk. She broke the kiss and looked over toward the front door, where the floor to ceiling windows were.

"We can't do this here," she said, in between heavy breaths. "Someone could see us. Come on, let's go to the workout room."

"Okay," Ollie said. "Take me there."

Elsie took his hand and led him to the back. The room was dark, except for the beams of moonlight that shone through the three small windows near the top of the walls. It was just enough light to see where she was going and she led him over to the massage table near the back.

I can't believe I'm doing this, she thought. *But who in their right mind would turn him down?*

Before she could even turn around, Ollie brought his hands to her hips and spun her to face him. Then he lifted her up onto the massage table. She laid down on her back, biting her bottom lip flirtatiously.

"You are so beautiful," he whispered, as he crawled onto the table with her.

His hands were above her shoulders, holding himself over her. The moonlight fell across his face, illuminating his blue irises. This was happening and any previous doubts that she'd held were quickly fading away.

"I wanted you since the minute I met you," she said.

"You should have told me," he replied. "I felt the same thing."

He leaned in and resumed the kiss. Elsie's body tingled all over. Something about the randomness of the moment, and the privacy they had, and the sexual tension she'd been repressing. It all came together and turned her on more than ever. She became wet with desire and began to crave having him inside of her.

"Take me, Oliver," she begged, as soon as he pulled away from the kiss. "Just take me."

Ollie sat up and pulled off his shirt, revealing his muscular figure. His chest and abs flexed as he reached forward and brought his hands to the top of Elsie's thighs. His touch sent a wave of anticipation into her and her pussy throbbed desperately underneath her pajamas.

"Let's get these off," he said, slipping his fingers into the waist strap of her pants.

Elsie lifted her butt up from the massage table as Oliver slid her pajamas down, taking her panties with them. He pulled them all the way to her ankles and she kicked them the rest of the way off. Her gaze moved down Ollie's body, noticing a thick bulge that was now protruding from the front of his athletic pants. She licked her lips when she saw it and her pussy clenched. She'd never wanted anything so badly.

"Take yours off, too," she ordered, and Ollie immediately did what she asked.

He stepped down from the table and slipped off his pants, releasing his shaft. Now naked, Oliver resumed his position over Elsie. He held her legs up, draping her knees over his shoulders. The head of his cock hovered just outside of her opening.

"Do it," she whispered. "Take me, Oliver. Take me."

Oliver clenched his jaw and slowly bucked his hips forward, pressing toward her. Elsie moaned, as his crown touched her entrance.

"Are you sure you want to do this?" he asked. His blue eyes met hers and his pupils dilated. His fingers tightened against her skin.

She reached forward, grabbing Oliver's hips. She looked him in the eyes and whispered, "Yes."

"The weather outside remains dangerous, so stay inside your homes," Ollie informed her.

Elsie sat straight up and looked at him. "What?"

"Lows today will be around five degrees with a high of only twenty-seven," he replied smoothly, looking her directly in they eyes as his fingers caressed her skin. "Tomorrow is looking slightly more sunny, with highs in the thirties. This is Iowa radio at six in the morning."

Elsie blinked hard, not understanding what in the world was going on. When she opened them again, Ollie was gone. She slowly sat up, expecting to see the workout equipment surrounding her and the massage table underneath her. But she wasn't downstairs in the clinic. She was still in her bed.

What the hell? She thought, looking around her room. Beside her the alarm on her radio continued to describe the top news stories of the day. She hit the off button with a little more force than was necessary.

Elsie threw the covers off of her. She was breathing hard and a layer of sweat covered her skin. Her body tingled and it felt like she'd just had an orgasm.

"It was a dream?" she said out loud. "Oh my God."

She glanced out of her bedroom window to see that the storm was still raging outside. The house was silent besides the wind. There was no rumbling of an engine or a knocking on the door. Oliver hadn't shown up to the clinic in the middle of the night in a snow storm. She should have known that it was just a dream.

It had been one of those dreams that was so intricate in detail that it felt more like a memory than a figment of her imagination. She could still taste his kiss and smell his cologne. She could still feel the sensation of him pressed against her and her fingertips still tickled from touching his beard stubble. It had seemed so real. A part of her wished that she could fall back asleep so they could finish what they'd started.

This is going too far, she thought, as she went to the bathroom to splash some cold water on her face. *I can't allow myself to think of Oliver this way. It's a level of unprofessional that I didn't think I was capable of. I'm having dreams of him now? This is insane. I'm insane.*

After a few minutes of pacing around, and even taking a second to go downstairs to make sure that she actually *had* been dreaming, she finally crawled back in bed. But as she tried to force herself back to sleep, the image of Oliver's naked body stayed at the forefront of her mind. It tempted her, making her want to peel her panties off and touch herself. But she refused. She couldn't let that happen. She had to ignore these feelings before they got the best of her.

"What am I going to do?" she asked the empty room. She knew the answer. She was going to ignore these feelings completely. She was going to stay professional and not give into her body's urges. She would just pretend that Ollie was married. And gay. And diseased. And actually a swamp monster in disguise.

She took a deep breath in and out knowing that it wasn't going to be easy. She pushed a lock of sweat-soaked hair off her temple and remembered just how good the dream had been.

It was going to be a rough couple of weeks

Chapter Twelve

Ollie

Several weeks later
Mid-May

Spring had finally come. There was still snow on the ground surrounding the cabin, but it was beginning to melt. Water poured out of the gutters, splashing into mud puddles below. Oliver opened the front door, squinting against the bright sunlight that reflected against the remaining snow. He drew in a long breath, letting the crisp and clean air fill his lungs.

The long winter appeared to be over, which had him feeling a bit blue, despite the nice weather. It had been almost twelve weeks since his arrival and soon, he'd be going back home. In fact, he guessed that he only had a few more sessions with Elsie before Coach sent for him. Then it would be time to pack up his bags and head back to California to resume his normal life.

Oliver leaned against the door jam as he gazed across the plains. When he'd first arrived there, he hated it. This little podunk town in the middle of nowhere was the opposite of what he was used to. It was isolated country that offered little to no entertainment. But after three full months, he'd actually begun to really enjoy the quiet and the solitude. It had grown on him and he understood the appeal now and how people could live like that.

I might actually miss this place, he thought with a chuckle.

In his heart, though, he knew that it wasn't really the farmhouse or the surroundings that he was going to miss. It was Elsie. His time with her was almost up. One more physical training session and she'd be able to sign him off to continue recovery on his own.

With a sigh, he turned around and walked back into the cabin, letting the door close behind him. His step was pretty much normal now. The hobbling that he'd once become accustomed to was now nothing more than a bad memory. He was able to walk perfectly and only experienced a tinge of pain if he stayed standing for too long. It was truly a miracle, at least Ollie thought so. And he owed it all to Elsie. Her infinite patience, focus and expertise had given him a distinct advantage in his recovery that he wouldn't have had otherwise.

"I owe her a lot." Ollie whispered to himself, as he strolled into the kitchen to make a pot of coffee.

He wasn't sure how he'd ever repay her. He'd been sending messages to the team manager, asking if there was a PT opening for the team. Oliver really wanted to get Elsie a job. She was made for sports medicine and her talents were being wasted here. The manager continued to say that there might be an opening, but they wouldn't know for sure until the beginning of the next season, or at least pre-season training.

Realistically, it was a long shot that something like that would pan out, but Ollie kept his fingers crossed. If Elsie had a job working for his team, not only would she make three times as much money, but he'd also get to see her every day.

Once the coffee had brewed, Ollie filled his mug and then walked across the house. He stepped into the makeshift gym, which he'd unofficially named "The Torture Chamber." After three months of relentless training, the new equipment was now very broken in. The mats on the floor were worn and the padding on the machines were indented. It was the sign of a lot of hard work.

I guess I'll need to figure out what to do with all of this stuff, he thought. *There's no way I'm packing all of it up and taking it back to California.*

He'd hardly finished the thought before someone came knocking on his door. His eyes lit up out of reaction. The only person who ever came to his place was Elsie. He thought it could be her, until he glanced at his watch. It was only nine in the morning and his final session wasn't until later that afternoon. Oliver spun around and went to the front of the house. From the living room window, he saw a car in the driveway that he didn't recognize.

That's odd, he thought.

He pulled the door open and did a double take when he saw who was standing there.

"Nikki?" he said, taking a step back.

She pushed her sunglasses to the top of her head and smiled wide. "Hi, Ollie."

Nikki was wearing her business suit, which meant she had likely flown in on first class. She looked amazing, all curves and sultry lines. She looked incredibly sexy, just the way Nikki wanted.

"What are you doing here?" he asked.

"I came to see you," she replied, as though the answer should have been obvious. She pushed her hand playfully against his chest. "I told you a few weeks ago that I had bought tickets."

Oh, my God, he thought. *I didn't think she was actually serious.*

"Nikki, I'm going to be going home soon," he said, backing away from her touch. "Why would you fly all the way out here if you knew that I was coming back?"

"I just couldn't wait to see you." Nikki walked up and gave Oliver a hug. He held his hands at his side, though, refusing to embrace her.

After a moment, she released him and then walked into the living room. She looked around, poking her head into each room. Oliver closed the front door, shaking his head. "Nikki, what are you doing?"

She slid back into the living room, shrugging innocently. "Just taking a look to see how you've been living for the past couple of months. Is it really this small? I don't know how you tolerated it all this time."

"Is that really what you were looking for?" Oliver asked, as he walked toward the couch and sat down.

"I might have also been checking to see if your personal trainer was here," she admitted, fiddling with a blond curl.

"No, she's not here, Nikki. Because I'm not having a session right now."

"That's good." She sat next to him on the couch, leaning her head onto his shoulder. "Speaking of your trainer, though, how is your recovery coming along?"

"I'm feeling great," Oliver said, slowly scooting away from Nikki. It didn't do any good, though. She clung onto him like a magnet.

"Yeah?" she asked. "You're ready for spring training?"

"More or less," he said. "I've got a session with Elsie today and she'll be able to tell me then whether or not I can start training right away."

"You're starting right away regardless," Nikki informed him. "It's not up to her any more."

"What are you talking about, Nikki?" Oliver frowned.

"Coach wants you back," she said, flipping her hair behind her. "He wants you back right now."

"I *can't* go back right now," Oliver said. His eyes narrowed. "And besides, is it Coach who wants me back or is it you?"

Nikki sat up and faced him. Her blue eyes were illuminated by the sunshine that poured into the living room. Ollie thought she looked pretty, but the way she was acting made her completely unattractive.

"Ollie, baby," she said, bringing her hand to the side of his face. "I want you home, of course. I wasn't joking when I said I missed you. But Coach says he wants you back in California, too. He said you need to begin training. Your team needs you."

"I'll come home when I'm ready. Coach can talk to me himself," Oliver told her. He moved his face away from her touch.

"Why don't we leave right now? We can escape this place," Nikki said. "I have tickets for both of us. We need to leave here within the hour to catch our flight."

Ollie shook his head. "Are you joking?"

"No," she replied with a frown. She pouted. "I bought return tickets because I knew you'd want to come back with me and leave this hellhole. I even reserved the suite at that hotel you like, just so you could get back to feeling like yourself."

"First off, it's *not* a hellhole," he said, through gritted teeth. "And second, I can't leave yet. I've got another session. You can't expect me to just uproot myself because you got antsy to have me back home. I'm not going."

Nikki's jaw dropped as she stood up from the couch. "Please God, don't tell me that you actually *like* it here. Have you become one of these *hillbillies*?"

Her tone made Oliver cringe. He looked up, meeting her gaze. "Don't call them that."

"What? Hillbillies?" she placed her hand on her hip and cocked her head to the side.

"I'm serious, Nikki," he said. "Don't insult a place that you know nothing about."

She rolled her eyes. "Whatever, Ollie. You didn't want to come here at first because you felt the same way."

"Yeah, but I learned that it's actually not so bad," he said. "In fact, people here are more friendly than anybody I know in California. It's nice, actually."

"I hope you enjoyed it," Nikki said, taking a few steps toward Oliver's bedroom. "Because you're leaving now."

"Nikki, I'm not a child so don't try to treat me like one." Oliver got up and followed her down the hallway. "I'll leave when I want to leave. Besides, if Coach really wanted me back, he could call me himself. I doubt it's as urgent as you're letting on."

"Look, you're right." She bit her lip and smiled coyly at him. "Coach doesn't want you back today. He wants you back next week. I just wanted you to come home, because it's not the same without you there."

Oliver sighed, as he let down his guard a bit. "I had a feeling you were stretching the truth."

"I just miss you." Nikki stepped close to him and placed her hands onto his chest.

"Look, if Coach wants me back next week, then I'll be back next week," Oliver said. "But I'm not going home with you today. Sorry, but there's no way."

"There no way?" she asked, flirtatiously. She looked up at him through her eyelashes. "Are you sure about that?"

Nikki gently bit her bottom lip and stood up on her tiptoes. She leaned in, bringing her face toward Oliver's to attempt a kiss. Right as their lips grazed, though, Ollie turned away.

"Nikki, stop," he said, taking a step back. "What are you doing? We're not together any more."

"What's one kiss?" she asked, her voice seductive.

"We can't keep going over this," he told her firmly. "I'm not having this conversation again."

She pouted out her lower lip and pushed past him. Oliver watched as she walked into the living room. This was how she would normally make him feel bad, but it wasn't working. The guilt trip and the silent treatment that would inevitably ensue were not threatening to him anymore. He just plain didn't care. He wasn't going to get lured into Nikki's manipulations, because there was another woman who was on his mind. Elsie was the one who had his heart. This fact alone took away all power from Nikki's attempts at making him feel bad.

Oliver walked out to the living room and leaned against the wall with his arms crossed. "You're welcome to wait here for an hour until you need to leave for the airport, but that's all I can offer."

She snarled at him, but didn't budge from the couch. "I thought we were friends."

"We *are* friends," Ollie said. "But that's all. Nothing else. Look, Nikki, I care about you and I always will. But not in the same way as you're hoping for. Our relationship is strictly professional now. I realize that it might hurt to hear that, but we both know that it has to be that way. We tried this once and it didn't work. It blew up right in our faces. What's the point of going through all of that again?"

Nikki's face crumpled and she held her arms tight against her body while refusing to look at him. "I guess you're right."

They were silent for a moment. Ollie felt bad for having to draw a clear line with Nikki, but it seemed like that was the only way to get through to her.

"Sorry, Nikki," he said. "I hope you understand."

She sighed and stood up from the couch.

"I do," she replied. A fake smile filled her face. "I guess I'll head back to the airport. I'll tell Coach that you'll be there next week."

Ollie was suddenly hesitant of Nikki's willingness to comply. Something was up with her and he could sense it. He knew her well enough.

"Are you sure you're okay with things?" Oliver asked, keeping his distance.

"Yes, I said I was," Nikki replied. She didn't stop as she approached Oliver and pulled him in for a hug. This time, he hugged her back. She smelled like hairspray and fancy perfume.

"Alright, well I'm glad you understand. There aren't any hard feelings." He pulled back from the hug. "I just can't have a personal relationship with you again. Business only."

She pulled away and faked a smile, clearly trying to keep from crying. "I just really care about you. I've been worrying about you, living out here in the sticks."

Oliver chuckled. "I'm totally fine. Safe and sound."

"Good." Nikki sighed, obviously stalling. "I wish you were coming back with me, but I guess I'll see you next week."

"Yep, I'll be there," he said, going to the front door and holding it open. "Tell Coach he can count on it."

"He'll be happy to hear that." Nikki slowly walked out the front door. She paused before making it to the steps of the deck. Then she glanced over her shoulder. "You sure you won't come with me? The hotel is ready for us."

"Bye, Nikki," Oliver replied, motioning to her car.

She pouted. "Take care of yourself, Ollie."

"Bye, Nikki," he said, closing the door.

Oliver listened as she started her car and backed down the driveway. The strongest feeling of relief swept over him now that she had gone.

It's funny, he thought. *It wasn't all that long ago when I never wanted that girl to leave. Today, her leaving was the only thing I could think about.*

As the sound of her car faded into the distance, Oliver let out a sigh. Nikki had flown all the way out there to try to rekindle things with him. But she'd failed miserably. Her visit had only really made him realize just how much he liked Elsie. She was the one for him, but with only seven days left in Iowa, he feared that he wouldn't get the chance to express that to her.

Chapter Thirteen

Elsie

"**O**kay, Oliver, I want you to walk across the room. When you get to the wall, run back toward me."

"Sure thing," Ollie said, with a grin for her.

Elsie stood in Oliver's gym, holding her clipboard. She needed to evaluate him to see how far along his progress was. He looked like he was healing pretty well overall, but there were things she needed to see him do in order to drop her physical training sessions down to one visit per week. She watched as Oliver walked across the room. His stride looked fairly normal. In fact, to the untrained eye, it would have appeared that he'd never had an injury in his life. But Elsie saw something.

"You're still favoring your good leg, Ollie," she said, jotting it down in her notes. "I can tell."

He made it to the other side of the room and turned around. "You can see that?"

"I can see everything," she said, with a smirk. "Now run back to me."

Oliver drew in a breath and brought one foot forward, getting ready to sprint the length of the room. He looked at Elsie and then took off, running quickly toward her. In about ten steps he was there and slid to a stop just inches from her feet.

"How was that?" he asked.

"It was fine, but I'm not convinced that you're ready for once-per-week sessions," she said. "I think we need to keep up the training until you can run and walk without favoring your good knee at all. I can see it in your step. You put more weight on your other leg. It's not a huge deal, but if you're wanting to play at a professional level, then we need to make sure that the strength in both limbs are equal."

Ollie ran his fingers through his blonde hair, keeping his gaze locked with Elsie. She wasn't lying to him. She really did see him favoring one of his legs while walking and running. But there was a part of her that wondered if her real intention of wanting him do more sessions was so that she could continue seeing him.

"Unfortunately, I don't think I can do any more training with you after today," he said, with a sigh.

Elsie's eyes widened. "What?"

"Do you remember, Nikki?" he asked, leaning against a piece of exercise equipment and crossing his arms. "The one who interviewed you."

"Yes, how could I forget?"

"She stopped by this morning," he said, his eyes watching her.

"And?" Elsie asked, urging him to continue.

"She came by to tell me that I have to go back to California," he replied. Elsie felt like she might be sick.

"When?" Elsie took a seat on the weight bench and Ollie sat next to her.

"She wanted me to leave today, but I told her there was no way I could do that," he explained, and Elsie could see sadness in his eyes. "But Coach wants me back by next week. I have to go home."

Elsie's heart sank. She knew it was coming, but she didn't think it would be here so soon. She had always realized that her time with Oliver would be coming to an end at *some point,* but didn't think it would be so soon and happen so suddenly. She still needed a few more weeks with him. She wanted months.

"I'm not done with your recovery work, though," she said. "I had more things planned for you."

Oliver shrugged. "I'm not sure that I have much of a choice. Coach needs me and so does my team. They've been without me for months and they want me back. Nikki said that if I'm not able to start training with the team next week, then Coach may not want to put me in as a starting quarterback. If that happens, I can be pretty sure that I'll lose most of my endorsements."

She was silent as she listened to him. It was tough news to hear. Oliver going home was heart breaking. It wasn't just the loss of a good patient either. It was the loss of a very good friend. He'd become her confidant. In just a handful of weeks, she grown more fond of him than she was of most people.

"Are you okay?" he asked. "You're not saying anything."

"Yeah, I'm fine." Elsie nodded, swallowing down her emotion. "I just didn't expect to hear this today. Kind of caught me off guard is all."

Oliver placed his hand onto the top of her knee. His touch send a pleasurable tingle through her body, causing her to take a quick breath. She was going to miss that.

"It took me off guard as well," he told her, his voice soft. "I had no clue that Nikki was going to show up today."

"So, that's that then?" Elsie asked. She sighed looking around the gym where they'd spent so many hours together. "I guess we're done with therapy?"

Oliver nodded. "I guess so. I've got to be honest, I didn't think I'd fear leaving this town as much as I do now. When I got here, I thought it was the last place on earth I'd ever like. But I was wrong. It's grown on me quite a bit."

"It's the Thai chili pizza, isn't it?" Elsie said, with a wink. "It does that to everyone."

Oliver laughed. "Yeah, that might be part of it. But it's certainly not all of it."

His gaze was locked with hers and she knew what he meant. She knew that there was mutual attraction between them. That had been confirmed when he had tried to kiss her that night she'd come over to his place, the same night she'd dyed his hair.

She'd made sure to stay as professional as possible for the weeks after that. No touching unless it was clinically needed. They'd still talked, though. She knew him better than she knew several of her closest friends.

But there was still that physical connection that thrummed through her bones whenever he looked at her. He made her vibrate with just a simple touch and she found herself dreaming of him nearly every night and waking up in a pleasant sweat.

Is it possible that he wants this as badly as I do? She asked herself.

It was as if Ollie had heard her thoughts. He scooted close, bringing his hand to the side of her face. His fingers gently touched her cheek as he gazed at her. His beautiful blue eyes caused her to melt into the weight bench.

He's going to try to kiss me again. I want this, but I shouldn't. I shouldn't... her thoughts trailed off as Oliver leaned in. He brought his lips to hers, before she could even consider turning away. There was a brief moment of hesitation, where Elsie wondered if she should allow this to happen.

This kiss was definitely crossing the patient barrier, but the feelings it filled her with seemed to trump all of her doubt about the situation. Still, though, she only allowed herself a moment to enjoy it before she pulled away.

Wide eyed and trying not to smile, she gently pushed her hand against Ollie's shoulder. "You can't do that. I'm your provider and you're my patient!"

Oliver simply shrugged and flashed a relaxed smile. "*Technically*, not any more. As of now, we are just two regular people. I'm not a patient at all."

Elsie's heart was thumping loudly inside her rib cage. Her mind whirled. The kiss had sent a tidal wave of emotion inside of her. It was exciting and made her feel young. It reminded her of her first kiss, or at least the way her first kiss had made her feel.

"I guess you're *technically* right," she said, nervously fidgeting her hands.

"Look, Elsie, I know that we both feel something for each other, and it's more than just friendship," Oliver said. "I felt drawn to you from the moment I met you."

"I know, Ollie. I feel the same way," she said. "It's just horrible timing. For the last few months you've been my patient, so I haven't been able to express my feelings. But now that you're not my patient and I finally can express how I feel, you're leaving to go home. I like you a lot. I really do. There's nobody else who I feel I can talk to the way I talk to you. But you're not going to be here for very much longer. And after that, then what?"

"Elsie, if I learned anything from that car accident, it was that life can change suddenly and when you least expect it," he said, pushing a strand of her hair off of her forehead. "I don't know what tomorrow will bring and either do you. Nobody does. But I do know how you make me feel and that's something that's not up for debate. I'm happiest when I'm with you. I may only have a week left here, but I want to make it the best week ever. I don't want to hold back any more. There's something special between us and I want to explore that. As far as the future, why not just let the chips fall as they may? Because regardless, none of it is guaranteed."

"I had no idea you were so deep," she said, smirking. "Seriously, Ollie. I've never heard you say anything so poetic."

He smiled. "I was lucky enough to get a few smarts from my brother. He didn't take all of the intelligence."

Maybe he's right. Maybe there's something to be said for just letting go and having fun. The future is never certain. Uncle Frank's cancer has taught me that. But still, I don't want to get hurt. I don't want to just be another fling or a notch in Ollie's bed post, she thought.

"What are you thinking?" he asked, his blue eyes on her face.

"How do you know I'm thinking something?" she replied.

"I can just tell. You do this thing with your eyes when you're deep in thought," he said, placing his hand on top of hers. "You squint ever so slightly and look up. You do it all the time."

"I'd be a horrible poker player, wouldn't I?" Elsie giggled, feeling embarrassed about how obvious she was.

"Horrible," he agreed, with a smile. "So what were you thinking?"

Elsie sighed. "I was thinking that I really like you and have since our first session."

"Is that all?" Ollie asked. His thumb made small circles on her hand, creating warmth that coiled in her belly and begged for more.

"No, there's more," she said. "I was thinking about how badly I wanted you that time you took your shirt off for your massage and how much will power it took for me to maintain self-control. I was also thinking about how nice it was to have you there to talk to when my uncle was diagnosed with cancer. But that's still not all."

Oliver raised his eyebrows, waiting for her to finish.

"It's just that... I don't want to end up being some statistic for Oliver Lance's scoreboard," she confessed. "I don't want to be someone you just have fun with and then go home, never to think about again. I've been that girl before and it hurts. It hurts bad. I can't do that again."

"I'd never hurt you," he said, with deep sincerity. "Besides, all I'm asking is if I can take you out on one date this weekend. A real date. Not just having you come over so we can watch TV, but a legitimate date. If you don't want to, I understand. But I have to ask, because if I don't, I'll kick myself for the rest of my life."

She narrowed her eyes, evaluating him for a moment. *How can I possibly turn that down? Plus, it's just a date. A casual, fun date. And anyway, it might be nice to get to spend a little bit of relaxing time with him before he goes on his way.*

"Okay. Yeah. I'd love to go on a date with you, Ollie," she finally said. "That sounds fun."

"Really?" he asked, his eyes widening. "You will?"

Elsie nodded. "Yes, of course I will. Besides, it's like you said, I'm not your doctor any more."

"I can still call you 'Doc' though, right?" he asked, chuckling. "I'll plan the whole thing. All you have to do is be ready by six o'clock Saturday evening. I'll pick you up."

Elsie looked confused. "Pick me up? How? You don't have a car and any rental place is sure to recognize you."

Ollie stood up from the weight bench and proudly put his hands onto his hips. "Hey, just because I've been slightly disabled over the past few months, doesn't mean I haven't made any friends. The nice farmer who lives next door stopped by a week or so ago and we chatted. He offered up his mode of transportation and I told him I might take him up on it if an opportunity arose. Well, here's the opportunity."

"Neighbor? There aren't any neighbors around here," Elsie said.

"By neighbor, I guess I mean the neighboring farm," he explained. "Johnny Jones was his name, I believe. He lives a few miles from here."

Elsie smiled while she watched Oliver's excitement. Somehow, he'd managed to make a connection in her small town. Apparently, it was a connection that offered him transportation too. He was nothing if not resourceful.

"I actually know Johnny," she said, standing up from her seat. "He's the old farmer who always has a piece of grass sticking out of his mouth, lodged between his front two teeth. I used to see him around town once in a while. He's a bit of a trickster."

"He seemed nice enough," Ollie said with a shrug. "He stopped by a while back to see if I needed anything. I was a little nervous answering the door, because I was afraid he might recognize me. But when he walked up, he saw me through the window of the living room, so I couldn't just hide. Funny enough, though, he didn't seem to have any clue who I was. I introduced myself as Oliver and he just shook my hand as though he were meeting anybody else. Didn't seem too impressed by much."

Elsie laughed, shaking her head. "Johnny is definitely not impressed by much. And he also doesn't believe in television, so I doubt he's ever even heard of your football team. Anyway, that's really nice of him that he said you could use his car."

"It's awesome, because it wouldn't feel much like a date if you had to come pick me up for it," Ollie said. "And I want it to be perfect. I was willing to risk having someone deliver one, but this is easier. Johnny assures me that she's 'a beauty.'"

There was no denying that Elsie's crush on Oliver was shifting into high gear. She decided that she'd just relax and go with the flow with him, see where things went.

A date does sound like so much fun, she thought. *It's been a while since I've had that happen.*

"So Saturday, then?" Elsie asked, as the two of them walked toward the front door.

"Yep. Text me your address and I'll be there at seven," he said, as he opened the door for her.

"I live above above the physical therapy clinic at the edge of town," Elsie said. "You can't miss it."

"Perfect. I'll be there." Ollie took Elsie's hands in his. She stood in front of him, feeling butterflies fill her belly. The ice had been broken since they'd kissed, but there was still that fun tension between them.

"I guess I'll see you then," Elsie said, before gently biting her lower lip.

"I can't wait," Ollie said.

Then he leaned in and kissed her again. It took Elsie's breath away, but this time, she didn't hesitate. She pressed into him, letting their lips collide with a kind of need that could only be present after months of suppressing their true feelings. It was electric. Sparks flew around them and her body burst into flames. She brought her hands to his chest, enjoying the sensation of his firm muscles. His taste, his smell, everything about him turned her on and made this the best kiss she'd ever had in her life. It had been a long time coming.

The two of them stayed embraced in the doorway. Their hands drifted over each other as their tongues danced. Elsie's knees turned to jello, her legs trembling beneath her. Outside, the sun poured down onto the farm. The warmth of spring was on its way, and the bitter winter was coming to an end. She couldn't say for sure, but it was quite possible that this was the most perfect moment she'd ever experienced. She savored it for as long as she could.

Elsie slowly broke the kiss. The two of them gazed and each other. She smiled. It was as though she was seeing Oliver for the first time. No longer was he a patient. The stigma that had held her from expressing her feelings was gone, finally. Now, he was officially a crush. And in the back of her mind, she knew it was even more than that.

Chapter Fourteen

Elsie

Elsie stood in her bedroom, surrounded by a hundred outfits that she'd tried on. It looked like a clothes bomb had gone off. Shirts, blouses, dresses and pants were strewn about, covering nearly every possible surface. It was Saturday afternoon and she was trying desperately to find the perfect thing to wear for her date with Oliver.

Why am I nervous right now? She asked herself. *It's not like I'm going on a blind date or something. It's just Oliver. I've known him for months.*

She couldn't shake the nerves, though. The excitement of going on an actual date and with a very gorgeous man made her heart beat quickly and her palms sweaty. It reminded her of when she was getting ready for senior prom in high school. But at least then, she'd had a dress picked out and knew exactly where she'd be going. Now she had no clue. It had been some time since she'd gone out on a date and felt very ill prepared.

"I wish I knew where he was taking me," she said to herself, standing nearly naked in front of the mirror. She was only wearing black panties and a black bra. "If he had told me where we were going, that would have at least helped narrow down the options for what I should wear."

With only a half an hour left until Oliver picked her up, she didn't have time to dilly dally any longer.

It's not like there are any fancy restaurants in town, so that rules out the little black dress, she thought, sifting through her closet. *And I certainly don't need to dress really nice if we're going to the diner. That would be awkward to go there wearing anything more than ripped jeans and a t-shirt.*

It took a while longer, but she finally settled on something. She slipped on her nicest pair of jeans, which were dark enough to be considered dressy, but light enough in case they did something casual. The weather, though nicer than it had been in months, was still breezy and cool. So she wore a light blue sweater, which she knew would have looked good regardless of the setting of the date. And for shoes, she wore black pumps. When she gazed into the mirror again, a satisfied grin crossed her face.

That should work, she thought. *Finally. Geez.*

She quickly brushed out her hair. For the first time ever, she would be around Oliver with her hair down. It was so rare that she'd almost forgotten what she looked like. Her chocolate curls looked great, though, better than she remembered. And after a few sprays of her favorite perfume, she was ready to go.

I still can't believe I'm about to go on a real date, she thought, gathering her cell phone and lipstick to put into her purse. *And with an ex-patient of mine, of all people. Who'd have thought?*

It would be a nice distraction from things, that was for sure. And she needed a distraction. Uncle Frank's health was always on her mind. His prognosis from the brain tumor was still unknown, but they were planning on doing surgery within the week.

She thought about him all the time, but he assured her that he would be fine and that there was nothing to worry about. Frank saying that obviously didn't help her from worrying. But somehow, spending time with Ollie really did. Ollie soothed her worries better than anything else. Which was just another reason why she didn't want to see him move back home.

By the time she looked at the clock again, it was only five minutes until seven. She glanced out her apartment window, the one that looked over Main Street. In the past few days, all of the remaining winter show had melted. The streets were wet, but it was clear that summer was on the way. The changing season was a reminder of time passing. Soon, Oliver would be back home and her life would go back to the way it was before he arrived. She figured she'd continue treating her usual patients and things would exist as they always had. The status quo would appear untouched, just the way a small town like hers liked it.

With a sigh, she turned and walked to her living room. Taking a seat on the couch, she kicked her feet onto the coffee table. Before she could even take a breathe, her cell phone buzzed in the front pocket of her jeans. It was a text from Ollie that read, "Hey, I'll be there in less than a minute. Wanted to let you know. See you soon."

She couldn't stop the excited smile from lighting up her face. She hopped up from her couch, suddenly more nervous than ever. After a few deep breaths to calm herself, she went to her mirror one last time to make sure she looked good. Her makeup, hair, lipstick and clothing was all in order.

Remember, Elsie, he's not your patient any more, she thought. *Don't act all weird and awkward. Just go have fun.*

A knocking came on her door and her eyes widened.

"He's here," she whispered.

Elsie grabbed her purse and walked toward the front of her apartment. She paused for a second to collect herself, then opened it up the door. Oliver was standing at the top of the stairs, with his usual smile. He'd combed his hair back and shaved his face, making him look even more handsome than she'd ever seen him.

"Hi," she said. "You found it."

"I did." Ollie stepped toward her. "It wasn't too hard, though. There's only one physical therapy clinic in town."

Elsie laughed, giving him a once over. "I don't think I've ever seen you dressed up in anything but a t-shirt and workout shorts."

"Oh, this?" Oliver rubbed his hands over his red and black, buttoned down plaid shirt. "Yeah, I didn't really have anything to wear tonight so I stopped by the country store. Turns out they have a lot of options for men's shirts. They have plaid, cotton plain, wool plaid and probably some other plaids that I've forgotten."

"In that case, I think plaid was a wise choice. You look good," she said, putting her purse over her shoulder. "A little bit country, but I suppose that's a good thing, given where we are."

"Yeah, it's different, but I think I can pull off the look," he said. "Did you happen to notice my shoes?"

Her eyes drifted downward, past Ollie's jeans and to his brand new cowboy boots. They were brown and shiny, and had obviously never seen a day of work.

"Oh, my gosh," she said, putting her hand over her mouth and trying not to giggle. "You went all out."

Oliver shrugged. "Hey, if you're going to do something, do it one hundred percent. That's what Coach always says, anyway."

Elsie was surprised to see him dressed like that, but found herself liking it more than she should. He looked buff and masculine, like something out of an old cigarette ad in a magazine. He was like a young version of the Marlboro man. A legitimate cowboy. Although she knew he'd spent more time with his feet on perfectly trimmed grass than on country dirt.

"By the way, you look beautiful," he said. "Thank you for letting me take you out."

He leaned in and gave her a quick kiss. Her lips tingled and she found herself smiling like an idiot, lost in her crush for her quarterback date.

"Are you ready?" he asked. "This should be fun."

Elsie closed her apartment door and locked it. "Yeah, I'm all set. Where are we going?"

"It's a surprise," he said, taking her hand and leading her down the stairs.

"A surprise, huh?" she asked. "You can't even give me a hint?"

"Nope," he said.

When they got to the bottom of the stairs, Elsie looked around. "Where did you park?"

Ollie chuckled and let out a sigh. "You're going to laugh."

She raised an eyebrow. "What happened? Did Johnny not come through on letting you borrow his car?"

"Oh no, he came through," Ollie said. "Only, he never specified 'car'. He'd said I could borrow his 'mode of transportation' which I had wrongfully assumed was a car. Turns out, the old man only owns a tractor."

"You're kidding me," she said, trying to hold back her laughter. Knowing Johnny, the old man had planned on this.

Oliver shook his head. "I'm not. I hope you don't mind that I'm picking you up for our date on a John Deere."

Ollie led her to the front of the building. Sure enough, parked next to the sidewalk on Main Street was a giant, front-loading John Deere tractor. It was easily twice the size of Elsie's car.

She chuckled, shaking her head in disbelief. "Ollie, you drove this thing here?"

"Yep," Oliver said. "It took me a few minutes to figure it out, but it's actually kind of fun, once you learn how how to use the brakes. I know, I know, it's ridiculous. But I told you that I'd take you out on a proper date and part of that means that I have to pick you up. I thought you'd find it funny."

Her smile continued to widened as she approached the metal machine that was parked in front of her physical therapy practice. The seat of it was at the same height as her head and the back wheels were taller than she was.

"I'm not mad at all," she said, glancing toward him. "This is perfect!"

He grinned. "I thought if anyone would enjoy a unique ride, it would be you."

"Honestly, I love it," she said, climbing up into the seat, which looked like it would barely hold the two of them. "Anybody can take a girl on a date in a car. How many guys are willing to drive a tractor?"

Oliver laughed and climbed into the seat beside her. He grabbed the steering wheel and turned the key. The engine roared the life, rumbling underneath them.

"All I need now is a piece of grass sticking out of my mouth and I'll fit right in," he said, putting the tractor into gear.

Elsie held onto his arm as they pulled away from the curb. She couldn't stop giggling. She sincerely loved the lengths that Ollie was willing to go in order to pick her up. It made her feel so special. Sure, she was being driven across town on an old tractor, but it didn't matter. It could have been an old bicycle for all she cared. What mattered was that he'd worked hard to make it happen and he'd done it all just for her.

"You still aren't going to tell me where we're going?" she asked, having to talk loudly over the firing of the diesel engine.

Oliver looked over. Then he did his best country boy impression. It was terrible. "Well, little lady, I reckon you and I will be moseying on over to the county fair. Last I heard, they're going to have them a merry-go-round and one of them sledge hammer games. What'dya think about that?"

"I think the County Fair sounds like fun!" she said, laughing at his impression. "But I think you'd better work on your country accent a bit. It's a little off. People might realize that you're not from around these parts."

"I've got something for that," he said, pulling a ball cap out of his back pocket. He slipped it on over his hair and pulled it down tight. "Or at the very least, they might not recognize me as Oliver Lance."

"It might work." Elsie pulled the bill of his cap down a little further onto his forehead. "You better keep that on, though. If word gets out that Mr. Lance is in town, you're going to get swarmed by people who want your autograph."

The two of them continued their journey on the tractor. Elsie was smiling on the inside as she sat next to him in the small bucket seat, which seemed to bounce up and down regardless of the fact that they weren't going over any bumps.

I haven't been to the county fair in ages, she thought. *I think the last time I went was with my Uncle Frank when I was ten.*

"Do you know where you're going?" Elsie asked, as Ollie turned the tractor onto a dirt road.

"Not exactly," he said. "I thought I did, but I'm starting to wonder if this is the correct road."

Elsie chuckled. "We can take this road. The county fair grounds are just east of town. I'll tell you when to turn."

"Sounds good," he said, then paused before adding, "Doc."

She just smiled and leaned her against against his shoulder. The nickname was really starting to grow on her.

Chapter Fifteen

Ollie

Oliver steered the tractor into the dirt parking lot near the fair. He had to park all the way in the back because it was so busy. It seemed like everybody in town was there.

"I had no idea it would be so popular," he said, as he turned off the engine. "This must be the thing to do when the weather gets nice."

"Oh, it is," Elsie said. "It's a pretty big deal. I'm willing to bet that nearly every single person in town is here. Don't be surprised if I run into people that I know that want to talk my ear off. If anyone asks, you're a friend from college."

The two of them got off of the tractor and walked hand in hand toward the fair. Ollie smiled as the sounds of the fair became louder. There were children laughing, people talking and the constant drone of the machines that powered the rides. It reminded him of his brother and how they obsessed over the rides when they were kids.

He glanced at Elsie, still shocked at how she'd slowly stolen his heart over the past few months. It hurt to think that he might not see her again after his return home. There was still the ever-lingering *possibility* that he could land her a job on the team, but he hadn't brought that up to her yet. He didn't want to give her false hope. He didn't want to give himself false hope, either.

"What ride do you want to go on first?" Elsie asked, squeezing his hand. "I should probably tell you right now that I'm not a huge fan of heights. So if you were thinking about doing every ride in the park, I might have to sit some out."

"I think that the very first thing we should do is get some cotton candy," he said, smiling like an excited kid. "Then we can figure out which rides to go on."

"Cotton candy?" she asked, raising an eyebrow. "I didn't know that was on your diet."

Oliver laughed. "Everything is on my diet when I'm at a fair. In fact, there are three main food groups here. There's cotton candy, funnel cakes and giant turkey legs. All of which we should partake in."

"You're not going to hear an argument from me," Elsie replied with a hearty laugh.

I love that she's here with me right now, he thought. *I truly feel like there's no place I'd rather be. If it wasn't for my career, I'd find a way to stay. Maybe I should just tear my ACL again. That would do it.*

As the two of them got closer to the fair entrance, Oliver noticed people turning heads. A few older men glanced at him and then whispered something to themselves. He pulled his hat down and his collar up, in an effort to hide as much of himself as possible. It didn't help, though. The plump young woman at the ticket counter recognized him immediately.

"Oliver Lance?" she said. "Oh, my God. Number seven. The Bandits. Is that really you?"

Crap. I had a feeling this would happen, he thought.

Ollie cleared his throat and shook his head. "I get that all the time. I'm not him, though. Oliver Lance is a lot taller than me. Plus, do I really look like the type of guy who can throw a football as fast as he does?"

The girl paused for a moment, cocking her head to the side. Then she shrugged. "I guess not. It's uncanny how much you look like him, though. Anyway, that will be five dollars each."

Oliver paid and the two of them stepped into the fair.

"That was close," Elsie said with a chuckle. "I'm surprised she recognized you, given the cowboy outfit and the hair."

"Who would have thought?" Ollie laughed, leading his date across the dirt path to the cotton candy stand. He ordered a blueberry one for himself and a grape one for Elsie. They then began their stroll through the fair as they ate. But they hardly made it ten feet before people starting coming up to say "hi" to Elsie. Everybody knew her and she knew everyone. And of course, all of that attention only brought more eyes onto Ollie.

"Oliver Lance? Really? In our town?" One older man said, after quickly greeting Elsie.

"No, no," Elsie said. "This is my friend from college, but I assure you, he just happens to look like Oliver Lance."

Oliver did his best to smile and shrug whenever anyone mentioned who they thought he was. Ollie didn't really mind all that much. He wasn't focused on that and at this point, wasn't as concerned with people knowing who he was. Sure, the news would spread like wildfire in a small town if anybody actually believed he was *the* Oliver Lance. But he thought he was doing a pretty good job of convincing everyone otherwise. Regardless, his real focus of the evening was his beautiful date, not a bunch of strangers.

"What do you say we do the Ferris wheel?" Ollie suggested. "It would give us a little privacy."

Elsie looked across the fair, toward the turning wheel. "It's pretty big. I don't know, Ollie. I don't like heights."

"You'll be with me," he said. "You'll be safe, I promise. Please?"

She looked a little nervous, but finally nodded in agreement. "Okay, just don't let me die."

Ollie laughed. "I won't. Trust me, that thing is safe as can be. I'm pretty sure that not one single person has ever even been injured on a Ferris wheel before."

"I think you just made up that little statistic," she said. "Actually, I'm quite positive you did."

"You're technically right. I *did* make that up," he admitted, with a boyish smirk. "But that doesn't mean it might not be true."

Elsie shook her head and smiled. "Come on. Let's go."

The two made their way to the Ferris wheel. The seat was fairly small, just enough for the two of them to squeeze in next to each other. Ollie put his arm around her shoulder as the wheel turned and lifted them into the air.

"See, it's not that bad," he said.

"Yeah, you're right. It's not that scary. "Elsie faced him. "At least with you here with me. I don't think I'd want to do this by myself."

As the wheel turned and sent them higher up into the air, they kissed. It was the kind of kiss that caused the surrounding carnival noises to become mute and distant. For a moment, Oliver felt like the two of them were the center of the entire world. Everything faded to sparkling lights and gentle laughter.

She's so perfect for me, he thought. *I know that I can't have her. It just wouldn't work. But God, I'd love it if I could.*

Time seemed to stop as they two of them continued to kiss on the Ferris wheel. Oliver didn't even notice the movement of the ride. The next thing he knew, they'd gone full circle and the attendant was tapping him on the shoulder. He broke his kiss with Elsie and looked over.

"Sir, the ride is over, please step out." The greasy-haired teenage boy who was working the ride opened door of the cart. He looked annoyed.

"Whoops," Ollie said, flashing a smile toward Elsie.

"Sorry," Elsie said to the attendant. She was bright red. "We'll be on our way now."

"Well, that was awkward," Oliver chuckled, as he took Elsie's hand and walked away from the Ferris Wheel.

"That kid looked a little bit freaked out," Elsie said, giggling. "That was a fun ride, though. I think maybe that's how I can get over my fear of heights. I just have to do everything while kissing you."

"You know, I think that could be arranged." Oliver smiled and squeezed her hand. They made their way across the dirt path that weaved through the events and the multitude of food stands. For being a smaller fair, it still had everything. Lots of rides, tons of food and an entire town of people scurrying throughout enjoying themselves, but the only thing that really had Oliver's attention was Elsie.

She looked incredible. Her tight jeans hugged her curves and accentuated her long legs. The smell of her perfume was intoxicating and the taste of her kiss lingered on his lips. He wanted her. He wanted her so badly it made his whole body ache.

"Hey, Mr. Quarterback," Elsie said, pointing toward one of the stands along the path. "Look, it's a one of those ball throwing games. You think you can win?"

Oliver glanced over. There were two stands to their right. One of them was a dunk tank. Next to that, was a stand with a wooden sign above it that read "milk bottle toss". That was the one Elsie was pointing to. His eyes lit up as soon as he saw it. He popped his knuckles and nodded. "I can certainly give it a try."

A group of kids were standing in front, and they had just finished their turn. One of them spoke to Ollie as soon as he approached.

"I wouldn't even bother with this game," the kid said. "It's impossible. I swear, it's rigged."

"I'll give it a try," Ollie said said with a shrug. "I'm just here to have fun."

"I guess. Good luck, man." The kid shrugged as he walked off. "I'm pretty sure those bottles are glued together or something."

"Don't listen to him." The game's attendant, a young blonde girl in a yellow summer dress, spoke up. "He's just bitter because he didn't have a good throw."

Oliver laughed, turning toward his girl. "Elsie, I'm going to win you that giant teddy bear."

Elsie grinned, bringing her attention toward the giant stuffed bear that was seated on a stool next to the game's attendant. The bear was bright pink and nearly as tall as she was.

"If anyone can win this game, it's you," Elsie said, stepping close to Oliver.

I hope she's right, he thought. *How embarrassing would it be to lose this in front of her?*

"You get three balls to throw," the attendant said, handing the balls to Oliver. "If you're able to knock them all down with just those balls, you can have the giant teddy bear. I'll tell you right now, though, it's harder than you think. Not one person has pulled it off today."

Okay, I got this, Ollie thought, as he lined up to throw. *I hope that kid wasn't right about the bottles being glued together.*

The milk bottles were arranged into a giant pyramid and were a surprising distance away. Nothing he couldn't handle, but pretty far for a kid's game. Oliver figured it to be at least fifteen yards. Good pass for a first down.

"It's been a while since I've thrown a ball," he said, glancing toward Elsie. "Don't judge me if I don't get this."

"You'll get it," she assured him. "I know you can."

Ollie let out a slow breath and then threw the first ball. It rocketed out of his hand, careening toward the milk bottles. He was used to a throwing a football, though and the spin he put on it caused this ball to curve, crashing into the very top bottle. It fell off the stack, but the rest of the pyramid stayed put.

"Damn," he whispered. Second down.

"It's okay, you've got two more tries," Elsie said, encouragingly. "Hit the bottom of the stack."

Ollie wound up and threw the second ball, this one took out the lower right of the pyramid, leaving just two bottles standing. He was understanding what the kid had said about it being nearly impossible. Here was Oliver, a professional quarterback, and even he was unable to get it as easily as he had hoped. He thought he could get them all down in the first ball, but that was clearly not the case.

Alright, he thought. *One more ball. I'm not leaving here without that teddy bear.*

He tossed the final ball, watching as it dropped down directly onto the remaining milk bottles. They split apart, flying in opposite directions and crashing to the ground. Elsie yelped in excitement and wrapped her arms around Ollie's neck, kissing his cheek.

"You did it!" she squealed.

"Wow, you actually *did* do it," the attendant echoed, handing him the over-sized bear. "I've been here all day and I haven't seen anyone get close. You might have quite an arm on you."

"It's all in the wrist," Ollie said, with a wink. He then turned to Elsie, handing her the bear.

"Awww," Elsie said, cuddling into it with a happy grin.

"It's as big as you are." Oliver laughed, as he watched her wrap her arms around it.

"I know, I love it," she said, giving it a squeeze. "Nobody has ever won me anything before. Thank you."

He loved the way her eyes sparkled when she smiled at him like that. It made him feel like the center of the world. It was better than lifting a trophy over his head, or at least pretty darn close. He felt like the MVP with her.

Oliver smiled, putting an arm around her shoulder. Then they just walked. They didn't run to any rides or sprint to the food, they just strolled next to each other enjoying themselves. The sounds and smells and their company was enough. It was all they needed. It was so simple, yet so perfect. Oliver couldn't have asked for a better date.

It's funny, a few months ago, I would have thought doing something like this would be dumb, he thought. *I'd have called this a waste of time and probably said I'd rather be out at a club, getting drinks with my boys and any beautiful women who wanted to join. But now, all of that seems dumb. This county fair with Elsie is so much better than any of that.*

Oliver knew that it wasn't really the fair he was enjoying, it was Elsie's company. Her smile, her laugh, her lighthearted sense of humor. That was what made the fair so much fun. They could have been anywhere and he would have been having a great time, as long as she was with him.

I think I could even enjoy myself at the DMV with her, he thought to himself with a chuckle.

The sun had dipped over the horizon and the air was beginning to cool. He considered suggesting to Elsie about going on some more rides or maybe getting a funnel cake or two, but what he really wanted was to spend some alone time with her.

The fair was fun, but the constant onslaught of people approaching the two of them had become just too much to handle. It was either somebody coming up to say that he looked an awful lot like Oliver Lance, or it was someone who knew Elsie and wanted to say hi. Either way, it seemed like the only time they had gotten a chance to breathe was when they were on the Ferris wheel.

"So, want to check out any more rides?" Oliver asked, hoping she was ready to be alone with him too.

"No, not really." Her response was music to his ears. "To be honest, I was wondering if you wanted to maybe get some take out Chinese or something. I'm starving for food with at least a little bit of nutrition. We could eat at my place."

"Chinese?" he repeated, his own stomach rumbling in response to the word.

"I mean, you're probably used to going to fancy restaurants and clubs, but there aren't any around here, and-"

"Chinese sounds perfect," he interrupted her. He loved that she relaxed into a big smile. "But you *do* remember that we drove a tractor here, right? You don't think they'll mind if we park in front of the restaurant in the John Deere?"

Elsie leaned her head against Ollie's shoulder, as they made their way toward the parking lot and the tractor they rode in on. "You have to remember just how small of a town this is. I doubt it will be the first time a tractor has pulled up into the Chinese restaurant's parking lot."

"It's settled then," Ollie said, as he helped Elsie and her bear onto the seat of the tractor, before sliding in himself.

He started up the engine and pointed the tractor back toward town. More than a few people turned their heads to watch as the Oliver Lance look-a-like, a town's physical therapist and a giant pink teddy bear pulled out of the parking lot on a John Deere tractor. Oliver knew it would be a story that many of the town's people would enjoy chatting about for the next few weeks.

Chapter Sixteen

Elsie

Elsie smiled from ear to ear as she unlocked her front door. Oliver was next to her, his arms overflowing with takeout boxes from the Chinese restaurant. The smell of sesame chicken and fried rice filled her nostrils, making her stomach rumble.

"I still can't believe the expression on the restaurant owner's faces when they saw us pull up in the tractor," Elsie said, as she stepped into her apartment and set her new teddy bear down on the chair near the front door. "They looked as us like we had come from another planet."

"We definitely made an impression," Oliver said. "They're probably still talking about it."

"Sorry, my house is kind of a mess." Elsie quickly picked up her living room area. "If you want, you can grab plates from the kitchen. We'll eat at that small table in the corner."

"You got it," Ollie said, kicking off his shoes and walking toward the kitchen.

Elsie couldn't remember the last time she had had company at her place that wasn't family. She wasn't used to having to keep things in order. As soon as she had picked up the living room, she went straight to her bedroom. The after-effects of her indecision on what to wear that evening was still there. Clothes were scattered on every possible surface.

Crap, she thought. *It looks like a tornado came through here.*

She had a couple of choices. She could either take the time to put everything back on the hangars and get it all organized, or she could do the quick option.

It's all going in the closet, she thought, picking up armfuls of clothes. She dropped them into a pile in the closet and repeated the process until everything was picked up. The mess was at least hidden now. It was good enough so that she wouldn't look like a total slob if Oliver saw her room, and she was really hoping that he would.

"Sorry about that," she said, stepping out of the bedroom and putting on a big smile.

Oliver was already seated at her small table in the corner of what she called her "dining room". It was hardly a dining room, though. More like a few square feet of unusable space that was wedged between the living room and kitchen. It was just enough to fit her table and two chairs.

"No problem," Ollie said, pushing his bangs off of his forehead. "Your place is great. I like it."

"It's tiny," Elsie said. "Someday I'll get a house."

"It's small, but nice." Ollie glanced around, then refocused his gaze onto Elsie. "Plus, it's close to where you work. Can't get much better than that."

"Living above your business is a mixed blessing," she said, taking a seat in the chair across from Ollie. "Sometimes it feels like I can never get away from work. It was actually really nice getting to treat you over the past few months. I got out of this building for a few hours."

"I enjoyed it, too," he said, as he put a plate in front of her. "It's been a nice little vacation. And I use the term 'vacation' lightly, since you put me through some of the hardest workouts of my entire life."

"I'd say it paid off, though. We whipped you into shape." Elsie smiled warmly, but her heart sank a little bit. She was going to miss those workouts and all of that time with him.

"You sure did," he said, patting the top of his once-injured knee. "You fixed me and I was pretty sure I'd never be fixed. Thank you, Elsie. Seriously. I honestly don't know what I would have done if it wasn't for you."

Elsie blushed at the compliment. "Just doing my job."

"No, the attendants at the fair, *they* were just doing their jobs. Not you, though. It was more than that," Ollie opened up the takeout boxes while he spoke. "You work miracles. Something about your touch and your passion for what you do. I hope that you see your work as more than just a job. Because what you did for me was nothing short of incredible."

"You're making me blush," Elsie said, sweeping her hair over her ear. "Don't stop."

"You deserve it," he said. "And also, you deserve some of this sesame chicken. It smells amazing."

"It really does," she agreed, as she put some of it on her plate. Her stomach grumbled and her mouth watered. Cotton candy was great, but it wasn't exactly filling.

She was about to take a bite, but Ollie stopped her. "Wait, hold on a second. We should do a toast. Do you have anything to drink?"

"Yes, a toast is in order." Elsie nodded as she stood up from her chair. "I have some boxed wine in the fridge, but I think that's about it."

"That will work," he said. "But you sit down. Let me get it. I want to spoil you tonight."

She smiled and stopped in her tracks. "Are you sure? I can get it."

"Nonsense." Ollie got up and led Elsie back to her seat. "You just relax and eat. I'll get the wine. This is supposed to be a date."

She sat back down in front of her plate, watching as Oliver disappeared into the kitchen. Her heart ached with how much she was really starting to like the guy. The more she got to know him, the more she realized he was perfect for her. It wasn't just his good looks, though that definitely didn't hurt. It was the way he made her feel. Especially now that the whole patient/provider stigma was gone. Ollie treated her like a princess and made her feel like she was his whole world.

To think, this is only the first date we've been on, she thought. *I can't imagine how great things could be if he didn't have to leave.*

In a flash, Oliver was back. He had in his hands two wine glasses, filled with the best boxed wine money could buy. Which also turned out to be the most inexpensive wine that could be purchased at the corner store. He handed one of the glasses to Elsie and then took his seat. Holding his drink in the air, he paused and gazed into her eyes.

"What should we cheers to?" he asked.

How about... how freaking gorgeous you look when you're dressed up like a cowboy? She thought, quietly to herself.

"I don't know," she replied. "Your recovery?"

Ollie nodded slowly. "Yeah, my recovery. But also, let's do a cheers to the car accident that brought me here."

Elsie raised her eyebrows. "You want to toast to your car wreck?"

He shrugged. "Don't get me wrong, I'd be happy to live my life without having to experience another one. But if it wasn't for that wreck, I wouldn't be sitting here right now with you. Seems to me like that's something worth praising."

"I guess I never thought of it that way," she said, as she slowly twirled the wine in her glass. "So how about this: here's to happy accidents, the kind that bring you some place that you'd never have expected. The kind that transform our lives for the better."

Oliver stared into her eyes as she spoke, causing her to melt.

"I couldn't have said it better than that if I'd spent weeks rehearsing," he said. "Cheers."

"Cheers." Elsie lifted her glass and clinked it against his.

"This is the first sip of alcohol I've had in quite awhile," Ollie said, after taking a drink of the wine. "In fact, the last drink I had was the night of the wreck, right before we left the club."

Elsie drank some of hers and set the glass down. With a smile, she said, "They have boxed wine at the club? That must have been a fancy place you were partying at."

Oliver laughed, seeming relieved by her joke. "Oh yeah, we only party at the best places. If they don't have boxed wine in the VIP section, we get the hell out of there."

"A VIP section without boxed wine?" Elsie asked, playing along. "I can't imagine a place so barbaric."

The two of them laughed and then began to eat their meals. There was a pleasant tension between them. Elsie could feel it in the air. There was a magnetic pull, drawing her toward the man across the table from her. It caused a tingling to shoot through her body, radiating from her core. It felt familiar. It was a similar sensation as the one she'd experienced when she'd given Oliver his back massage.

Maybe it was the sip of wine kicking in, or maybe it was the fact that they had the privacy of her apartment. Or, she thought, it could have simply been that the moment was finally right. But as she ate her meal, she couldn't stop thinking about how badly she wanted Oliver physically. And she knew that if it was going to happen between them, then this night would be the final chance.

"How's your food?" Ollie asked, interrupting her thoughts.

She swallowed her bite of sesame chicken, followed by another sip of red wine. "It's really good. Nothing is as good as the Thai chili pizza we had, though."

"Agreed," Ollie replied. "That pizza was amazing. I remember that night so well. It was the first time you came over that wasn't for therapy."

"That was a strange evening for me," she admitted. "It was the same night that I found out about my uncle's diagnosis."

"How is he doing anyway?" Oliver asked.

"He's doing alright, given the circumstances," Elsie said. "The doctors are trying to decide whether or not they should do surgery, or try chemo first and see if it shrinks the tumor. But, as is always the case with Uncle Frank, he's somehow in good spirits about the whole thing."

"I wish him the best," Ollie said. "I didn't get to meet him, but you've painted him as an amazing person."

"Maybe you can meet him before you leave, if it works out." Elsie swallowed another sip of her wine. It made her stomach feel warm and fuzzy, helping her to relax.

"I'm really going to miss you, Elsie," Ollie said, setting down his fork. "It's kind of crazy how fast this time has flown by. I hope that we can stay in touch after I leave."

"I hope so, too," she said. "But I know you've got a pretty complicated life back home, so I understand if it doesn't happen. I'm well aware that most people don't live the simple, small-town life that I do."

Elsie fought back some tears. Every minute she spent with Ollie was another minute closer to him leaving. It was a double-edged sword. She wished she had some magic powers, something that could allow her to stop time and live in the moment forever. But forever wasn't an option. Not for anyone.

"Are you finished?" she asked, looking at his empty plate.

Ollie patted his belly. "Yes, I'm stuffed."

He stood up and cleared the table, while Elsie finished her wine.

I could seriously get used to having a man around the house, she joked to herself. *I feel so spoiled right now.*

"What do you want to do next?" she asked. "I can put some music on and we can pretend it's the club? As long as we turn it down by ten, the neighbors won't mind."

Oliver popped back into the living room. "How about we just relax on the couch for a minute and decide? I'd be up for watching a movie here. Just something simple. I don't really care what we do, I just want to spend the time with you."

"That sounds great," Elsie said, standing up from her chair.

They walked over to the couch and sat down. Oliver scooted close and placed a hand on top of her knee, while Elsie grabbed the remote and clicked on the TV, turning it to a movie channel. She didn't recognize the movie that was on, but didn't really care. It was really just background noise. Her body was on fire, burning with three months of subdued passion. That was all she could focus on.

This is likely our last night ever, she thought. *I'm not usually a one-night stand kind of girl, but this is different. It's our only chance to be together. I'd kick myself if I didn't express my true feelings.*

"Ollie," Elsie said, turning to face him. "Kiss me."

Her words fell out of her mouth in one desperate exhale. Oliver turned and brought his lips to hers. No hesitation. Not any more. She moaned softly as their tongues danced. Elsie slowly crawled over the top of him, straddling him, without breaking their kiss. His hands gripped the outside of her thighs as he pulled her firmly over his lap. In an instant, she became wet with desire.

This may or may not be the smartest move, she thought. *I might fall for him even harder by getting this close to him. But God help me, because I don't care right now. This is all I want.*

Elsie brought her hands down to the front of his shirt, gently pressing against his muscular pecks. His firm muscles tightened beneath her hands, making her want him so badly that her legs trembled with anticipation. The kissing became more passionate by the second, like an upward roller coaster. Their tongues continued their sensual dance. There was an eagerness in their kiss, one that hadn't been there previously. It made it very clear to Elsie that he wanted this just as badly as she did.

Oliver's strong hands moved up her thighs. He placed them onto her hips, holding her firmly against him. His touch felt amazing. It was strong and sexual. Elsie slowly broke the kiss. She was practically panting.

She gazed at Oliver, noticing that his eyes had dilated and his breathing had quickened. They only looked at each other for a brief moment, before leaning in and resuming their kiss. It was like neither of them could get enough of each other. It was desperate and passionate, and Elsie began to ache with a kind of desire she hadn't experienced before.

Her hands drifted to the buttons of his plaid shirt. She undid the top one, letting her fingers slide underneath the cloth and to his bare skin. She could feel his breathing and his heart beat quicken. Elsie continued moving her hands downward, unbuttoning Ollie's shirt a little at a time, until his entire front was exposed. Then she broke their kiss, letting her gaze move down his torso.

His ripped chest and washboard abs flexed with his breathing. Every muscle was accentuated. The word 'perfection' wouldn't have done him any justice. Elsie touched him, letting her fingers trace over the lines of his stomach. Ollie kept his eyes locked onto her and his hands firmly on her hips.

"Can I tell you something?" Ollie asked, in a whisper. "I wanted you from the first moment I saw you in those green scrubs. I didn't say anything, but it's how I felt."

Elsie gently bit her bottom lip before responding. "I wanted you then, too."

Oliver reached forward and grabbed the bottom of Elsie's sweater. He lifted it upward and Elsie raised her arms in the air, letting him take it off completely. As soon as it was off, Ollie's eyes refocused on her and his jaw dropped.

"God, you're beautiful," he whispered, as he leaned forward and brought his lips to her neck.

Elsie dipped her head back, pressing her chest toward him. Oliver kissed the outside of her neck, just below her ear. Then he inched downward, dragging his lips on her sensitive skin, all the way to her collarbone. Ollie's touch sent goose bumps popping up all over her arms.

He let out a low growl, moving his face to her cleavage. He kissed the top of her breasts and fondled them over her bra at the same time. Elsie drew in a slow breath and pressed her chest toward him. She wanted him as close as possible. She needed to feel him.

"Yes," she mouthed, though no actual noise came out.

While he continued to kiss her cleavage, Elsie reached back and unclasped her bra. It fell loosely off of her shoulders. She shimmied it the rest of the way, letting it fall down onto Oliver's lap. Oliver growled in approval and then immediately brought his lips over one of her nipples. As soon as he did, a shudder of pleasure burst through Elsie's body. She ran her hands through Oliver's hair and pulled his face against her. The sensation increased, taking her breath away.

Ollie clearly knew how to pleasure a woman. He was delicate with his tongue as he flicked it against her firm nipple. Then he'd gently bite on it, slowly dragging away until it fell out of his mouth. Then he'd lick it again, soothing the pleasurable pain he'd just created.

Without even realizing it, Elsie had begun to buck her hips forward. Now, though, it wasn't just Ollie's jeans that she could feel between her thighs. His cock had grown hard and she noticed it as she moved her body over his lap.

As if she wasn't already turned on enough, the feel of his manhood intensified things. Her body tingled with anticipation. She *craved* him now, aching to have him deep inside of her.

Oliver slowly pulled his face away from her chest, creating a wet kissing noise. He moved to her other breast and began giving it equal attention. Elsie was writhing on top of him, moving her body in a way that intensified the friction against her jeans. She felt so naughty, so bad. It was a side of her that she didn't get to express very often.

"I want you so bad," Ollie said, pulling away from her breasts. "I need you right now."

Elsie nodded in agreement. "Then take me."

The side of his mouth curled up into a smirk and his pupils dilated. With his hands on her hips, he lifted her off of him and set her back down on the couch. Elsie giggled, surprised by how strong he was. She'd seen him lift some pretty significant weight in the gym, but was still shocked at how easily he could move her. It was as though she weighed less than a feather.

She watched as Oliver stood up from the couch. He faced her with his shirt open. Her eyes moved from his chest, downward along his abs, all the way until they landed on the bulge that was protruding from the front of his jeans. His erection was thick and firm, looking like it was about to rip through the denim.

Oliver let his shirt fall off of his shoulders, where it landed on the floor behind him. Then he placed his hands onto the couch cushion on either side of Elsie, hovering over her. Their lips grazed, but he quickly brought his face down, kissing the side of her neck. She leaned her head back and placed her hands over his shoulders. His muscles flexed under her fingers as he held himself over her. Those muscles, which she'd once massaged. The same muscles that had been turning her on for months. Now she could finally touch them guilt-free.

He kissed between her breasts as he moved his face downward, making his way past her belly button and to the waist of her jeans. When he got there, he undid the silver button that held them together. As soon as it popped open, Ollie pulled her zipper down.

With his fingers in the waist of her jeans, Oliver gently tugged them downward. She helped him shimmy them off by bringing her legs together and lifting them into the air. He tossed her jeans to the side, then looked her up and down, shaking his head in awe. She watched as his breathing quickened and the expression of lust on his face intensified. Underneath her panties, a desperate throbbing had come to live, creating a heat that radiated outward. It was a fire that could only be extinguished by Ollie.

"Take your pants off, too," Elsie said, with a smirk. She was surprised to find herself being so assertive, but something about the moment just brought it out of her.

"Anything for you, Doc." Ollie smiled, as he slipped off his jeans.

As soon as he kicked them away, Elsie's jaw dropped and a burst of passion filled her. Wearing only his boxer briefs, she could now see the outline of his cock as it pressed against the thin material.

He's big, she thought. *He's big and gorgeous and sweet and perfect in every way. If I'm dreaming right now, then I don't want to wake up. At least not until this is over. Please don't be a dream.*

Oliver dropped to his knees in front of the couch and lifted up Elsie's legs so that they could rest over his shoulders. The position put his face directly in front of her most sensitive area. It caused her hands to tremble with anticipation. She'd already learned just how skilled he was with the use of his tongue, and the thought of him doing that down there caused her to bite her lip.

He looked up toward her, then licked his lips as he pulled her panties off. He tossed them to the side then immediately brought his face to the inside of Elsie's leg, just below her knee. He gently bit the skin, then kissed it, making his way upward. She reached forward and gripped his hair, urging him closer. She wanted his touch.

But he didn't change his pace. He just slowly kissed a straight line down from her knee. Elsie's heart beat rapidly in her chest, pounding her ear drums. Her entire body tingled as he neared. He hadn't even touched her pussy yet and she already felt like she could climax.

"Please," she whispered, her words drowned in desperation. "Ollie, please. Stop teasing me."

He let out a soft chuckle, as he eased his way forward. Finally, after what felt like an eternity to Elsie, he got to the top of her thigh. He kissed the crease and then moved his face over, bringing his tongue to her. As soon as he did, her world exploded in ecstasy. With her fingers still intertwined in his hair, she squeezed her hands into fists. Ollie let out a deep moan as she pulled his tongue into her. The vibration from his throat traveled through his lips and into her flesh, making the pleasure intensify.

Ellie was panting now. The tingling in her body radiated outward, all the way to her fingertips. Each lap of

Ollie's tongue sent another wave of bliss into her, and each wave built on the last one until it all came to one glorious climax. She shuddered, biting her bottom lip. Her legs clamped over Ollie's ears. She arched her back, pressing her chest in the air. Then she drew in a quick breath, holding it as a powerful orgasm pumped through her.

Oliver kept pace, using his tongue in the most miraculous of ways. He continued until Elsie finally released her breath and relaxed her back. The climax had passed, but it had done nothing to slow the lust pumping through her veins.

"That was amazing," she whispered, in a daze.

In that moment, she had no worries at all. Nothing else in her life that usually ate at her mind was present. All she could feel and think about was the pleasure that lingered in her, even after Ollie pulled away and slowly stood up in front of her. Her eyes focused and she watched as he slipped his thumbs into the elastic waist strap of his underwear.

Oliver peeled his boxer briefs off quickly. Elsie's jaw dropped at the same speed. He was as hard as could be. And big. He slowly stroked himself as he took a step forward. He seemed eager to enter her, but paused before doing so.

"We should use a condom," he said.

Elsie reached over, pulling one out of her purse. "Here." She tossed it to him and he slipped it on. As he did that, Elsie laid down on the couch, bringing her head to the red velvet pillow at the end. Oliver crawled over the top of her, placing his hands above her shoulders. She watched him breath, admiring the muscles in his arms as they flickered with the tiniest of his movements.

Ollie gently clenched his jaw. Then he slowly bucked his hips forward, sliding between her thighs.

"Yes," she groaned, gripping her fingers into his shoulders.

Her eyes rolled into the back of her head as he entered her completely. Pleasure overwhelmed her, drowning her in ecstasy. With her legs wrapped around his waist, Ollie began to thrust his body. He started slowly, easing in and out, almost teasing Elsie with his pace. Then his movements quickened.

Elsie lifted her head, watching as he made love to her. His abs flexed with each thrust and the muscles in his arms continue to ripple as he held himself above her. Wave after wave of sensation penetrated her. Her body exploded in pleasure, making it difficult not to moan. She bit her bottom lip, once again closing her eyes and leaning her head back. Her hands stayed on Ollie, though. Her fingers drifted over his body, up and down his back, and then across his shoulders.

When Elsie finally opened her eyes and focused, she saw that Ollie's skin was covered in a light layer of glimmering sweat. His hair had fallen down over his forehead, nearly covering his blue eyes. He was breathing harder and nearly every one of his thrusts was accompanied by an animalistic grunt.

"My turn," she said, bringing her hand to Ollie's chin and lifting his gaze. "Sit back."

He did as she asked. He sat back, bringing his feet to the floor and his arms over the back of the couch. Elsie crawled over him, straddling his lap. Hovering above him, she moved her hips side to side, letting his crown float just below her, teasing him.

"You just *love* torturing me, don't you?" he asked, with a playful smirk.

Elsie shrugged. "I've just gotten used to it."

She eased her weight down, but only a little ways. Then she brought her body back up, taking away the pleasure from Ollie.

"You're killing me," he groaned, bringing his hands up to fondle her chest.

Elsie enjoyed being in control and teasing Oliver. It made her feel powerful and desired, but at the same time, she was also teasing herself and she couldn't take it for much longer. She needed him back inside. She almost felt empty without him.

"Kiss me," she whispered.

Ollie leaned forward and brought his lips to hers. As soon as they touched, Elsie brought her weight down over his lap, wrapping herself over his cock once again. The pleasure was back instantly. Her jaw dropped and she broke their kiss with a moan. With her hands gripping Oliver's shoulders, she began to ride him.

Ollie's eyes were half open and his lips were parted. The look of utter bliss was written all over his face. His expression mirrored how Elsie felt. It was perfect pleasure. It wasn't just the fact that she was having sex. It was that she was having sex with someone she really cared about and was truly attracted to. That fact alone multiplied every sensation in her body, making the moment that much more intense.

Elsie leaned forward, bringing her chest toward Ollie's face as she rode him. He began to pleasure her breasts with his mouth, gently biting and licking her nipples. The combination of that, and having him inside of her, caused the waves of ecstasy to increase in intensity. She moved faster, riding him harder and harder. Each drop of her weight caused another pulse of sensation to enter her and each pulse sent her closer to orgasm. Within a few seconds, she was climaxing again.

She clenched around him as she rode the final wave of ecstasy. A moan escaped her lips and her fingers dug into Ollie's arms. When the pleasure passed, her legs were trembling. She began to slow down, but then changed her mind as Oliver whispered, "I'm coming."

"Yes," she responded, her body coming alive at his words. "Come for me."

Keeping pace, Elsie rode Oliver's cock as hard as she could. She watched as his face contorted. His lips curled into a pleasurable grimace and he closed his eyes. The flesh of his cheeks turned red and he brought his hands to her thighs, squeezing them firmly. He let out an animal sounding grunt, followed by a quick exhale. She stayed straddled over him until he finally opened his eyes, looking dazed and content.

"You're incredible," he said, between heavy breaths.

She leaned in and gave him a kiss. "You are, too."

Elsie slowly crawled next to Ollie on the couch. He put his arm around her, holding her close. The two of them relaxed for a while. The movie that had been on in the background continued playing, but neither of them were paying it any attention. Especially Elsie. Her hands and legs were still shaking.

That was absolutely amazing, she thought. *A week ago, he was my patient. Now he's my lover, at least for the night. It's crazy how fast life can change.*

Oliver kissed the top of her head as he stroked her shoulder. His touch was soothing and she found her eyelids getting heavy.

"Are you falling asleep on me, beautiful?" Ollie asked, causing Elsie to look up.

"Just resting my eyes," she said, with a smile.

"Come on, let's go to bed," he said.

Oliver stood up from the couch and took Elsie's hand. She followed him to the bedroom, where they crawled under the covers. She snuggled up next to him, resting her head onto his naked chest. The sound and cadence of his breathing quickly lulled her into a deep sleep. She felt so safe next to him and slept better than she had in years.

Chapter Seventeen

Oliver

Oliver sat in the back of the taxi. Two suitcases were next to him, stuffed with all of the clothes he'd brought with him to Iowa. In addition, he'd also packed a few mementos. One of which was the ticket stub from the fair. He wanted something to remember that very special day by. It was the first and last date with the best woman on the planet.

"I'll be back in a few minutes, okay?" Oliver said to the driver, opening the rear door.

"No problem," the cabby responded. "I'll wait right here."

"Thanks."

Ollie stepped out of the car and sighed as he looked at the building in front of him. The 'open' sign on the front window of the physical therapy office was lit up and inside, he saw Elsie behind the counter. Her head was down and it looked like she was either on the computer or doing paperwork.

"I guess this is it," he whispered to himself as he approached the door. His feet moved like lead.

His mind and heart had been a whirl of emotions for the past week. He and Elsie had been able to spend a lot of time together, which was amazing, but it didn't come without its consequences. Because of it, he'd grown substantially closer to her. The girl had stolen his heart. She was all he could think about.

Day and night, Elsie was on his mind. She was the most amazing woman he'd ever met, both physically and emotionally. He knew he'd never meet another girl like her. But regardless, it was time for him to go home. His team, his coach, his contracts, and all of the fans of the Bandits were counting on him to be there for training. It was a tough decision, but he didn't have much choice.

Oliver pulled on the door handle, causing a little electronic bell to ring. Elsie looked up from her desk and smiled as soon as she saw him. Her smile faded almost immediately, though, when she looked past Ollie to see the taxi cab waiting outside.

"Hey," she said, standing up from her desk. She ran a hand over her hair, smoothing her ponytail.

She was wearing her lime green scrubs, Oliver's favorite.

"Hey, gorgeous," he said, with a sigh. "Come here."

Elsie walked into his open arms and he held her close. He kissed the top of her head, breathing in the scent of her rose shampoo. It made his heart ache. The smell was surprisingly nostalgic, bringing back a wave of memories and emotions from the previous few months. When Elsie pulled away, he saw tears in her eyes.

"I knew this day was coming, but I guess didn't expect it to be this hard," she said, looking away. "It suddenly feels real."

A tear streamed down her cheek as she spoke and Ollie gently wiped it away with his thumb.

"I know. This is a lot more difficult than I thought it would be," he said, keeping his hand on her cheek. "Who would have thought that I'd grow to love this town and the people in it?"

Elsie smiled, but it wasn't genuine. He could tell she was trying to force herself not to cry. But he could see through it. He knew her well enough to know what her real smile looked like and this wasn't it. Not even close.

"It's going to feel weird without you here." Elsie gazed at him, making Ollie's heart sink even further. He was going to miss those beautiful eyes of hers.

"I'm really going to miss you," he said.

As the words tumbled out of his mouth, a tear welled up in his eye and slid down his cheek. He wiped it away with his sleeve, surprised by how much emotion the moment was bringing out of him. It wasn't like him to feel this way. The only other thing in the world that had ever caused him to shed a tear was his brother's cancer.

"Do you think we'll be able to stay in touch?" Elsie asked, her voice just a little to chipper to be real. "I know you'll be busier than I will be, but I'd like to check in at some point and see how you're doing."

"Yes, we can stay in touch," he said, then let out a defeated sigh. "But I don't see it bringing anything but heartache. If we keep talking then it'll only make me wish I didn't have to be in California. And it'll only make you wish you didn't have to be in Iowa. Maybe it'll hurt less if we just move forward from here."

Saying the words stung his heart. It had crossed Oliver's mind several times to suggest the idea of a long distance relationship with Elsie. He had money, so flying out to see her wouldn't have been that big of a deal. But after much consideration, he realized that it would only end up hurting her.

She needed someone who could really *be* with her, not just someone who could see her every other month in person and talk with her on the phone every few days. She deserved better than that. As much as he didn't want to let her go, he knew that he had to. In the long run, it was the right thing, for *her*.

Elsie nodded slowly. "Yeah, I guess you're right. It's probably for the best."

"I have something for you, though," Oliver said, hoping that he could shed a little optimism on the situation.

Her eyes widened a bit, but he could still see the sadness in them. Ollie reached into the front pocket of his jeans and pulled out a single silver key, pressing into Elsie's palm.

"What's this for?" she asked.

"It's the key to the farmhouse," he said. "I'm on the lease for another three weeks, but wanted to give you access. Your real gift is inside the house."

Elsie cocked her head to the side. "What is it?"

"I want you to have all of the medical and workout equipment," he said, unable to keep himself from smiling. "Every piece of it is yours now."

Her jaw dropped. "Ollie, that's over a million dollars worth of equipment. I can't accept that."

"Yes, you can." He grinned as he cradled her chin in his hand. "I *want* you to have it. You deserve every bit of it and more. I've hired movers to bring it from the farmhouse to here. They'll come tomorrow, but you'll have to let them in the house. That's why I gave you the key."

Elsie looked like she was about to fall over from surprise, so Oliver wrapped his arms around her to hold her up.

"Oliver, that equipment is going to turn this physical therapy office into the most advanced clinic in the county," she said, shaking her head in awe as she looked at the key in her hand. "Thank you. Thank you so much. I can't believe how generous you are."

"It's the least I can do," he said, kissing her cheek. "If it wasn't for you, I wouldn't be walking right now. And I sure as hell wouldn't be about to jump into training again. If not for you, Elsie, my life would be over. There's one more thing, though."

She lifted her gaze, seeming surprised that there could possibly be something else he could give her. "What's that?"

"I know that when I got here, it was kind of a secret," Ollie said. "We didn't want people to know the severity of my injury and all that. But since I'm up and running again, I want you to use my name to help grow your business. As long as it's never known just how bad of shape I was in when I first came here. Feel free to advertise your business as 'the clinic that has served Oliver Lance' or something along those lines. Keep it vague and it'll be fine."

"You're serious?" she asked. "You really wouldn't mind?"

"Not at all," he said, watching as Elsie finally began to smile for real. "It should help drum up some business. I'd imagine that people will start coming from all over once they hear how you helped me out. I already asked my publicist to make you up some posters."

"You're amazing, you know that?" Elsie said, as she brought her hands to Oliver's chest. "What you've just given me has the capacity to turn my Uncle's business completely around."

"I hope you make millions," Ollie said, with a soft smile.

Outside, the taxi cab honked his horn. Oliver spun around and waved at the driver. It was clear the man behind the wheel was getting impatient. Ollie wasn't too concerned about that, but he did need to hurry if he wanted to catch his flight.

"You need to go," Elsie said, as he turned back around to face her.

Never in his life, had his heart ached as much as it did right then, standing there with Elsie. The moment was tender and beautiful, but it was also fleeting. This would be the last time he'd lay eyes on her.

"I wish you the best of everything," Ollie said, holding back his own tears. "Truly, Elsie. I hope that life gives you absolutely everything you want and more. You deserve it. You deserve the world. Thank you again for all that you've done for me. I wouldn't be able to repay you in a thousand lifetimes."

Elsie sobbed as she wrapped her arms around Ollie's neck. She brought her lips to his and they kissed. Ollie savored the moment the best he could. He placed his hands onto her hips and held her body close. He wanted the kiss to last forever. Her smell, her taste. He was going to miss everything about her.

When she pulled away, there were fresh tears on her cheeks and she wiped them off with the back of her hand.

"It was three of the best months I've ever had in this town," she said. "I'll never forget you, Ollie."

"Me either." The strings on Oliver's heart pulled in every direction as he spoke, shredding it to pieces. "I couldn't forget you if I tried, Elsie."

The cabby honked the horn again, this time holding down on it for more than just a few seconds. Elsie drew in a long breath and exhaled. "You should go, Ollie. He's waiting."

Oliver nodded slowly, not wanting to turn away even though he had to. "Okay. I'll see you, Elsie. Take care."

"You too," she replied, then quickly turned away, obviously devastated.

Ollie took a few steps backward, until his butt hit the door. He pushed it open and then stepped outside. He felt numb, sad and confused. It felt like his heart had been pulled out of his body, stomped on by his cleat-wearing offensive line, and then pushed back into the space behind his rib cage. He'd never felt so much heartache in his life.

He crawled into the back seat of the taxi and closed the door. Then he took one last glance at the physical therapy clinic. Through the window, he saw Elsie. She was standing inside behind the counter, drying her tears with a tissue.

"Take me to the airport," Ollie said, facing forward.

He didn't speak another word the entire day.

***

It was only ten o'clock and the line of people standing outside the club was so long that it spilled out onto the street. Oliver followed his teammates to the front of the line. The bouncers recognized them immediately and ushered them inside. No wait and no cover charge. Just like always.

Joseph wrapped an arm around Oliver's shoulder and they stepped inside, making their way toward the reserved

VIP booth in the back. "You don't seem too excited tonight, Ollie. We're here to celebrate the return of our quarterback, so you better get ready to have some fun."

Ollie nodded and forced a smile. "Yeah, I'm ready. Still just getting used to being back in California, that's all. It feels kind of strange after being gone for so long."

"Cali is your home," Joseph said. "You'll get used to it again. Once we get a few drinks in you, you'll be back to yourself in no time."

The group made their way toward the VIP and took their seats. People scrambled around them, trying to catch a glimpse of the team. Girls screamed out, guys tried to get high fives. Everybody in there acted like they knew Ollie, but he didn't know a single one of them besides his teammates. The crowd was filled with nothing but strangers.

Once they sat down, Ollie put his feet up onto the table in the middle. Before he could say a word, Adam, The Bandits' running back, pushed a glass of whiskey into his hand.

"Drink up, man," he said. "Here's to you finally being back in the game."

Ollie held up his glass and then took a sip, letting the harsh liquid slide down his throat. He cringed and set the drink on the table.

"Been a while since you've had the good stuff, huh?" Adam asked, laughing. "Man, what happened to you out there in the sticks?"

"Sticks?" Oliver asked. "What do you mean?"

"Come on, man. Everybody knows you went out to the middle of nowhere for your recovery," he said. "Well, the *public* doesn't know. But everyone on the team does. That accident that you and Sean were in was pretty brutal. You were lucky to live through that. But you weren't fooling any of us when you said you were fine. We all knew your leg was messed up and that you went halfway across the country to get it fixed. I heard you went to some little redneck town where nobody would recognize you."

These grown men gossip like school children, Ollie thought. *You'd think they would at least have the decency not to pry into my business.*

"It *wasn't* a redneck town," Ollie replied harshly. "It was just a place that had a very good physical therapist who happened to specialize in my type of injury."

Adam held his hands up in the air defensively. "Okay, man. I wasn't trying to offend whatever town you've been in for the past three months. Just trying to catch up."

"I know, sorry," Oliver said, patting Adam on the shoulder. "But all that anybody needs to know is that I'm healed up and ready for training. In fact, I'm better and stronger than ever. This next season is going to be one for the books. You watch."

"That's what I like to hear," Adam said, before taking a sip of his drink. "And that's worth celebrating, if you ask me."

Oliver hadn't been sure that he even wanted to go out tonight. His buddies had talked him into it, saying that it would be good for him. He wanted to believe them. He wanted to think that there was something he could do that would actually get his mind off of Elsie, but she was the only thing he could think about, and being at the club didn't help at all. It only reminded him of the car wreck. The wreck that led him to meeting the girl of his dreams.

I should call her, he thought, then immediately changed his mind. *No, I can't. She's home with her family. As much as I want her right now, I can't to do anything that would hurt her. I can't give her false hope that a long-distance relationship could work. Because they never work.*

Sean came and sat down on the other side of Ollie. "How you been, bro?"

"Better now," Oliver greeted his friend. He clasped the other man on the shoulder in a friendly greeting.

"I was worried about you, man," Sean said. "It's good to see you in person and not just hear you on the phone."

"Likewise," Oliver explained. "Though I really appreciate our talks. It was great to have a link to the outside world."

"You're all healed up now, though?" Sean asked.

"Absolutely." Oliver patted the side of his own knee, the one that had been injured. "Better than ever."

"For *real*?" Sean raised his eyebrows in suspicion. "Or are you just saying that so coach will let you train?"

Ollie shook his head. "I'm dead serious. I'm a hundred percent. Honestly, I've never felt better."

"Good to hear," Sean said, reaching for a drink. "Because I'd be worried sick about the Bandit's future if it wasn't for you. We've been running drills with our second and third string quarterback and it's not the same. They've got good arms and a tight throw, but they just aren't consistent like you are. They're missing that intuitive element. I'll be glad to have you throwing me the ball again this next season."

"Me too, man," Oliver said. "Me too."

While Ollie caught up with his friends, the crowd that surrounded their VIP became more and more chaotic. The club was packed now and the news that The Bandits were in the house had spread faster than a Colorado wildfire. A few girls clamored over the ropes that separated them from the crowd. One of the bouncers tried to stop them, but Adam allowed them over.

"Pretty girls can hang with us," Adam told the security guy. "Everybody else can leave us alone."

There were three of them. Two brunettes and one blonde. They all looked like they could have been models if they'd wanted to. They were tall and skinny, with high cheek bones and glowing skin. They were wearing next to nothing and what was there left little to the imagination. A slight breeze would have exposed them. Normally, Oliver would have been delighted to have girls like these come and sit next to him. But for some reason, as they approached, he felt more repulsed than attracted.

"Oh, my God, it really *is* Oliver Lance?" He heard the blonde girl say to her friends. "I thought it was him, but couldn't believe it until I got close."

The girl sat on Oliver's lap, wrapping an arm around his shoulder. She smelled like over-priced perfume and tequila. She was beautiful, though. No doubt about it. A so-called "ten" in most men's books.

She's nothing compared to Elsie, he thought.

"I love your new hair," the woman said, running her fingers through his hair. It made him pull away. She looked more confused than annoyed.

"Everything okay?" she asked. "Why so blue?"

"It's a long story that I'm positive you wouldn't want to hear," he said, his words barely audible over the increasing volume of noise in the club.

"I'm all ears," she replied. "Just let me take this shot first."

Ollie rolled his eyes as the girl took shots with everyone in the VIP section. He looked around at his surroundings. His best friends were there, his wallet was full of cash, expensive alcohol was on the table. Beautiful women surrounded him and he knew that any one of them would have gone home with him at the slightest suggestion.

It was everything that he should have wanted. These things used to satisfy him completely. And yet, as he scanned the room, all he could think about was the physical therapy girl in Iowa. The girl who had entered his life out of nowhere. She'd not only stolen his heart, but her simple existence had changed his perception on everything that he thought he knew. What he had once perceived as valuable; the club, the girls, the money, the fame. It all felt worthless now. Empty. It made him feel out of place, as his thoughts were hundreds of miles away. It made him wish he was back in the quiet of the farmhouse, waiting for Elsie to show up with a Thai chili pizza.

Ollie slid out from underneath the girl who was sitting on his lap. He got up and made his way toward the exit of the VIP area.

"Hey, where are you going?" Adam stepped in front of Oliver.

"Just heading outside real quick," Ollie said. "I'll be right back."

"Alright," Adam replied, taking a step to the side to allow him through. "But hurry back. I've got more girls coming by. You know they'll want to meet the great 'Oliver Lance'."

Oliver turned and stepped into the crowd. He pushed through, making his way across the club. He needed some fresh air. The club and all that it entailed weren't making him feel all that great. When he finally got outside, he turned away quickly from the line of people and went straight to the back alley of the building. For the first time that night, he was by himself. The only noise was the bass sound, rumbling from inside the club. He leaned against the brick wall and closed his eyes, taking a long breath.

I'm just not who I was before I left, he thought. *None of this is for me any more. I don't even want to be hanging out here right now. I'd rather be with Elsie. Cruising around on a tractor sounds more fun than this.*

His phone vibrated in his pocket and he quickly pulled it out. He had a fleeting moment of excitement, in the hopes that maybe it was a text from Elsie. But his initial excitement faded when he saw that it was just an email from the general manager of the Bandits.

Oliver nearly dismissed the email, until he saw the subject line. It read: "Position Opening for the Bandits, physical therapist". He opened it up and read the note.

To all members of The Bandits. Please note, we are currently looking for a new physical therapist to join our team. Our current therapist has moved onto another franchise, leaving us in need for our next season. Please, if you know of anyone who is qualified and interested, don't hesitate to recommend them. All eligible applicants will be considered. Thank you. GM.

It was the email that he'd hoped to receive weeks ago.

Is it too late to suggest this job to Elsie, though? He asked himself. *I told her we should go our separate ways. Would I only confuse her by bringing this opportunity up?*

He sighed and slipped his phone back into his pocket. As much as the logical side of his mind told him to just ignore it, his heart said otherwise. His heart told him that the job opening on his team was a sign, not to be overlooked.

Maybe I'll forward her the email in the morning, he thought. *I won't pressure her to apply. I'll just send her the email so that she knows. She can make her own decision from there.*

A few moments later, his phone began to blow up with texts from his buddies who were inside the club. They were wondering where he went and making sure that he was still up for celebrating. It had been so long since he'd seen them, that he knew he couldn't just go home as much as he wanted to. Part of being on a team, meant spending time with the boys outside of training. So, with a sigh, Oliver walked back to the front of the building and into the club.

I guess I can fake a smile for a couple of hours, he thought, as the swarm of people sucked him in. *There are worse things to fake.*

Chapter Eighteen

Elsie

Elsie laid the last padded mat onto the floor. She took a step back, admiring the new workout room that she'd created for her clients. The equipment that Oliver had given her barely fit into the small space, but she had managed to make it work. It had changed her business from run-of-the-mill to a high-end operation. She couldn't wait to start using it for some of her current clients and already had begun thinking about how she could let the community use it as a gym.

Of course, every piece of that equipment was nostalgic to her. The leg press, brought memories of Oliver, and the "torture" she'd inflicted on him in order to get him back into shape. The treadmill, which was a bit worn from the miles and miles that she'd made him walk during his three-month stint in her care. And of course, there was the massage table. She'd put that in the far corner of the room, where she wouldn't see it as often. Every time she noticed it, it reminded her of the first time she saw Ollie with his shirt off. That was the last thing she needed to be thinking about, though, while treating her other patients.

"I guess that's that," she said, taking a final glance around.

Time to get myself back on the schedule, she thought. *Time to get back to real life.*

Elsie went to the front desk and sat down, peering out the glass window in front. She chuckled, as she remembered the date with Oliver where he picked her up out there on the John Deere tractor. It was something she knew she'd never forget and would probably think of every time she looked out.

"Okay, where was I?" she whispered to herself, as she dusted off her laptop and turned on the scheduling program.

The sound of a car pulling up distracted her. She looked up to see her Uncle Frank's beat up brown Oldsmobile parked next to the curb. Elsie set her computer to the side and went out to greet him.

"Uncle!" she squealed, as he eased himself out of the driver's seat.

He looked more feeble than he used to, but still had enough strength to pull her in for a powerful bear hug.

"Hey, kiddo," he said, all smiles. "How've you been?"

Elsie shrugged. "I've been alright, I guess. Just getting things back to normal around here, now that that private patient of mine is fully recovered."

"He went back home then?" Frank asked.

"Yep, he's back home," she said, trying to hide the sadness in her voice. "I have a surprise for you, Uncle."

"I'm too old for surprises, you know that," Frank said, with a chuckle and a wink.

"This is a good one, though," Elsie assured him. She opened the front door for him and followed him into the clinic. "How are you feeling? I haven't talked to you in a while. Is your surgery still scheduled for next week?"

Frank sighed, as he leaned against the front desk. "Yeah, it's still next week and I'm still wondering if I should do it. The prognosis isn't great, no matter which way I go."

"I think you should go through with it," Elsie said quietly. "At least you're giving yourself the best possible chance."

"I suppose you're right," he said with a sigh.

Elsie could see the worry behind her uncle's eyes. The compassion she felt for his situation was overwhelming, but she knew that the best thing she could do was to assure him that things would be okay.

"I'm here for you if you want to talk," she said. "I'm always here."

Uncle Frank placed her hand onto Elsie's shoulder, giving it a firm squeeze. "Don't look so blue, kid. Everything is fine. And look, if it makes you feel any better, I'm pretty sure I'm going to go through with the surgery. I'm just not quite ready to admit that fact to myself yet. The whole idea of going under the knife makes me nervous, but I realize it's probably the best move. Besides, I'm not ready to throw in the towel quite yet."

Elsie's eyes lit up. "That's great news, Uncle Frank. I know things will be fine."

"I'm sure they will," Frank agreed. "Now, where's this little surprise you were telling me about? I think I'm ready, but I hope it's nothing too crazy. The last thing this old man needs is a heart attack on top of everything else."

Elsie chuckled. "Come on, it's in here," she said, leading him toward the back room where all of the new equipment was.

"What in tarnation?" he whispered, as he stepped into the exercise and recovery room. "Elsie, where did you get all of this? This is incredible."

Elsie proudly walked through the room, showing off all of the new things. "Isn't it amazing, Uncle?"

"This must have cost a fortune." Frank walked around the room, touching every piece of equipment as though he'd found the holy grail. Physical therapy was his life's work as much as hers.

"Didn't cost a penny," Elsie said, unable to hide her excitement. "That last patient of mine gave it all to me. Every bit of it."

Uncle Frank brought his gaze toward her, wide eyed with bewilderment. "He *gave* this all to you?"

"Yes." Elsie nodded. "He said that he owed so much to me for helping in his recovery. He said it was the least he could do."

She felt her smile fading as she talked about Ollie. Bringing him up forced her to remember the fact that she would never see him again. She turned away from her Uncle.

I can't let him see me cry, she thought, choking back the tears. *He's already got too much to worry about.*

But Elsie's uncle knew her better than she knew herself. He stepped beside her, wrapping a comforting arm around her shoulder.

"What's wrong, kiddo?" he asked. His voice was low and comforting, just like when she was a little girl. "Something is on your mind."

"No, I'm fine," she said, with a sniffle. "Just, uh, I don't know. Maybe a little stressed or something."

Frank gazed around the room. "Elsie, you just had a million dollars of equipment that landed in your lap. Patients will be coming from all over the state once they hear how state-of-the-art this place is. Financial worries will be a thing of the past. I'm having a hard time understanding what you're stressed about. I think it's something else."

He looked at her with discerning eyes. It was a look Elsie had seen from him a million times in her life. He could see right through her and she knew that there was no getting around that.

"I just miss him," she said, surprised at how the words felt as they tumbled out of her mouth. "I miss Oliver."

"The patient?" Frank asked.

Elsie nodded. "He and I became pretty close over the past few months. I knew he'd have to leave at some point, but it seemed so sudden when that time finally came."

Her uncle was silent as he listened, stroking the white beard stubble on his chin.

"I know what you're thinking, Uncle Frank." Elsie took a seat on one of the weight benches as she spoke. "It was wrong for me to become close to a patient. But I promise that it didn't happen until *after* I'd released him from my care."

"Elsie, I may be a crotchety old man, but that doesn't make me some kind of prude," he said, sitting next to her on the bench. "You don't need to justify anything to me, and you certainly don't need to fear getting into trouble for dating one of your patients. I know you did everything above board."

"I just don't know what to do," she said, turning to face him. "I've never met anyone like him. He's different. He's kind and sweet. We get along so well. Maybe I'm just overreacting, but I miss him so much right now."

Frank brought an arm around her shoulders and pulled her close, giving her a firm squeeze. "Elsie, I've noticed that you haven't been yourself over the past few days. You've seemed distant and distracted. There's a sadness in your eyes that I've never seen before. I had a feeling it had something to do with that patient of yours, but I never realized just how close you two were."

"What should I do?" Elsie asked, leaning her head against her uncle's shoulder. "I feel like I've been walking in circles ever since he left. I can't get organized, my thoughts are scattered. He's the only thing I can think about. I feel so uneasy without him here in town."

"You really want my advice?" Frank asked.

Elsie pulled away and looked him in the eyes. "Yes. You know how much your advice means to me."

It was true, too. She'd always looked up to her uncle in helping to make life decisions. This was the first time she'd ever sought out advice about a guy she liked, but she knew that her uncle's wisdom could apply to just about anything. He'd seen it all. He'd been to war as a young man, lost friends along the way and eventually lost his wife. Frank had lived and had lived deeply. The scars of his experiences showed up as wrinkles around his eyes.

"I'm eighty-two years old, Elsie," he said, after clearing his throat. "No matter what happens with my health because of this cancer, I only have so much time. I've lived a long life, though, and I've learned a very important lesson over the years. It's a lesson that I wish someone had taught me when I was younger. If you want something, you have to go after it. You *have* to, Elsie, because nothing in life that's worth having will fall into your lap. Your heart knows what you want, and you need to listen to it. If you ignore it, you'll survive. Sure. You'll live a long life and maybe even find some degree of happiness. But when you look back one day, I promise you, you will have wished that you followed your heart every step of the way. Because it always knows what is right for you and it never lies. Don't ignore it, just follow it."

Goosebumps popped up on Elsie's arms as she listened. She hadn't ever heard him speak about something so deep and it resonated with her. Her heart had been trying to tell her this whole time. From the moment she met Oliver, her heart had been knocking on the door of her mind, trying to tell her that he was the one. And for three months, she'd done her best to ignore the message. But now she couldn't any more. She couldn't let Ollie go, at least not without giving a legitimate effort first.

"What should I do?" she asked, wiping her tears from her cheek. "My heart tells me that I should be with Oliver, but he's hundreds of miles away and I'm here. My life is here."

"Your life is where you want it." Frank pushed his little round glasses further up on the bridge of his nose. "Go get him."

"Just... leave?" Elsie said, shaking her head. "You mean fly to California?"

He shrugged. "I mean you're welcome to walk, but I think flying might end up being a little faster."

"What about the clinic?" Elsie looked around the room. "My patients? *Our* patients?"

"You see, Elsie, that's your *mind* that's talking right now," he said, with a smile. "Your *heart* doesn't need to worry about the business. Let me handle that part. I know someone who can cover everything here. Besides, running this clinic was never your dream anyway. That was my dream and I had foisted it on you."

"But...Uncle..." she began to say.

Frank gently grabbed her hands. "Look, Elsie, this is a beautiful moment in your life. Please, just grab it. Run. Follow your heart. If you don't, you'll live out your years here and be miserable. I don't want that for you."

"What if I go out there and Oliver wants nothing to do with me?" Elsie asked, putting voice to her fears. "What if it's all for nothing?"

"What if it's *not*?" Frank asked. "Besides, you know this old place isn't going anywhere and either am I. It's not like you couldn't come back, if push came to shove. You do have an in with the owner."

For the first time since Ollie had left, Elsie's lips curled up into a smile. A *real* smile. One that wasn't forced or fake, but a genuine beam of happiness written all across her face.

"You're serious, aren't you?" she said, squeezing his hands. "You know someone who can handle things around here for a while?"

Uncle Frank nodded. "I do. I'll give him a call and arrange everything."

Elsie dropped his hands and then wrapped her arms around his neck, hugging him so hard that she squeezed the air out of his lungs. "Thank you, Uncle Frank. Thank you so much."

He patted her back and when she finally released him, she noticed that a tear had streamed down his cheek. "Why are you crying, Uncle?"

"Because it's nice to finally see you happy again," he said. "Now go. The clock is running. Buy a plane ticket and get on that flight to California. Call me when you get there."

"Okay. Yes, okay. I'll call you." Elsie nodded eagerly. "Oh, my gosh, I'm really doing this. Thank you, Uncle."

She gave him one more hug and a quick kiss on the cheek. Her uncle's talk was exactly what she needed. It had given her the confidence to get out there and pursue the only thing that could possibly ease her anxieties; Ollie.

"I'll call you as soon as I land to let you know that I got there safely," she promised. She stood up and started organizing things in a last minute need to put everything away before she left. "If you need anything at all, just pick up the phone, okay?"

"I will," Frank said, watching her with a wry smile. "But I don't expect that to happen. Everything will be fine around here. You know that nothing too dramatic ever happens in this town and I highly doubt that anything will while you're gone."

Elsie gave Uncle Frank one more hug. He laughed as he patted her back.

"Now get going," he chastised. "Go pack!"

She went straight upstairs to her apartment, where she quickly threw some clothes into an old dusty suitcase that she hadn't used since college. With no idea how long she'd be gone, she ended up packing another suitcase in addition to that one, just in case. Then she hopped on the computer and ordered a plane ticket for that very afternoon.

I can't believe I'm actually doing this, she thought. *But Uncle Frank is right. If I stay here, I'll just be moping around forever. I have no idea if Oliver even wants to see me again, but at least if I go out there, then I'll know for sure. At least then, I can rest. Because I tried.*

Chapter Nineteen

Elsie

After driving around San Francisco in her rental car for nearly an hour, Elsie finally pulled into the parking lot of The Bandit's training stadium. She wasn't used to spending time in such a big city and it had taken her forever to find it. Luckily, the three gas stations she'd stopped at had very helpful people working there who were happy to point her in the right direction even when her GPS said otherwise.

Elsie's plane had landed the evening before and she'd spent most of the night pacing her hotel room. She'd considered calling Oliver at least a hundred times, but talked herself out of it each time. Finally, she'd gone to sleep, with the decision that she'd just show up at his practice the following day and see his reaction. Now, as she walked across the parking lot, she wondered if that was the right choice. Her palms were sweaty and anxiety burned in her chest.

Calm down, Elsie, she told herself. *It'll be fine, no matter what happens.*

It didn't cost anything to get in, since pre-season training was free to watch. Elsie stepped into the stadium. The sound of the small crowd talking and clapping filled the halls, as she made her way toward the seating area. There were a surprising amount of people in the stands, all wearing orange and red to support the team. She spotted an empty seat a few rows back from the front, and squeezed her way over everyone's feet until she made it there. As soon as she sat down, she looked straight ahead.

Covering the perfectly trimmed grass were at least forty football players, many of them wearing full gear and helmets. Scattered among them were the coaches, dressed in orange polo shirts. They were blowing their whistles and calling out plays for the men to run. Elsie scanned the field, looking for Oliver. It didn't take long to find him. He wasn't wearing a helmet and his blonde hair reflected the sun.

She exhaled as a wave of excitement filled her. It had only been a few days since she'd seen him, but laying eyes on Oliver again made her tingle all over. It was a sign that she'd made the right decision in coming there.

"Lance, I was to see you throw that slant route again." One of the coaches jogged up to Oliver. "This time, send the ball to Smith as soon as he's open. Even if Harris looks like he's not being defended, don't break the play. Run the route."

"Sure thing, Coach," Lance replied.

Where Elsie sat, she could hear everything. It was much different than it would have been during a real game, with tens of thousands of people all shouting and screaming at the top of their lungs. For the most part, the crowd was quiet, with just the occasional clapping and chatter. It allowed for Elsie to hear everything that was said on the field.

She relaxed into her chair, watching as Oliver signaled for the center to snap the ball. He took a few steps back, waiting for his receiver to get open. As soon as he had the shot, Ollie threw the ball. It whipped out of his hand, spiraling perfectly toward the open man. It made a slapping sound as it landed in the receiver's hands.

"Yes, like that," the coach said, patting Ollie on the back. "Good job. That's the kind of route we need to run if our opponent keeps blitzing us. It'll throw them off every time."

Oliver nodded, pushing his blonde hair across his forehead. He was sweaty and looked sexier than ever. Elsie thought he looked even better in his football uniform than he had in his cowboy outfit on the night of their first date. It suited him in a way the country clothing didn't.

As Ollie continued to run plays, Elsie just smiled and watched from her little spot on the bleachers. It didn't even bother her that she was wedged between two overweight guys, one eating hot dogs and the other stuffing nachos in his mouth. Her heart swelled with every minute that passed, as she watched Oliver do his thing on the field. Just knowing that he was close made her feel a little better.

She was also happy to see him moving around so well. He'd run and stop, then spin around to avoid a tackle. It seemed as though he was coming along quite nicely with the final stages of his recovery. In fact, if she hadn't known better, it would be nearly impossible to tell that he was ever injured at all.

It was fun to watch. Over the course of their getting to know each other, Elsie had heard many football stories from Oliver. But getting to actually see him play the game was eye opening. He was good. *Really* good. He threw the football so hard that it was just a brown blur across her vision, until it stopped into his receiver's hands. He'd put the ball wherever the coach told him to, with the accuracy of a Marine sniper. She was starting to see why he was idolized by so many. There was talent inside of him that was most certainly of the rarest kind.

A half hour went by, but it seemed like only a few seconds. The next thing Elsie knew, coach was blowing his whistle and telling the team to take a break. Her heart jumped up into her throat as the football players took off their helmets and started walking toward the stands. She kept her eyes locked on Ollie, feeling her pulse pounding in her ears as he neared.

A few people in the front row got up and approached Oliver, squealing with excitement. Elsie stood up from her seat and lifted her hand in the air, gently waiving. It was enough to catch Ollie's attention. He glanced up and as soon as he saw Elsie, he dropped his helmet to the ground at his feet. His lips curled into the widest smile she'd ever seen.

"Elsie!" he shouted, pushing through the crowd that surrounded him. "Oh, my God."

Oliver ran to the stands and then up the stairs. Elsie stepped over the robust man to her right, causing the second half of his hot dog to spill from his hand and to the ground.

"Sorry," she muttered. "I'll buy you another one. Sorry."

She didn't even stop to pick it up, she just continued climbing over everyone until she got to the stairs. Ollie skipped three steps at a time, making his way toward her as fast as he could. They nearly collided at the end of the aisle. They gazed at each other for a moment. It was as though Oliver couldn't believe his eyes.

"Elsie," he said, in the middle of catching his breath.

"Hi," she replied. "I was in the neighborhood."

Oliver laughed, then pulled her in for a hug.

"God, I missed you," he said.

"I missed you, too." Elsie closed her eyes as he held her close. He hugged her so tightly. It felt like he never wanted to let her go.

"I can't believe you're here right now," he said. "Am I dreaming? Please don't tell me I'm actually knocked out on the field and this is all some post-concussion illusion."

Elsie laughed, as she looking up at him. "No, it's real. I found myself missing you so much. I know we said that we'd go our separate ways, but I just couldn't move forward. I've spent the last couple of days pacing around, trying to decide what to do. So, here I am."

"I've felt the same way. It's taken every bit of energy I have just to focus enough to get through practice." Ollie cradled her chin in his hand as he looked at her. "I'm so glad you're here right now. I thought I'd never see you again."

He leaned in and kissed her. Their lips touched, immediately soothing any anxiety she'd been feeling ever since he left. The surrounding crowd cheered and clapped as they embraced. Elsie didn't mind. It made no difference that there were a few hundred people watching. She could have been surrounded by a few thousand and it wouldn't have mattered. The only person who really existed in her world, at least in that moment, was Oliver.

When they finally stopped kissing, Elsie looked around to see that The Bandit's fans had already gotten bored with watching the public display of affection. Most of them were staring down at their cell phones, mindlessly scanning through social media.

Out on the field, Coach began blowing his whistle. Oliver looked over his shoulder and then back to Elsie.

"I guess the break is over already," he said, his hand still touching her cheek. "I've got another half an hour of practice. Will you wait for me?"

Elsie nodded. "Of course I'll wait for you. I didn't fly all the way out here for just one kiss."

Oliver grinned. "How about we go out on a nice date tonight? Something special?"

"That would be amazing," she agreed before forcing her face into a frown. "But there's one problem."

Ollie's smile faded. "What's that?"

"Johnny's tractor is back in Iowa. What are you going to pick me up in?" Elsie giggled as she asked the question.

"Well shoot, little lady," Ollie replied, in his fake cowboy accent. "I reckon I'll have to pick you up in my four-wheeled driving machine, that some refer to as a 'car'."

"I reckon that'll do just fine," Elsie said, patting his chest pads.

The coach continued to blow the whistle impatiently in the background.

"You better go, before Coach gets even more mad." Elsie stood on her tip toes and kissed Oliver one more time, just a quick peck on the lips.

"Okay, I'll meet you right here after practice," Ollie said, as he turned around and began jogging down the stairs. He looked back when he got to the bottom. "Promise you'll wait."

"I promise!" Elsie called back.

As Oliver ran onto the field to meet his teammates, something caught Elsie's eye. A woman, standing on the grass near the edge of the field. Her blonde hair was nearly fluorescent as the bright sun reflected on it. It contrasted her black suit skirt. How she hadn't noticed her before, she couldn't be sure.

Maybe the woman had just arrived or maybe it the scowl she wore on her face that finally garnered Elsie's attention. But there, standing with her arms crossed and looking straight up at Elsie, was Nikki. As soon as their eyes met, Nikki turned away. She didn't wave, or smile, or anything. She just turned away, obviously pissed.

Uh oh, Elsie thought. *I'm guessing that kiss with Oliver just now didn't go over so well with her.*

She hadn't even considered the fact that Nikki would likely be there at training. It wasn't that Elsie had done anything wrong by kissing Ollie, but she was well aware of the fact that he and Nikki did have some kind of history. But, she believed Ollie when he said it was long over and that Nikki and he only had a professional relationship.

Still, though, she had traveled hundreds of miles to see the man who had her heart. She couldn't allow a jealous ex-girlfriend of his to make her feel uncomfortable about things.

I just hope that she's not as crazy as Ollie has led me to believe, she thought. *The last thing I need is to get caught up in some kind of public drama.*

After buying her neighboring stranger another hot dog to replace the one she'd ruined, Elsie took her seat. It was a few plays before Nikki caught her attention again. With a walk that should have dislocated her hips, Nikki sashayed over to where Ollie was standing getting some water.

Nikki said something to him that Elsie couldn't hear. Ollie tipped his head back and laughed, a full body laugh that made his eyes sparkle. Nikki grinned and touched his arm, standing intimately close to him. She grabbed a towel from the bench and wiped some grass from his cheek. The gesture was incredibly friendly, almost romantic, but Ollie didn't react at all.

Elsie tried not to worry. Ollie had told her that they'd had a thing in the past, but he swore it was in the past. Even though that little cheek-wipe didn't look very past-ish. She thought of all the images she'd seen when she looked him up that one time. He always had a beautiful lady on his arm. It had always been someone with beauty like Nikki, not like her.

Her lip was between her teeth before Elsie realized it, as she chewed on it nervously. Was Ollie really happy to see her? Or was he back to his old ways and his old girl now that he was back home? Would he decide that their attraction was just because she was the only female he'd seen for three months?

Elsie suddenly wasn't so sure that this was the best idea. Maybe she should have just left things where they were in her memory: happy and perfect. Being here, there was now a chance that those beautiful memories would turn into something much more painful.

Oliver looked over at her and waved and she did her best to smile and wave back.

"Don't doubt him," she said to herself. "He's a good guy and he really is into you."

The stranger sitting next to her gave her an odd look, but didn't say anything. Elsie took a deep breath in and tried her best to ignore Nikki and how she was making Ollie smile.

Chapter Twenty

Ollie

Oliver sat at the table across from Elsie. He adjusted his blue tie, loosening it a bit around his neck so that he didn't feel like he was choking. He wore suits for games and as part of his duties as a professional spokesman for the team, but he tried to avoid wearing a tie. Ties felt too formal and fancy for him.

But tonight was different. His girl was in town and he'd taken her to finest restaurant within fifty miles, a place called The Ruse. It was located on the beach, just a few hundred feet from the San Francisco Bay. Ollie had never been there, but when he asked his teammates where to take the most beautiful girl in the world to dinner, this was the place that they'd unanimously agreed on.

The interior was beautiful. From the tables, to the chairs, to the art work on the wall. Everything was crafted with perfection. He hoped the food would be just as good. Even if it wasn't, he'd still consider it to be a great night, though, because the girl of his dreams was there with him.

I'd probably be just as happy at a McDonald's right now. As long as she was with me, he thought, as he gazed across the table to his date. *God, she looks beautiful. She always does, but tonight...wow.*

Elsie had worn a tight fitting black dress. It hugged her body perfectly, accentuating her womanly curves in all the right places. He'd never seen her wearing anything like it before, but hoped that he'd get the chance to many more times in the future.

"You look beautiful," Ollie said, unable to take his eyes off of her. "I know I've already told you that at least ten times since I picked you up from the hotel room. But seriously, Elsie. You look like a model."

"You're too sweet, Ollie. I have to admit that I feel a little weird wearing this dress, though," Elsie said, as she played with the pearl bracelet that hung loosely on her wrist. "But I'm flattered that you like it."

"Please wear it every single time I see you," he joked. "It's either that, or the green scrubs. You can choose."

Elsie chuckled as she swirled the red wine in her glass. She may have been a country girl from a small farm town in the middle of nowhere, but she sure as hell knew how to look and act classy.

"Tell you what, I'll wear this dress every time you wear your suit," she said, before taking a sip of her wine.

"I have to wear a suit for all my away games," he replied. "You'll just have to come to all of them."

She grinned. "Don't tempt me."

A surge of hope filled him as he taking a sip of his whiskey and ginger ale. He didn't want to hope for things he couldn't have. He cleared his throat.

"Still, I still can't believe I'm sitting across the table from you right now," he said with a smile. "Seeing you today at practice was honestly the best surprise I've ever had in my entire life."

Elsie smiled, which of course made Oliver's heart melt like butter.

"To be honest, I wasn't sure how you were going to react when I showed up." She shrugged, pushing a strand of hair behind her ear. "A part of me worried that you'd be mad."

"Mad? Not a chance," Oliver said, shaking his head. "I'd never be mad at you. The reason I thought it was best that we move forward, was because I didn't want to hurt you. I thought that if we started something more serious, then it would distract you from the life that you've built in

Iowa. I didn't want that. But the fact that you flew all the way out here to see me says so much about you. I can't let you go again. Even if I have to fly out to Iowa every week, I will. I'll do whatever it takes."

Oliver had never said anything like that to a woman before. He'd never felt that way about anyone. Not even Nikki. But he realized that Elsie was worth fighting for. She was worth sacrificing whatever he had to in order to be with her. For years, he'd been looking for his "why". Why does he work so hard at his career? Why does he wake up every morning and give the day one hundred and ten percent? Why does he keep going, even when everything seems lost?

Maybe she's my reason, he thought. *Maybe she's who I've been looking for my entire life, but didn't even realize it.*

"I wouldn't expect you to fly out to Iowa every week," Elsie said. "That would be insane. I'm not saying that a long distance relationship couldn't work, though. To be honest, I didn't come out here to etch anything in stone. I just needed to see you again. I don't know what the future holds, all I know is that I was pretty damn miserable without you around."

"Me too," Ollie said. He reached out across the table and took her hand. "I wish that you never had to go back."

He paused after speaking.

The job, he thought. *Oh my God, the physical therapist opening!*

"Elsie, did you get my email from the other day?" he asked. "I'd sent you something important."

Elsie shook her head, shaking the strand of hair out from behind her ear. "I've been a little busy and have a million emails to answer right now. Was it important?"

"This would be one worth reading," he said, leaning toward her. "There's a job opening on the team. It's for a physical therapist. Full time, with benefits and a nice salary."

Elsie nearly dropped her glass of wine from surprise. She set it to the side and Ollie watched as her eyes widened. "Are you serious? The Bandits are looking for a sports therapist?"

Oliver nodded slowly. "The general manager sent an email to everyone two nights ago. I forwarded it to you, thinking you might be interested in it. What do you say? You'd be perfect for it, Elsie."

"Wow." Elsie pushed her hair back over her ear. "I don't know what to say. I mean I guess I could apply."

"If I vouch for you, which of course I will, they'd hire you." Ollie squeezed her hand in his. "You're exactly what they're looking for and I'm walking proof of that. If you want the job, you'll get it. Trust me."

"That's a lot to think about," she said, still smiling. "But Uncle Frank did say yesterday that I didn't need to worry about the clinic any more if I didn't want to. I guess he's got someone who can run it if I'm not there."

"There you go," Ollie said, gently squeezing her hands. "It's meant to be."

"I don't want to say 'yes' without thinking it over. I have to think about my nephews and my uncle," she said, with a sigh. "It *does* sound like an amazing opportunity, though. Ever since I graduated college, all I wanted to do was work with sports injuries. Plus, the added bonus, is that I'd get to see you every day."

"How awesome would that be?" Oliver asked, with a wink. "Look, I'm not usually one who believes in the aligning of the stars or any of that mystical mumbo jumbo. But everything seems to be lining up. First, that job opening. Then you show up. Things do happen for a reason."

Elsie nodded and Ollie could see in her eyes that she was legitimately considering it. The idea of getting to spend time with her every day sounded like heaven to him. It would almost be too perfect of a situation. He hoped she'd take it, but only if it was something she truly wanted to do.

"Okay," she said, after a moment of silence. "I'll apply for it and we'll go from there. How does that sound?"

Oliver couldn't have smiled wider if he'd tried. "That sounds like cause for celebration. Waiter, another glass of Cabernet for my beautiful date and a glass of your finest Irish whiskey for me, on the rocks."

The suited waiter was standing nearby and spun around when he'd heard Oliver's requests. "Of course, sir," he said. "I'll return momentarily with your drinks. And your food will be here shortly."

"Perfect," Oliver said. "Thank you."

"You're quite welcome, sir," the waiter replied, before swiftly making his way toward the bar to get the drinks.

Oliver felt like he'd been wearing a goofy smile since they'd sat down, and maybe he had. But he was suddenly so overwhelmingly happy that he couldn't help himself. The aching in his heart that had started when he left Iowa had finally subsided. Just the idea of Elsie living in California with him eased the pain.

The waiter returned with the drinks. He set the on the table and shuffled off to tend to the other patrons. Oliver took his drink and held it in the air. Elsie did the same.

"To us," he said. "In whatever shape or form our relationship ends up being, may it make us both happy and content."

"I like that," Elsie said, clinking her glass against his. "Cheers."

They sipped their drinks and not more than a minute later, their food arrived. Ollie had ordered the filet mignon, cooked medium rare, with a side of potatoes and asparagus. Elsie went with the teriyaki salmon, with brown rice and broccoli. The plates looked amazing. Perfectly portioned and cooked.

"It's been a long time since I've eaten anything this fancy," Elsie said, picking up her fork. "It looks so good."

They dug in. The food was incredible, but all Ollie could think about was Elsie and how badly he wanted her. He wanted to peel that dress off of her and kiss her from head to toe. He wanted to taste her, every inch of her. He wanted to feel her once again in the most intimate of ways. The meal was good, sure, but nothing compared to her.

"So is this a better date than the one where I picked you up on a tractor?" he asked, with a chuckle.

Elsie shrugged. "I like them both. But I'll never forget the John Deere date. That was strangely romantic. That was the night when I knew for sure that there was something special about you, something different."

"I really missed you, Elsie." Ollie set his fork down and reached across the table to take her hands once again. "You were all I could think about since I left. When I should have been rehearsing game plays in my mind, all I could see was you."

"You should have called me," she said, frowning slightly.

"I would have," he admitted. "I know that I wouldn't have been able to help myself if much more time had passed."

"Next time, don't hesitate." Elsie squeezed his hands.

"I won't, I promise," Ollie assured her.

They went back to eating and finished their plates quickly. It seemed that both of them were eager to finish. Oliver was especially having a hard time being patient. He couldn't wait to be alone with her again.

"Are you all done?" Elsie asked, looking toward his plate.

Ollie nodded. "Yeah, I'm full."

"What do you say we get out of here?" she asked, her words like music to Oliver's ears. Her eyes dilated slightly as she gazed at him from across the table. It was the same look she'd given him right before they made love at her apartment after their first date.

"I'd say that's a great idea." Ollie held his hand up, waiving the waiter over. "Check, please."

"Of course, sir," the waiter said. "I'll be right back with that."

"Please hurry," Oliver said. "We don't want to leave this beautiful woman waiting."

The waiter raised his eyebrows. "I can't blame you, sir. I'll be back in a flash."

The way that Oliver and Elsie were staring at each other was intense and filled with lust. It was as though they were tearing off each others clothes using only their eyes. He couldn't wait to get her to his bed to do it for real, because as good as she looked in that dress, he knew that she looked even better wearing nothing at all.

Chapter Twenty-One

Ollie

O liver walked next to Elsie as the two made their way down the hallway to her hotel room. He'd offered to drive them to his place, but she had insisted on going to her hotel instead. She said it was closer than his house and she didn't want to wait any longer than she had to. Of course, Oliver wasn't about to complain. Just watching her walk in that tight black dress of hers made him ache to have her once again. The way her butt moved underneath the thin material was almost too much for him to handle. He couldn't wait to get that dress off of her.

Elsie unlocked the door with her room key and they stepped inside. As soon as the door closed behind them, Ollie spun her around to face him. Their lips collided, sending a spark of electricity into the air that should have lit the place up like the Fourth of July. He stepped forward, pressing her against the wall in the entry way. She let out a soft moan and Oliver felt her hands drift up his back. He pulled away, just long enough to see the desire in her eyes before resuming the kiss.

The soft smell of her perfume floated up to his nostrils and he breathed it in without breaking the kiss. The scent turned him on even more and he let out a soft growl as he pressed his body into hers. It had only been a week since they'd made love, but it might as well have been a year.

The way he craved her in that moment was unlike anything he'd ever experienced before.

There was a fire inside of him that scorched him from the core, radiating outward. It was a deep desire. The kind of desperate ache that could only be experienced between two couples that truly loved each other. This wasn't just physical for Oliver. No, not with Elsie. This was the culmination of all that he felt for her, both emotionally and spiritually.

"God, I missed you," he said, breaking the kiss.

Elsie was breathing heavily as she licked her lips. Her hair was a bit messy now, but it looked sexy as hell.

"I missed you, too," she whispered, between breaths. "Now get over here."

She reached forward and grabbed his tie, jerking him back toward her. They kissed again, this time with even more aggression and fire than before. Their tongues slipped in and out of each others mouths, as their moans of passion became louder. Ollie slowly pulled away, then brought his lips to the outside of her neck. She leaned her head back against the wall and he could hear her breathing as he moved his lips down to the top of her bare shoulder.

"Oliver," she whispered. "Take me to the bed."

Oliver didn't hesitate. He picked her up with one arm and put her over his shoulder. She let out a playful giggle as he carried her with ease to the bed and laid her down on her back. Elsie grabbed his tie once again and gently pulled him over the top of her.

"I'm glad you're with me right now," she whispered. "Flying out here was the best decision I've made in a long time."

"I couldn't agree more," Ollie said, before leaning in to resume kissing her neck.

She let out a soft groan as soon as his lips touched her skin. He could feel her warmth as it radiated against the growing bulge in the front of his slacks as she wrapped her legs around his waist, causing her dress to slide up a bit.

Oliver slowly pulled away. He gazed at Elsie and watched as she gently bit her bottom lip. She looked so innocent and vulnerable as she laid there, waiting for him to make his next move. He brought his hands to her legs, and drifted his fingers all the way up until they landed on her panties. Elsie moaned approvingly, as she helped Oliver pull them off completely.

He held the black lace panties in the air, like some kind of trophy, then tossed them to the other side of the bed. Her dress was still bunched up at her waist and with her underwear now off, it was clear that she was wet with desire, aching with the same desperation that filled Oliver.

"Don't ever leave," Ollie said, staring at her in wonder.

Elsie laughed, spreading her legs just a bit in an effort to tease Oliver.

"Oh yeah?" she asked. "Why's that?"

"You know why," he said, unable to take his eyes off of her. "You're perfect."

Ollie crawled off of the bed and removed his suit coat. He quickly loosened his tie, tossing it onto the comforter next to Elsie before eagerly taking of his white dress shirt. By the time he looked back up, Elsie was holding the tie in her hands and there was a playful smirk on her face.

"I could think of a few things to do with this," she said. "Why don't you lay down on your back with your hands up?"

The implication was obvious. Elsie wanted to tie up Oliver and tease him. Dominate him. In other words, he wanted to torture him, but in the best of ways. He wasn't about to say 'no' to that.

"Should I get undressed the rest of the way?" he asked.

Elsie shook her head and grinned. "No. I'll take care of that."

Ollie crawled back onto the bed, now wearing only his slacks. He did as Elsie asked and laid on his back, placing his head onto a pillow. He brought his hands up, feeling the cold metal of the wrought iron headboard. Elsie straddled over his lap and wrapped his blue tie around his wrists.

"You're so bad," he whispered. "I had no idea."

Elsie smirked. "I just like having a little fun once in a while."

She pulled on the knot, clinching his wrists firmly together, then attached the tie to the headboard. Oliver had his hands above his head and unable to move them. He gently pulled downward, but it was clear that she'd done a good job with the knot.

"Jesus, Elsie," he said, with a chuckle. "I didn't know you had been in Boy Scouts. You really know how to tie a knot."

Elsie leaned forward and gave Ollie a quick peck on the lips. She didn't respond to his joke, instead, she placed her hands onto his bare chest and began to slowly move her hips back and forth over the front of his slacks. He could feel her warmth, as she pressed her weight down on top of him, and because she wasn't wearing any panties, he could feel just about everything.

"Oh, my God," he whispered, as he watched her move over the top of him.

She bit her bottom lip and closed her eyes, quickening her movements. The friction against his cock sent waves of pleasure through him. He got so hard that his shaft throbbed, desperately wanting to be released from the confines of his slacks.

Elsie opened her eyes. She was breathing harder now. Her nipples had grown firm and pressed out against her dress. She looked so hot that Ollie could hardly stand it. He wanted to reach forward and touch her, but as soon as he tried, he was reminded that he and the headboard had become one. He couldn't move an inch.

"Just relax," Elsie said, as she leaned forward and kissed his chest.

"I want you so bad right now, though," Ollie said, as he pictured himself sliding inside of her.

She sat back up and Oliver watched as she reached her hands behind her back. She pulled down on the zipper of her dress, causing the front of it to fall a bit. The top of her breasts were released, but still not enough for him to see her completely.

"Please take it off," Ollie begged, wishing so badly he could just pull the dress down for her.

Elsie crawled off of the bed and faced him. He watched her intently. The slowness of her movements increased the sexual tension and he felt like he was about to explode. He enjoyed it, though. It made the moment intense and interesting.

I'm going to make love to her like she's never felt before, he thought. *Just as soon as she unties me.*

Elsie breathed in through her teeth, creating a hissing noise. Then she slipped her fingers into the top of the dress and gently pulled it down. Her naked breasts were revealed, and her nipples grew even harder as they hit the cool air of the room. Ollie was practically drooling now.

"You're killing me," he said, shaking his head. He checked the restraints again, wanting nothing more than to have her in his hands.

She just giggled as she shimmed the dress the rest of the way off. It slid down her smooth skin, all the way to the floor, rendering her completely naked. Ollie looked her up and down. She was perfect from head to toe.

"Please, come here and get me undressed," he said, breathing hard. His blood was pounding through his veins with a primal urge that he could barely control.

Elsie made her way back onto the bed and straddled over Ollie's lap once again. She positioned herself just below the bulge in the front of his pants. Then she undid his belt and tugged his slacks down, taking his boxers with them. His dick, fully erect, popped straight up as she pulled his pants all the way down to his ankles. Ollie kicked them the rest of the way off.

"I kind of like having you like this," she said, looking him over. "I can do whatever I want."

"You can do whatever you want whether I'm tied up or not," Ollie replied, with a wink.

"I like that you say that." Elsie resumed her position, straddling over his lap. His cock stood tall, pressed against the lower part of her belly. She reached down and began to slowly stroke his shaft. Ollie pressed his head back into the pillow and let out a low moan, as pleasure filled him. She had the perfect grip. Not too firm and not too weak. She moved slowly and steadily, sending waves of pleasure into Ollie's body.

Oliver closed his eyes, just enjoying the pleasure. The sensation changed. Something wet and warm wrapped around his tip. He opened his eyes, to see that Elsie had gone down on him. He was in her mouth and she was bobbing her head down onto him.

"Oh, God yes," he whispered, his eyes rolling into the back of his head as Elsie worked her tongue in the most miraculous of ways.

Ollie found himself bucking his hips upward, wishing for her to allow him deeper into her mouth. But she pulled away and looked him in the eye, wagging a finger.

"No, you have to be a good boy," she said, with a smirk.

"I don't want to be good," he said, tugging on his restraints.

"Doctor's orders," she replied.

"I thought you hated when I called you 'Doc'," Ollie said, chuckling.

Elsie shook her head and grinned. "Maybe I do. Maybe I don't."

She took his shaft in her hand and once again began to stroke it. All thought about her nickname flew out of his head and was replaced with pleasurable need.

"Elsie, please, get on me," he pleaded. "I'm going to explode."

Elsie smiled at his words, then glanced to the side of the bed where her luggage was. "Hold on. I need to get something."

Ollie watched as she hopped off of the bed. She dug a condom out of her bag and opened it up. "I came prepared."

"That's what I love about you," he joked. "You're always thinking."

Elsie slipped the condom onto Oliver's cock, then brought her legs over him once again. This time, she held her body so that her opening was just over his tip. She dropped her weight down, just a little. He let out a groan, as she filled his body with deep sensation.

"Does that feel good?" she asked, pressing her weight down a little more.

Oliver could only nod. The synapses in his brain were only focused on one thing: the pleasure. He couldn't even formulate a sentence in that moment. Elsie slowly dropped her hips down until he was all the way inside. Ollie groaned, as ecstasy pumped through him.

Elsie began riding him, causing her breasts to bounce in cadence with her movements. He wanted to touch her so bad. He wanted to lean forward to lick and bite on those perfect nipples of hers. Tugging on his restraints only made them tighter, though, and it seemed he was going to have to get used to ignoring his desires. At least for the time being.

Elsie moved perfectly. Her eyes were closed and by the moans she made, it was clear to Oliver that she was enjoying herself. She arched her back slightly, pressing her chest into the air. She quickened her pace, letting out a soft squeal with each drop of her weight.

After a while, she slowed down and opened her eyes. She leaned forward, giving Oliver a quick kiss on the lips. "Do you like it?"

"Yes," he replied. "God yes."

"Good," she said.

As soon as she spoke, she stood up. He was about to beg her not to, but before he could, Elsie turned around and straddled him once again. She was now facing away from him and he had the perfect view of her backside. He shook his head in awe. She was so amazing to look at.

Instantly, the pleasure was back. Her movements were slow and precise, like a sensual dance. She held her hands above her head, bucking her hips back and forth over his shaft. Her movement brought friction to his sensitive tip, filling him from head to toe with waves of bliss. The combination of that, plus the amazing view in front of him, was enough to make him climax.

"I could come right now," he grunted.

Elsie slowed down to a stop, then looked back over her shoulder. "Not yet."

She then crawled off of him and spun around. She reached above his head, undoing the restraints that had been keeping him attached to the headboard.

"Your turn," she whispered, with a playful grin.

Oliver sat up and the two of them kissed. His hands, now free to roam, danced along the outside of her thighs and along her back. A thin layer of sweat covered her smooth skin, making it so that his fingers slid over it with ease. When he broke the kiss, he immediately laid Elsie onto her back. He put her hands above her head and tied her up in the same way she had done to him. She didn't resist at all. She seemed eager.

"I like this side of you," Ollie said, as he finished tying the knot. "Was it the nice dinner that did it? Because I'd like to make this an every day occurrence."

Elsie chuckled. "Maybe it was the suit you were wearing tonight. I don't know. It just turned me on."

Oliver kissed her as soon as she finished speaking. He dragged his lips down the front of her neck. His hands drifted to her firm breasts, where he fondled them gently. When his mouth got to her cleavage, he brought it over one of her nipples. As soon as he made contact, Elsie gasped and the sensitive nub grew hard in his mouth.

"Yes..." she whispered.

He pleasured her with his tongue, lapping it quickly around her nipple before moving to her other breast to give it equal attention. Elsie wrapped her legs around Oliver's waist and gently pulled his hips toward her. As soon as his tip pressed into her sex, he bucked forward, sliding between her thighs. Her heat surrounded him and the sensation was back.

Something surfaced inside of him. It was a combination of lust and love, an expression of sexual tension that he'd been keeping inside since he'd left Iowa.

It was powerful and out of his control. Like a carnal *need* to give her all of the sexual energy he could muster. He lifted his face away from her chest and began to pound his body against hers.

Elsie cried out in pleasure with each thrust. She was writhing underneath him. A blissful smile was frozen on her face and her eyes were half-closed. It looked like she was in heaven. And she wasn't the only one. Oliver's body began to tingle with ecstasy. It was only a few minutes before he felt himself rising quickly to orgasm.

He pressed deep inside of her as his balls clenched, releasing everything he had all at once. It felt incredible. It was the most intense orgasm Ollie had experienced in years. He held himself in that position for a few moments, as the world came back into focus for him. Then he took a few exhausted breaths and gazed up at Elsie. She was smirking back at him, gently biting her bottom lip.

"Kiss me," she whispered.

Oliver leaned in and they kissed. Without breaking the kiss, he brought his hands up and undid the knot that had held her in restraint. Elsie immediately wrapped her arms around Ollie's back. The two of them made out with passion, still breathing hard from the sex.

Oliver crawled up next to her and Elsie laid her head on his chest. She began drawing imaginary circles over his pecks with her index finger.

Neither of them said anything for a while. It wasn't for lack of things to say. It was just that, the moment was so perfect as it was. The two of them, laying there in each others arms after the amazing sex, was all that they needed right then.

"You know, Elsie, you don't have to stay at the hotel while you're in town," he said, while affectionately massaging her shoulder with one hand. "I've got a house not far from here."

She looked up at him, meeting his gaze with those beautiful eyes of hers that always made him smile. "I know that. I just don't want my presence here to bring too much attention to you."

"What do you mean?" Oliver asked.

"Something happened when you first saw me in the stands at your practice and we kissed," she said. "I looked over when you were going back down to the field and I saw Nikki. She gave me a pretty nasty look. There's a lot of girls out there that would give me that nasty look. You're kind of a hot commodity."

"That's just Nikki," Ollie said with a sigh. "You've got to ignore her. And everyone else."

"And I will," Elsie assured him. "I just don't want to step on any toes or make anybody mad."

"That's why you don't want to stay at my house?" Oliver asked.

"I don't want to attract unnecessary attention. Plus, what if Nikki were to show up while I'm there? She'd flip out and I know it." Elsie sighed, still looking into his eyes. "I just think it's easier if I stay at the hotel for now."

Oliver's heart sank a bit. He wished she'd stay with him while she was in town. It would make him feel like they were a real couple. They'd get to play house for a while. He could make her dinner and they'd get to wake up together in the morning. It would have been so much fun, but he also had to respect Elsie's need for a boundary, being that Nikki had already made her presence known and didn't seem too happy about it.

"Okay," he finally said. "I guess I can understand that. Can I ask you something, though?"

"Of course." Elsie slowly sat up and crossed her legs.

"How long are you in town?" he asked. "You haven't told me."

Elsie shrugged. "I wasn't sure how things would turn out, so I just bought a one-way ticket. I can go home whenever."

"That's the best news I've heard all day," Ollie said, with a smile. "By the way, I've got practice tomorrow and it will be a long one. Coach is running us through offensive drills again and they usually go until late in the evening."

"That's okay," Elsie replied. "I can find something to do around here."

"No, I've got a better idea," he said. He had an idea. "How would you feel about a day at the spa tomorrow?"

Her eyes lit up immediately.

"Really?" she asked.

Oliver nodded. "Yes, really. I feel bad that I won't be able to spend time with you tomorrow. Plus, you deserve some spoiling."

"You're too sweet to me, Ollie," Elsie said.

"Anything for my girl," he replied, as he leaned in to kiss her.

I mean that, too, he thought. *Anything.*

Chapter Twenty-Two

Ollie

After a brutal workout and several hours of grueling training with his team, Oliver was finally home. It was almost nine at night, but it felt much later. Every muscle in his body was sore and the intensity of the drills had renewed a bit of pain in his recovering knee. He did his best to keep his weight off of it as he took a shower and crawled into bed. Sleep was coming soon. He could feel it. But he didn't want to close his eyes until he at least called Elsie to see how her day was.

He dialed her up and relaxed into his pillows as the phone rang.

"Hello, handsome," Elsie said, picking up after just two rings.

"Hi, beautiful," Oliver replied. "How was your day?"

"Let's see. I was picked up this morning at my hotel by a limousine and taken to a spa," she said. "I then spent the better part of the day getting massaged and pampered. I don't think I have a single knot in any one of my muscles right now. So my day was beyond amazing, to say the least. Thank you again for spoiling me. It was really nice."

"You're very welcome," Ollie said, as he scooted himself up to a seated position with his back leaning against the headboard. "I'm glad to hear that you enjoyed it. A massage sounds pretty amazing right now."

"Did you have a tough training today?" she asked, sounding concerned. He loved that she cared.

"Yeah, harder than I was expecting. Coach ran us ragged and I learned that I'm still not one hundred percent." Ollie put a pillow underneath his right leg to elevate it, helping to ease the throbbing a bit. "My knee is a little sore actually. First time in a while."

"That's normal," Elsie said. "You're still healing. It could take months before you don't feel any pain at all. As long as it's not excruciating, then it's nothing to worry about. Take some ibuprofen and relax."

"Are those the doctor's orders?" Ollie joked.

"Yep, you know it," she said, laughing.

"I wish I could see you tonight," Ollie said. "But I'm afraid I'd fall asleep before I made it out of the front door."

"It's okay. I'm so relaxed and already curled up under the covers here at the hotel," she said, letting out a yawn. "Can I see you tomorrow, though?"

"Definitely," Ollie said, feeling his eyes get heavier by the second. "I've got a meeting with one of my sponsors in the morning, but that should only go until eleven. After that, I'm all yours. I'll take you out to lunch and a movie. How does that sound?"

"Sounds like a date," she said. "I'll check to see if there are any good movies playing. In the meantime, get some rest and elevate that leg."

"One step ahead of you," Ollie replied. "I've had a pillow under my knee the whole time we've been talking. You've trained me well, Doc."

"That's what I like to hear," Elsie said. "You know, I was thinking about you today and I've got to say, it's much more fun dating you than it is treating you as a patient."

Oliver smiled, recalling the night before and the amazing sex they'd had. It almost got him hard just thinking about it.

"That's an understatement," he replied, with a chuckle. "Way more fun."

"Okay, well have a good night," Elsie said. "Sleep tight."

"You, too, gorgeous." Ollie's eyes were almost fully closed now, but he managed to at least end the conversation before falling asleep. "Goodnight. I'll see you tomorrow."

He hung up and then set his phone on the night stand. Within seconds, he was sound asleep.

***

It was still dark in Oliver's room when something woke him up. A beam of light entered through the open crack of his bedroom door. The brightness washed over his face, pulling him out of his deep sleep. Someone was standing in the doorway. He could only see their silhouette, but it was clearly a female. Tall and skinny. Oliver sat up in his bed and squinted against the incoming light.

"Elsie?" he asked.

The response he received was immediate. "No, sorry to disappoint you."

The woman flipped the light switch, illuminating Oliver's bedroom. Standing there, wearing sweat pants and a loose-fitting tank top, was Nikki.

"Nikki? What are you doing here?" Oliver asked, his voice still groggy.

"I just came by to see how you were doing," she said, in her most innocent voice. "I had heard you guys had a pretty ruthless training session last night."

Ollie rubbed the sleep out of his eyes with the back of his hands. "So you show up in my house in the middle of the night?"

"It's not that late," she scoffed. "And actually, I was just about to leave. I tried to wake you up, but it seemed you were out like a light. I'm actually surprised you're awake right now."

This has got to be the weirdest thing she's ever done, he thought.

"What are you doing here?" he asked. His brain was still groggy with sleep and all he wanted to do was go back to it.

"I brought you those muffins you like on recovery day," she said, leaning against the door frame. "And, I guess I just felt like seeing you and didn't want to wait until tomorrow."

"Nikki, you see me almost every day," he said, beginning to lose his patience. "You can't just come in my house whenever you feel like it. That's beyond weird and I don't like it."

"What? Your old friend can't come surprise you?" Nikki asked the question as though showing up to someone's house in the middle of the night was something that normal people did.

"No, Nikki," he replied. "You can't."

A part of him wondered if he was dreaming. Although, Nikki standing in his room uninvited would be something he'd likely consider to be more of a nightmare than a dream. She was there, alright. Bad intentions and all. She was always up to something and in his gut, he had a feeling that this was no exception.

"Look, you need to leave." Ollie pointed toward the door she was already standing in front of. "I've got to get some sleep and there's no reason for you to be here right now. Unless there's a business emergency, then it's best you go."

Nikki pouted out her lower lip, seeking a bit of empathy from Ollie. It didn't phase him in the least, though. Her little tricks had no power over him any more. She gave it her best effort though, for full minute. Just standing there, with the most innocent and attention seeking expression on the planet. But Oliver didn't budge. He just sat in his bed with his arms crossed and his eyes half-closed, wishing for nothing more than to be able to fall back asleep.

"Fine," she finally said, realizing that Ollie would not be swayed. "I guess have a good night. See you tomorrow morning for the sponsorship meeting."

"Sounds good," he replied, abruptly. "See you then."

Nikki turned and began to walk out of the bedroom, but Ollie called out, stopping her in her tracks.

"Hey, Nikki," he said. "Hold up."

She stopped and looked over her shoulder. "Yeah? What is it, Oliver?"

"Do I need to amend your contract?" he asked. "I don't want you coming over without permission ever again."

"I won't do it again." Nikki nodded in agreement, but there was a gleam in her eye and the outside of her lips curled into an evil-looking grin. Ollie had seen the expression before. It was usually when Nikki was pissed off beyond belief but trying her best to hide it.

"Sleep tight," she said, as she stepped the rest of the way out and closed the bedroom door behind her.

That woman is crazy, he thought, listening to Nikki's steps as she made her way downstairs and out the front door. *And not the good kind of crazy. Whatever, though. I'm going back to sleep. I'll just pretend this weird incident didn't happen. Besides, I've got a lot to look forward to tomorrow. I get to see Elsie.*

Chapter Twenty-Three

Ollie

After a few hours of schmoozing with the new sponsors, Oliver and Nikki stepped out the front doors of The Bandit's manager's office. Ollie was still a bit tired from the night before. He hadn't slept well after Nikki had left his home. He'd tossed and turned the rest of the evening, trying to figure out why she'd really been there in the first place. It just didn't make sense.

"Oliver, why are you being so quiet?" Nikki asked, as the two walked across the parking lot.

"Just a little bit tired, I guess," he said.

He considered bringing up the weird midnight visit from the evening before, but knew that he wasn't going to get any answers from her. She'd just tell him what she had said then, which was basically that she had missed him and wanted to see him and muffins. But he knew there was more to it than that. In his gut, he *knew*.

"I hope you're excited about how well that meeting just went with the sponsors," Nikki said, her face beaming. "We just tagged another million dollars onto your contract and all you have to do is wear that company's brand of glove when you're playing."

"Yeah, can't argue with that," he said, unlocking the driver's door of his SUV. "Nothing wrong with easy money."

Nikki's car was parked next to his, but she didn't walk up to it. Instead, she stood next to Oliver as though she was expecting something.

"I guess have a good day," Ollie said, hopping into the driver's seat.

Nikki held the door open, moving in close to Oliver.

"Can I spend the rest of the afternoon with you?" she asked, batting her eyelashes.

"No, sorry, I can't," he said. "I've got plans."

"With *Elsie?*" she growled.

"Yes, actually," he replied. "With Elsie."

"Whatever." Nikki spun around and marched over to her car. She started it up and slammed on the gas, causing the tires to squeal on the concrete as she sped out of the parking lot.

What has gotten into her? Ollie thought.

He pulled out his cell phone to see a handful of calls and texts that he had missed during the sponsorship meeting. One of the calls was from Sean. It was odd to get a call from him, since they spent so much time together during training anyway. Ollie decided to call him back right away.

"Hey, buddy." Sean sounded excited when he picked up Oliver's call. "Man, I thought you were famous before but now you're like the king of social media. Why didn't you tell me you were getting back together with Nikki? I thought you were with Elsie."

"Wait, what?" Oliver asked, in utter confusion. "What are you talking about?"

"Seriously?" Sean laughed. "Nikki posted that picture of you guys last night and it's gone viral. Over a million 'likes' in one day. That's one way to tell the world who you're dating, I guess."

Ollie sat silent for a moment, trying to absorb what his friend was telling him. But it didn't make any sense.

"I'm not dating Nikki," Oliver said. "I have no clue what you're talking about."

"Really? Because she put up a picture online of you guys laying together in bed. Nothing too risque. It was just you two cuddled up."

"What in the hell are you talking about, man?" Oliver was overwhelmed with confusion, but desperately trying to put the pieces together.

"You really don't know?" Sean asked, his voice loosing the upbeat quality he usually had. "The picture was a selfie she'd taken. She posted it with a comment that said something about how she was waking up from a nap with her boyfriend."

"Are you joking me?" Ollie asked. "You better be messing with me right now, Sean."

"No, I'm not," he said. "Why would I do that? I was kind of excited that you guys were back together, so I was calling to say congratulations. You liked the picture, so I thought it was legit."

"We *aren't* back together. Nikki and I haven't been back together since I broke it off a year ago." Oliver's confusion was quickly turning into anger. His heart was beating quickly. "Can you send me what Nikki posted? She has access to all my social media."

"I can, but like I said, all you have to do is go online," Sean explained. "Just type in your name and I'm sure it'll come up."

"Thanks," Ollie said. "I'll call you later."

He hung up the phone and immediately got online.

What has Nikki done? He thought, as he typed his name into the search engine.

Just like Sean had said, the Internet had blown up about "Oliver Lance's love affair with his personal assistant, Nikki." His eyes scanned down the screen of his phone. The headline of each article was similar, so he clicked on one of them. The first thing that popped up on the website was a photo. It was clearly the one that Sean had been referring to.

"What the hell," Ollie whispered, his eyes focusing. "No way."

On the left side of the photo was Nikki. Her arm was in the shot, as she held her phone to take the selfie. She was smiling playfully. Her hair was in disarray and she wasn't wearing make up. She was wearing a loose-fitting tank top that left little to the imagination. But that part of the image isn't what disturbed him the most. On the right side, laying directly next to Nikki, was Oliver. He was on his back with his blankets pulled up to his chin. He was sound asleep in his bed.

This has got to be some kind of joke, he thought.

His gaze moved down to the caption at the bottom of the photo, where Nikki had written, "Waking up with my amazing boyfriend, Ollie. He's still sleeping. Football season starts in two days! He needs his rest!"

The little heart was filled in with Oliver's name right next to it, indicating that he liked the picture. There was even a comment, "You're too good to me, babe!" from his account. He suddenly regretted giving Nikki access to his social media. She'd even pretended to be him for this little stunt.

Oliver's vision turned red and the phone dropped out of his hand and onto his lap. Everything began to add up. The weird visit from Nikki the night before was no random occurrence, just as he had suspected. He recognized her tank top in the photo and it was the same one she had been wearing when he'd woken up to find her standing in the doorway of his bedroom. She hadn't been stopping by for just a visit, though. She'd come in to snap a picture of the two of them in bed. Nikki was trying to sabotage him.

He picked up his phone and quickly surfed the Internet for a bit, checking to see just how far this rumor had spread. Sean had been right. It was everywhere and already trending on social media sites. The public was eating up the story. It was juicy gossip and that's what people love. The juicier the better.

Oliver became deeply angry. His privacy had been invaded by Nikki. But then someone else entered his mind. Someone who would be just as affected by this gossip as he was.

"Shit," he whispered. "Elsie. She's going to see this."

Ollie started up his car and pointed it in the direction of her hotel. It was a twenty-minute drive and he feared he was already too late. Even so, he had to talk to her and explain things.

His heart raced as he pulled onto the highway. His hands were shaking with emotion.

That crazy bitch, Nikki, he thought. *She's finally gone too far.*

As Ollie made his way across town, he called up the woman who'd started this mess. She answered her phone after just one ring, with a chirpy "Hello!"

"Nikki, what in the hell have you done?" he shouted, cutting off a car on the highway.

"What do you mean?" Nikki replied. Innocence dripped off every word.

"The photo," Ollie stated, abruptly. "The one you took last night when I was *asleep*. What's wrong with you? Are you insane?"

"Oh, no, honey," she said. "I'm not insane."

"I'm *not* your honey," Oliver snapped back.

"I just thought I'd get a cute picture of us together," she said. "I didn't see the harm."

"Nikki, your *cute picture* is all over the Internet and it's telling a lie," he growled. "I am not your boyfriend. I am your employer and that's all."

She was silent for a moment, but then spoke up. "It's not that big of a deal, Ollie. Who cares if people think I'm your girlfriend?"

"*I* care." Ollie was gripping the steering wheel so tightly that his knuckles had become white.

"Well then I'm sorry," she replied. "I wasn't trying to upset you."

This has to end, he thought. *I can't let this crap continue. She's ruining everything that's I care about in my life. I don't care how good of a manager she is. She's gone way too far this time.*

"Nikki, it's done," he said.

"What? What do you mean?" she asked. Fear trickled into her voice.

"You're done, Nikki," Oliver repeated. "You're fired. You no longer work for me. As of today I am not your employer."

"Are you joking, Ollie? Really? Come on, you aren't going to do that."

"I just did," he said. "You've pushed and you've pushed and you finally went over the line. You had no right coming into my home last night and doing what you did."

"It was just a silly picture. Don't overreact. Besides, we have a contract, Oliver," she said, her voice getting louder. "You *can't* fire me."

Oliver chucked, shaking his head. "You posted a photo of us online telling everyone that we are a couple. That's a total sham. By doing that, you've broken our contract. I have every right to let you go. If you want to try to fight it, then fine. But I'd recommend reading the fine print first and getting a damn good lawyer."

He knew the contract between Nikki and himself quite well. He'd spent the better part of an afternoon going over it with his lawyer before signing. He wanted to be quite sure that having Nikki work for him wouldn't end up biting him in the butt. It turned out that his concerns had not been in vain.

"You're really firing me?" she asked, sounding more angry than sad. "I thought we were friends, Ollie."

"Anyone who would want to deliberately sabotage my love life is no friend of mine," he said. "I'm going to hang up now, but not before I ask one question."

"What?" she growled.

"Why did you do it?" he asked. "Why would you do something like this? It doesn't make any sense to me."

"I was sick and tired of seeing you with that whore physical trainer," she said angrily. "I should have known when I'd hired her that you'd get starry eyed over the bitch. And look, I was right. Here you are, bowing down to her like some kind of loser. You're a loser, Ollie. That's all you are. You might be able to fool the general public, but you can't fool me. Of all the girls you could get, you choose some hillbilly from a podunk town in Iowa? Good choice, Oliver. You could have had me, but now you've gone and screwed it up."

"First off, Elsie is neither a whore nor a bitch," he said. He was lucky he could see straight enough to drive. Rage rippled through him in waves. "Don't you dare say anything like that ever again. And second off, you're right. I could have had you. But I didn't want you, Nikki. You're manipulative and cruel and I'm beginning to wonder if there's a soul underneath that skin of yours. It doesn't matter now, though. You're gone, Nikki. Forever."

He hung up the phone without waiting for her response and then tossed it over to the passenger seat. Immediately, Nikki tried calling back. Over and over again, his phone rang. She must have tried at least ten times before he reached over and muted the ringer. He pressed hard on the gas, urgently driving to Elsie's hotel.

"I hope she's still there and that she hasn't seen that picture yet," he whispered to himself. "Please, please, please..."

Chapter Twenty-Four

Elsie

Elsie had been waiting impatiently all morning. She was excited to see Oliver later that afternoon, once he was through with his meeting with the sponsors. In an effort to kill some time, she'd taken a walk around town, casually seeing the sights. She'd enjoyed a coffee and some breakfast at a little diner near the hotel, then strolled through the neighborhoods, soaking up the warm morning sunshine.

When she got back to her room at around eleven, she decided to get ready for her lunch date. Since it was just lunch and not a fancy dinner, she dressed in dark jeans and a light blue blouse. It wasn't too dressy, but also not too casual. Plus, she thought the blouse looked super sexy on her and she knew that Ollie would love the way her butt looked in the tight jeans.

I've got an hour, she thought, crawling onto the bed and picking up her cell phone from the nightstand. *What do I do for an hour?*

So she did what anybody would do if they had a little bit of time to kill and they were holding their phone in their hands. She went straight to the Internet to check her news feed on her social media accounts. It would be the same old thing, she knew, but it at least would entertain her for the time being. She read the latest updates from her friends, laughed at a few cat videos, and then sat up straight in the bed when she saw a trending post about The Bandit's star quarterback.

Elsie didn't even bother reading any more of the headline before clicking on the link. It sent her to a webpage where she was greeted with a picture. Not just any picture, though, but one of Oliver and Nikki. Her heart turned to lead and sunk into her stomach. Her throat went dry and she tried to swallow, but couldn't.

"What is this?" she whispered.

As if the picture itself wasn't enough, she then caught a glimpse of the comment that Nikki had written underneath.

Why is she calling Oliver her boyfriend? She thought. *This has to be an old photo.*

Elsie then scrolled back to the top of page to check the date. It had been posted just twelve hours before. It was as fresh as an open wound. Her chest tightened and she could suddenly hear her heart pumping blood past her eardrums. Pure, raw emotion filled her. It was jealousy, combined with anger and topped off with hurt, confusion and betrayal.

"This can't be," she said, out loud.

Elsie then backed out of the website and began searching the Internet for any information she could find on Oliver. She was welcomed by exactly what she feared; more of the same. She found the original photo and found that Oliver had liked it and even commented on it.

"You're too good to me, Babe!" Each word was a knife to her heart. It was suddenly impossible to breathe.

The photo was everywhere and so was the news that Nikki and Oliver Lance were a couple. It was obvious she'd been duped and lied to. She'd never felt so sick or used in her life.

It didn't take but a few minutes before the damn of dignity that was holding back her emotions finally broke. Tears burst out of her eyes and flowed down her cheeks, ruining the makeup that she'd spent so much time making perfect for Oliver.

They're all the same, she thought. *All guys. Even the ones who you think are something different.*

Heartbroken, the only thing Elsie wanted to do was go home. The thought of facing Oliver made her sick to her stomach. She didn't want to see him again. She didn't want to hear his name or see his face. The only thing she really wanted was to be able to move on with her life and do everything she could not to even think about him.

"I shouldn't have come out here," she said, as she hopped onto her computer. "I should have known better. I'm just a notch in Oliver's bedpost, just like I feared."

Once her laptop had started up, so went to the website to order a plane ticket back home. The flights were booked, though, at least for the next two days. So she bought the soonest ticket available, which had her leaving the day after next at five in the morning.

That'll have to do, she thought.

She wiped the tears from her cheek, but it didn't do any good. It would have been more effective to sweep the ocean back with a broom. They just kept coming and the agony inside of her only got worse with each passing minute. The more she thought about it, the more intense her emotions became.

How could he do this to me? She thought, as she paced her room. *Was he dating Nikki the whole time? I opened myself up and all he did was take advantage of me.*

Even though it was two days until her flight out of San Francisco, she went ahead and began packing her bags anyway. She wanted to be as ready as possible when the time finally came to leave. Her urge to be home was powerful, even more so than when she had left for college. She couldn't wait to see her parents and Uncle Frank. Suddenly, going back to work at her clinic seemed more like a vacation. Or at the very least, it was something familiar and didn't hurt.

She grabbed her phone and for a fleeting moment, considered calling Oliver and confronting him about the incident, but the idea left her mind as soon as it had come.

She decided she wouldn't give him the time of day. He didn't deserve it.

"Screw this," she said, tossing the phone onto her bed. "I need to go for a walk or something. Get some air."

Elsie stepped into her tennis shoes and opened the door to the room. She'd hardly had a chance to close the door behind her before the sound of footsteps caused her to look down the hallway. There, running toward her at breakneck speed, was Oliver. He was dressed in a black suit and his tie was over his shoulder, flowing back like a cape.

What the hell is he doing here? She asked herself.

Ollie ran up and slid to a halt, coming toe-to-toe with Elsie. He was panting and out of breath. A few drops of sweat ran down his forehead.

"Elsie, thank god you're here," he said. "We need to talk."

Seeing him in person made her even angrier and she felt like slapping him right across the face.

"We don't need to talk," she said, swallowing back her tears. "We don't need to do anything. We're done, Ollie. I saw your damn picture with Nikki. You're a disgusting dirt bag of a man and you have no business being in my life."

"Elsie, please. You have to let me explain," Ollie begged. "It's not what it looks like."

"Go away, Oliver," she said, crossing her arms. "I mean it. You've hurt me so badly. The fact that you'd sleep with Nikki and call her your girlfriend while you and I were dating me makes me sick. I've got enough going on in my life and I certainly don't need this. Please, just leave. Go home and don't ever call me again. I'm doing the same."

Ollie sighed, looking defeated. "Please. Let me tell you what happened. I wasn't sleeping with Nikki and I wasn't dating her. I haven't been with her for over a year. She snuck into my room last night and..."

Elsie cut him short. "Oh yeah, Oliver. That makes total sense. She 'snuck' into your room, huh? Did she also accidentally drop her panties and take off her shirt? Did she happen to sneak under your covers while she was at it? I hate when those kind of accidents happen."

She placed her hands onto Oliver's chest and pushed him hard. It forced him to take a few steps backwards.

"You have to trust me, Elsie," he said, moving back toward her. "Please. Nothing happened last night. Nikki is crazy. She's trying to ruin my life because she's jealous of you."

"You want me to trust you, Ollie?" Elsie felt another wave of tears coming on, but she did her best to ignore it. "How am I supposed to do that? You think I don't know your history with women? You're a player, Oliver. I knew that when I first looked you up online after we met."

"Elsie, it wasn't me-"

"But I wanted to give you the benefit of the doubt. So for three months, I ignored what everybody already knew about you. Do you know why I did that, Ollie? I ignored it because I thought I had gotten to know you. The *real* you. I thought I had gotten to know the Oliver Lance that the public didn't have a clue about. For the last couple of weeks, I was absolutely certain that you weren't the womanizing player that everybody had made you out to be." She was shouting now, but she didn't care. "But I had been duped. I guess I should only blame myself, though. I should have realized that guys like you never change."

Oliver stayed silent the entire time. His shoulders were slumped forward and he looked sadder than Elsie had ever seen him. She didn't care. There was no way that he was more upset than she was.

She pointed down the hallway. "You need to leave."

"What about you?" he asked, not moving a step. "Are you leaving?"

"Am I leaving?" she snapped back. "What do you care?"

"I don't want you to go home before you at least let me tell you the whole story of what happened," he begged. "Please."

"I don't need or want the story," she said, shaking her head. "I saw the story this morning on the web. Trust me, that was enough."

Two heads popped out of doors along the hallway.

"Please, just leave so I can get on with my life as you so obviously have with yours." Her hands were shaking she was so angry. "Good luck with your season. I hope your knee stays healthy."

After saying that, she turned and went back inside of her hotel room. She closed and locked the door, then leaned against it. The tears she'd been holding back exploded out of her. Oliver knocked on the door, but she ignored it and ran to her bed. With her face buried in her pillow, she just cried. She cried until her eyes were dry and the pillow case was soaked. By the time the waves of emotion had passed, Ollie had stopped knocking on the door and the room was silent.

Elsie rolled over and sighed. The word "heartbroken" wouldn't have done any justice to the way she was feeling now. The man that she was beginning to love had shattered her trust and stomped on her heart. Now, she was forced to wait for two miserable days until she could catch her flight back home.

I can't believe Oliver did this to me, she thought. *When I get back home, I'm throwing away everything that reminds me of him. That's all I can do, is just pretend this fling with him never happened.*

Chapter Twenty-Five

Elsie

Two days later...

It was early in the morning. Elsie had hardly left her hotel room since the run in with Oliver in the hallway. She practically locked herself in there and only opened the door to allow room service in. It wasn't because she was suddenly afraid of the outside world, it was just that she didn't want to deal with it right then. She didn't want to have to fake a smile when ordering at a cafe, or really even talk to anyone.

Most of her time had been spent in bed, eating junk food and crying. She had tried watching an old movie, but it only depressed her. Everything seemed to remind her of Ollie. It didn't help that he had continually tried to call her and had left a bunch of messages, all of which she had ignored.

Why is this eating me up so bad? It's not like I've known Oliver for that long. She thought, as she packed the rest of her belongings into her suitcase. *But this hurts. This hurts a lot.*

There was only about ten minutes before she needed to leave for her flight. It was time. It was time to move on and forget about everything to do with Oliver Lance. Elsie got out her cell phone and ordered up a ride from Uber. Then she gathered her bags, threw her purse over her shoulder and stepped out of her room. She went straight down to the lobby and then outside to wait for her ride.

The sun was shining and the birds were chirping, but she didn't feel like she could relate to their excitement. All that sounded good was curling up into a ball on the floor of her apartment and sleeping for a full day. She figured that would be all she'd need, or at least all that she'd allow herself to have in order to get over this.

I can't let this take any more time away from my life than it already has, she thought.

As the minutes ticked by, Elsie noticed many people walking in and out of the hotel. Most of them were wearing Bandit's jerseys and hats, or at the very least they were sporting the team colors. It was the beginning of football season. Oliver would be playing his first game today.

Dammit, Elsie, she told herself. *Don't even think about him.*

Within a few minutes, her ride pulled up in a large black SUV. She got into the back seat with her luggage and was greeted by a young man with dark hair and a wide smile.

"Good morning!" he said, sounding way too cheery for how early it was. "Looks like you're headed to the airport. Elizabeth? Is that right?"

"Yes, please," she replied, looking out the window.

"You got it," the driver said, pulling away from the curb.

Elsie watched as the hotel panned out of view. A single tear fell down her cheek, but she quickly wiped it away. She'd had break ups before and she knew it would hurt for a while, but eventually it would be okay. It would only be a matter of time before the pain that was currently in her heart would be nothing more than a memory. She just needed to get through the worst of it.

"Do you mind if I turn on the radio?" The man behind the steering wheel looked up into the rear view mirror as he spoke.

"No, of course not," Elsie said. "Go for it."

Talk radio filled the interior of the car and it only took a second for Elsie to realize they were talking about sports. And of course, since it was the first day of the season, the announcers were talking about football. She tried not to listen, but it was impossible not to.

My only concern this year, John, is about the Bandit's new receiver, Demitri Jameson. The kid is fast, there's no doubt. But does he have the ability to break tackles and simply run the football? We saw him make some major mistakes in pre-season and that concerns me.

Don't let it concern you, Peter. Oliver Lance can put the football into any player's hands. I don't care if it's Jameson or Frosty the Snowman. Lance has an arm unlike any player in the league. I say don't worry about the rookie receiver. He'll be fine. The Bandit's still have what it takes to make it to the play offs.

John, I understand that you think Oliver Lance is like Superman. But we both know that he's been dealing with some things off of the field. From what I've heard, he's recently fired his sponsorship manager, Nikki Roberts. I guess this was the same girl he was dating? I don't know. Sounds like a lot of drama to me.

Well, Peter, let's just hope that the drama doesn't effect his ability to play the game.

Elsie's eyes widened and she scooted forward on her seat.

"Hey, did they just say that Oliver Lance fired his sponsorship manager?" Elsie asked the driver.

He nodded. "Yeah, apparently. It's weird. Two days ago they were dating and now he's fired her. Sometimes I wonder why this sort of thing makes headlines. I think the media should just leave people alone."

She sat back in her seat and pulled out her phone. Within seconds, she was online and trying to confirm what the sports announcers had just said. Sure enough, according to every major site that she landed on, Oliver Lance had fired Nikki. Apparently, they had had a personal disagreement that had conflicted with business.

The announcers on the radio continued to speak and Elsie's ears perked as they began to interview a player of the team.

We're here with Bandit's running back, Logan Whitman. Logan, how do you feel about the upcoming season and today's game?

Hey Peter. Hey John. Glad to be here. You know, I feel really good about today's game. We've been training hard and we're going to play the best we can out there. We'll give it a hundred and ten percent. Same as last season.

Do you worry about Lance's injury at the end of last season? We know he had a couple of bumps and bruises. Do you think he's ready?

Absolutely, he's ready. Physically and in every other way, too. To be honest, ever since he got back from his vacation, he's been happier than ever before. Ollie is a positive guy in general anyway, but this year even more so. I think that will show in the game. If your quarterback is happy, then so is everyone else.

Elsie nearly dropped her phone onto the floor. Based on what she had just heard, Oliver had been noticeably happier since returning from his "vacation". She couldn't be sure if that was because of her, but it definitely made her wonder. Still, though, it didn't matter. It didn't matter that he'd apparently just fired Nikki either.

"What's done is done," she whispered.

"I'm sorry, ma'am. What did you say?" The driver looked into the rear view mirror again.

"Nothing," she said. "I was talking to myself. Do you mind turning the radio off? I'm sorry, I kind of have a headache."

"No problem," he replied, turning the volume all the way down.

The car was now quiet, so Elsie closed her eyes and tried to relax. She didn't know long she'd stayed like that, or whether or not she fell asleep. But the next thing she knew, she was awakened to the sensation of the car stopping and the sound of a crowd of people.

Are we at the airport already? She thought, as she opened her eyes and glanced out the window.

Elsie expected to be parked at the drop off point at the airport, but looming outside, was a building as wide as a city block. Surrounding it were people wearing jerseys and hats, just like the ones she'd seen outside of her hotel a fifteen minutes before.

Are we seriously outside of the Bandit's stadium right now? She thought.

"Sir, what are we doing here?" she asked, looking toward the driver. Anger flared in her stomach. "I told you that I needed to go to the airport. We need to hurry or else I'll miss my flight."

The young man unbuckled his safety belt and then grabbed a white envelope from the glove compartment. After that, he turned around in his seat and handed the envelope to Elsie.

"What is this?" she asked, with a confused expression. "I don't have time for this. We need to go to the airport. *Now.*"

"Please, ma'am, let me explain," he said. "Inside of that envelope are two tickets to today's opening game."

"What?" she asked. "I have no clue what you're talking about."

"The tickets are compliments of Mr. Lance," he explained. "He paid me to pick you up from your hotel and to surprise you with them."

Oliver set this up? She thought.

Elsie opened the envelope and sure enough, there was a club-level ticket inside with a printed ticket price of over a thousand dollars. There was also another slip of paper.

"What's this?" she asked, pulling it out.

"That would be a first class plane ticket," he said, pushing his sunglasses up onto his forehead. "It leaves about an hour after the game ends."

"Oliver Lance gave this stuff to you to give to me?" Elsie asked, shaking her head. "How is that possible? How did he know you'd be picking me up?"

"Mr. Lance has many connections," the driver said. "It's not difficult when you're famous, you know? He did want me to tell you one thing, though. He said, and I quote, 'Elsie, please come to my game. Even if you don't want to talk to me, you'll still get to finally watch a live football game. And also, you'll get to fly home in first class afterwards. Remember what I said? Anything for my girl'."

"He told you to say all that?" Elsie asked, raising her eyebrows.

"I assure you, ma'am, I couldn't have made that up. Oliver made me repeat it to him several times to make sure that I wouldn't screw it up."

Elsie looked out the window once again. A line outside of the stadium was beginning to form as the crowd made their way in. The game would soon be starting.

Wow, she thought. *This is most certainly not what I was expecting.*

She sighed, glancing back toward the driver.

"Did he say anything else?" she asked.

"That was it," he said. "So, what are you going to do?"

"Why can't I just skip the game and use the first class ticket for later this afternoon?" she asked.

The driver gently took the envelop and tickets back from her. "Unfortunately, that wasn't part of the deal. Mr. Lance specifically said to only give you the plane tickets if you attend the game."

That totally sounds like something he'd do, she thought with a huff.

Elsie felt torn. For two days, her mind had been set on leaving as quickly as possible and never looking back, but this little surprise from Oliver had reminded her of the side of him that she'd grown to love over their time together.

Maybe he cares about me more than I realized, she thought. *I suppose I could at least watch the game. I don't have to talk to him at all. He'll be playing anyway. All I need to do is relax and watch a football game, root for the other team because I'm still mad at him, and then fly home in the comfort of first class.*

"Fine," Elsie said, snatching the tickets back from the driver. "I'll go to the game. Thanks for the ride."

She grabbed her bags and stepped out of the car. Before she could close the door, the driver said, "Let me know if you need a ride to the airport afterward."

"I think I'll be okay," she said, with a forced smile. "I do appreciate it, but I'd rather find someone who doesn't work in secret for Oliver. By the way, you're not getting a tip."

"Fair enough," he said, with a chuckle. "You have a good day."

"You too." Elsie closed the door and then got in line.

**

As Elsie made her way toward the box seats, she expected a number of things. She expected to watch a football game, to see Oliver playing, to get mad about what Oliver had done to her and maybe have a few drinks because of it. She was also pretty certain that she'd leave immediately after the game was over and get on that plane and head back home, where she belonged.

But when she stepped into the club seating, everything that she had been expecting flew straight out of the window as fast as Oliver could throw a football. Elsie stopped in the doorway of the room that overlooked the field and felt her knees turn to jello.

"Mom? Dad? Uncle Frank? Sis?" she asked, using the door frame to hold herself up as she looked around the room to see familiar faces that she wasn't expecting. "What are you all doing here?"

They turned to look and her mom jumped up out of her seat in excitement.

"Elsie! There you are! We thought you were going to miss kick off," her mom squealed, running over to get a hug. "Isn't this amazing? Check out how good of a view we have of the field!"

Elsie must have looked like she'd seen a ghost. As her mom pulled her in for a hug, Elsie glanced around the club seats, which were filled only with people she knew. In addition to her uncle and her parents, both of her sisters and all of her nieces and nephews were there. The kids ran over and hugged her legs.

"Aunt Elsie!" they squealed in unison.

"What is happening right now?" Elsie asked her mom. "I'm so confused."

Her mother pulled away and looked her in the eyes, unable to contain her excitement. "Your boyfriend, Oliver, flew us out here. He paid for everything, including airfare and our hotel. We haven't officially met him yet, but we did talk on the phone. I'd say you found yourself a keeper, Elsie."

Elsie took a few breaths, letting the surroundings soak in. "Oh."

Ollie did this? She thought. *For my family and me? Okay, this is a whole new level of kissing butt to get out of the dog house.*

"Come on, honey," her mom said, leading her toward the seats. "Everyone is here. Oliver said this was supposed to be a surprise for you. You have no idea how hard it was not to call you!"

Elsie approached her uncle, giving him a hug.

"Uncle Frank, how are you?" she asked, taking a seat next to him.

"I'm doing well, all things considered. My surgery is in a couple of days, but I'm feeling good about it now." He cleared his throat. "I'm happy to be here, though. The weather is perfect. It'll be a nice little vacation before surgery. You okay?"

"I'm in shock right now," she replied. "I had no idea Oliver was going to do this."

"He's a very nice guy," Frank said. "I see now why you like him so much."

Elsie parted her lips to tell him that she didn't *actually* like Oliver any more and that she wasn't even dating him, but decided against it. Her family was around her and they were as happy as could be. There was no point in ruining the beautiful moment by telling them the news about their breakup. To say she was surprised would have been an understatement. It almost felt like she'd walked into an episode of the Twilight Zone.

Is it possible that Oliver is actually as good of a man as I thought he was initially? She asked herself. *Was I the one in the wrong by not letting him explain himself and that picture of he and Nikki?*

These kind of questions flooded her mind and were only interrupted when the stadium began to cheer. She got up and looked out of the Plexiglas to the perfect view of the field. The Bandit's players jogged out onto the grass and the crowd went insane. Leading the group, was Oliver. He had his helmet tucked under his arm and his blonde hair bounced over his forehead as he ran.

Even from way up in the club seats, Elsie could see his smile. Her heart reached for him. It was strange and confusing. A few minutes before she had hated the guy and now, after seeing what he'd done for her and her family, she began to love him again. It was an uncomfortable and odd combination of emotions.

I can't cry here, she thought. *Not in front of my family. For all they know, everything between Ollie and I is going really well.*

She breathed in and exhaled slowly, releasing her tension. When she glanced to her side, she saw that her two nephews had their faces pressed against the glass. They were watching with wide eyes and admiration. The two little league players were seeing their first real game and from the best seats in the entire stadium.

"Are you guys excited?" Elsie asked them.

They both looked over and nodded eagerly. The youngest one spoke up. "This is so awesome, Aunt Elsie!"

"Who do you think is going to win?" Elsie asked.

He shrugged. "The Bandits, of course. Nobody can beat Oliver Lance."

She couldn't help but to smile in response. The kid was probably right. Nobody *could* beat the great Oliver Lance. When Elsie looked back out toward the field, she saw a young man in a suit step out onto the grass to begin singing the national anthem.

Ollie was standing on the sidelines with his team, holding his helmet over his heart. He kept his head down for most of the song, except the part when the girl began to sing "...and the rocket's red glare." It was then that he glanced up toward the club seats, or at least that was where he appeared to be looking. It was difficult to tell, because he was quite a distance away, but Elsie thought she could feel his gaze. She took a step back from the glass and resumed her seat next to her uncle.

I don't want him to know I'm here, she thought. *I'm still mad at him.*

"Everything okay, Elsie?" Uncle Frank asked, patting her knee.

"Yeah, Uncle Frank. Everything is fine. I'm just still getting over the shock of this," she said. "Who are you rooting for?"

"You know the Bandit's aren't exactly my team, but I'm rooting for them because if it wasn't for Oliver, I wouldn't be sitting here right now," he said, with a smile.

"Fair enough." Elsie smiled back. It was nice to see her uncle happy. "They do have a pretty good quarterback. From what I hear anyway."

Frank laughed and pulled her in for a one-armed hug. "It's nice to see you again, Elsie. I missed you. I know you've only been gone for a few days but it has been strange not having you around."

"I missed you, too, Uncle Frank," she said, with a sigh.

"Aunt Elsie! Aunt Elsie! The game is starting!" Her nephews squealed. "They're about to kick off!"

I guess it's time to find out how well his recovery actually went by how well he plays today, she thought, bringing her attention forward. *And time for me to figure out what the hell I'm going to do about my relationship with him.*

Chapter Twenty-Six

Elsie

A lthough Elsie had made the decision to cheer for the other team, she couldn't stick to it for very long. Her family had instantly become Bandit's biggest fans and the entire room became a riot of celebration with every completed pass that Oliver threw. By the time the second half had started, Elsie was cheering right along with them, rooting for Ollie and his team.

He was playing well, besides the fact that he did seem kind of nervous. Even the commentators had taken notice of it. They'd said several times that he appeared to be distracted and they'd caught him looking up toward the box seats on more than one occasion.

Is he looking for me? She'd asked herself each time they mentioned it. *He must be, right?*

The game clock continued on and by the two-minute warning in the fourth quarter, it was clear that the Bandit's were going to win. With a fourteen point lead, they weren't going to be caught. As the game drew to a close, Elsie was forced to make a decision. She could either head back to Iowa or she could stay there and give Oliver a chance to explain himself.

I'm so torn, she thought wishing that the big clock on the screen would just stop counting down.

Her family and everyone in the stadium in the stadium but her cheered as the game clock went to zero. Ollie had just won the first game of the season, and the first game since his accident. Elsie's nephews ran up to her, each one wrapping their arms around one of her legs.

"They won, Aunt Elsie!" they squealed. "Told you Oliver couldn't be beat."

"Yeah, you were right." She ruffled up their hair, chuckling to herself. "I guess he's pretty good, isn't he?"

The door to the club seating opened up behind her and she glanced back to see a man in a black suit. He was wearing a white dress shirt with a narrow blue tie.

"Good afternoon, everyone," he said, after clearing his throat to get everyone's attention. "I hope you all enjoyed the game. I work for the Bandit's. Oliver Lance has invited all of you down to the locker room for a tour. If you'd please follow me."

Elsie froze. This was the moment of truth. This was where she had to make her decision.

"Come on, Aunt Elsie," her youngest nephew said, tugging on her hand as he attempted to drag her toward the door. "We get to meet the team!"

It seems my decision has just been made, she thought, automatically following her nephew.

Elsie glanced back to the rest of her family. "Are you guys coming?"

Her mom's eyes lit up and she nodded her head. "Of course we are! We need to meet this boyfriend of yours!"

Elsie sighed, forcing her lips to curl into a smile. "Okay. Let's do it."

The group followed the suited man out of the door. As they made their way downstairs toward the locker room, Elsie became nervous but also excited. She found herself actually looking forward to seeing Oliver again after all he had done for her and her family that day.

At the very least, maybe I can thank him for all of this before I go home, she thought, justifying it to herself.

"Alright, everyone, we're here," the man said, as he held open the door of the locker room. "The players are just getting off of the field, so give them a little space.

Oliver is in there and waiting for you guys. He'll show you around."

Elsie and her family stepped into the locker room, led by her nephews. She hadn't seen those two boys so excited in their entire lives. Even on Christmas mornings, their smiles were never as wide as when they walked into a room full of their heroes.

They passed through a group of football players, who all stood at least a foot and a half taller than Elsie. They were still wearing their pads, too, which made them seem even larger. Her heart was beating in her chest as she scanned the room for Oliver.

Oh God, there he is, she thought, as her eyes focused across the room.

Ollie stood there, with one foot up on the wooden bench. He was chatting with his teammates, but glanced toward Elsie as soon as she was in view. Her heart leaped into her throat as they locked eyes. She felt the same tingling inside of her that she had the very first time she met him. It was as though she was seeing him for the first time. She didn't know what to do. It was like her feet were suddenly stuck in a bucket of molasses.

"Elsie, there's Oliver!" her nephew cried out.

Oliver approached them, his smile wide and his eyes as blue as ever. He kept his gaze locked onto Elsie as he got close. Her nephews released her hand and ran straight up to him.

"Oliver Lance! Oliver Lance!" they shouted.

Ollie chuckled and dropped to one knee to give each of them a hug. "Hey, guys. Did you enjoy the game?"

"It was amazing!" the oldest replied. "You killed it out there."

"I couldn't have done it without you two cheering me on," Oliver told them. "Let me say hi to your Aunt really quick, then I'll show you guys around. In the mean time, my buddy Sean here has something for you."

Sean walked up holding two small-sized jerseys. "What do you think of these?"

Her nephews slipped into the jerseys and gave each other a high five. Then Sean walked with the kids, and the rest of Elsie's family, to begin their tour. Meanwhile, Oliver stood up and approached Elsie, who was still weak in the knees.

"Hi," he said softly.

"Hi." The tone in her voice was hesitant.

Oliver took her hands in his, but she pulled them away.

"Elsie, please, let me talk to you," he said. "I'm asking for five minutes. That's all."

"You want to talk here?" she asked, looking around the locker room filled with strangers.

"No, let's go outside," he said, holding out his hand. "Please."

Elsie sighed, but took his hand. She followed Oliver out into the hallway just outside of the locker room. The hall was empty, minus a reporter and her news crew who were packing up after the game. They didn't even give the two of them the time of day. Ollie was still wearing his pads and jersey. His hair was a total mess and it looked like he hadn't shaved since she last saw him. Still, though, he looked hot as hell.

"What do you want to tell me, Ollie?" she asked softly. "I mean, I appreciate the surprise you gave my family, but that doesn't make up for what you did."

Oliver sighed, gazing into her eyes. "I'm going to tell you exactly what happened that night. You may or may not believe me, but I would never lie to you. I want you to know the truth."

"Okay," she said, crossing her arms.

"I went home that night after training," he said. "I was beyond exhausted and my knee was sore, so I crawled into bed. You and I chatted on the phone for a bit and then I fell asleep right after. I woke up in the middle of the night, and Nikki was in my room."

Elsie watched him explain the story and it really seemed to her like he was being genuine.

"She and I hadn't done anything at all. I had been sound asleep," Ollie continued. "She was standing in my doorway when the light from the hallway woke me up. She'd taken that picture of us before I'd awaken. I didn't even know about it at the time."

"How did she get into your house?" Elsie asked, trying to break the story open.

"She's my manager, she has a key to get in and grab gear or drop off contracts," he explained. "I didn't know how crazy she was until that night, so I was never worried about her having access to the house. Plus, we work together. Or, well, we *did* work together. I fired her."

"I heard," Elsie said.

"You did?" he asked, hope rising in his voice.

"It was on the radio." She crossed her arms.

"News travels fast." Ollie shook his head. "But that's what happened. Nikki has had it out for me ever since we broke up a year ago. I never knew she'd stoop so low, but apparently I shouldn't have put it past her."

"What about your comments on it?" she asked, her voice nearly breaking. She could believe Nikki would post the picture, but that he would reply? That was the part that hurt so much.

Oliver's eyes were on hers. "As my manager, she had access to my social media accounts. She did that. I don't even know my own password. It's supposed to be just for promotion stuff."

His eyes remained true as she watched for any sign of a lie. All she could see was a desperate pain that mirrored her own. Elsie believed him. She had to. He was clearly telling the truth.

"So you didn't do anything with her?" Elsie asked. "No kissing, no nothing?"

"Nothing at all," Ollie said. "I swear on my brother Michael that I did not touch her. And I fired her immediately after I found out about the photo."

Oh man, so does this make me the one in the wrong for not letting him explain himself before? She asked herself.

"Oliver, I was about to go back to Iowa," she said, as a few tears trickled down her cheeks. "You have a reputation and I guess I let that cloud my judgment of you."

"Look, Elsie, I *do* have a reputation with women," he said, placing his hands gently onto her shoulders. "But if there's anything to be learned about what happened with Nikki and that stupid photo, it's that most of the time a reputation doesn't mean anything. It's contrived from gossip."

Elsie held her breath, not wanting to miss a word of what he had to say next. The feel of his hands on her shoulders were the only thing keeping her from floating away.

"Sure, there was a period in my career where I might have used my fame and power to meet women. I was young, though. A different man. I thought that getting drunk and meeting girls was the end that justified the means. But I was wrong, Elsie. When I met you, I learned that there's something in this world that I truly can't live without. Something that transcends the wants and needs of my previous life. It's you. It's you, Elsie. It always has been and it always will be. You're the only thing I need."

Elsie swallowed and the tears that streamed down her face became ones of joy. Ollie reached forward and gently wiped her cheek with his thumb.

"Do you understand now?" he asked. "I'd do anything for you. I'd go jump off of a building to break my leg, just so that I can go back to Iowa for rehab. I'd go to the end of the world. I'd..."

"Just stop talking," she said, reaching forward to grab his chest pads.

She pulled him toward her and stood up on her tip toes, bringing her lips to his. The kiss instantly washed away the torment that had been filling her for days. She pressed into him and Ollie held her close. His scent, his touch, his everything. He was all that she needed, too.

After a moment, she slowly broke the kiss, but kept his eyes locked with his. Oliver brought his hands to her cheeks. "Elsie, I love you," he said, and she watched as his eyes welled up with tears. "I love you so much."

Elsie felt the world shrink down and once again, the only people in the entire universe were the two of them. Her heart thumped behind her rib cage, reaching toward Oliver. She knew it right then, that this was the man she was meant to be with. Sure, she'd questioned it for a while. But maybe that was what it took for her to see just how much he cared and the lengths he'd go to keep her.

"I love you, too, Oliver Lance," she whispered.

He leaned and kissed her again. Her heart swelled as the two embraced in the hallway outside of the locker room. It was the perfect moment. The kind of moment that made her realize that all of the trials and tribulations in her life were not in vain and in fact, had a purpose. They'd brought her there.

Elsie felt someone grab her leg and she opened her eyes, pulling away from Ollie. She looked down to see her youngest nephew standing there in his new jersey, wearing an innocent smile.

"Aunt Elsie, can I please borrow Oliver Lance for a minute?" he asked. "I want him to take me out onto the field."

Elsie laughed, wiping away the tears of joy from her face.

"Yeah, you may borrow him," she said, smiling toward Oliver. "But you have to promise to bring him back."

"I promise," her nephew said, as he took Oliver's hand and began dragging him away.

Ollie beamed as he looked at Elsie.

"You're coming with, aren't you?" he asked. "You want to see the field up close and personal? I guess you could call it a tour of my office."

Elsie nodded. "I'd love nothing more."

She followed them out to the field, where her family and some of the players were already standing around. She watched as Ollie put one of her nephews on each of his shoulders and paraded them around the grass. Those boys were in a heaven that they didn't know existed until now and it was all because of Oliver, their hero.

Oliver Lance, she thought, smiling. *I think you might be my hero too.*

Epilogue

Four months later...

The Bandit's were behind by three points. With only thirty seconds left in the fourth quarter, it was starting to look like the championship trophy might end up being handed over to The Rockets instead. But after the hard fought season, Oliver wasn't about to throw in the towel. He couldn't. Not with his girl standing on the sidelines watching.

Come on, Ollie, Elsie thought, bundled inside of her Bandits trainer down coat.

The wind howled, adding to the noise of the crowd. It was bitter cold. The kind of January day that should have been spent indoors. If it wasn't for a game like this, that's where Elsie would have been, but no amount of cold weather or rain and thunder would have kept her from being on that sideline and rooting her boyfriend on. Besides, it was her job to be there now.

He needed her there. He'd told her that she was his lucky charm and she was starting to believe it. The Bandit's had won every season game that she'd attended, and had lost the few that she wasn't there for. The team had even joked that they should make it a job requirement to be on the field so that they would never lose again.

It was the Bandit's last possession of the game. Oliver huddled with his team and then they stepped up to the line.

"Blue, forty-two!" he shouted. "Hut. Hut. Hike!"

The ball was snapped and Ollie took a few steps back, scanning the field.

"Come on, Oliver," Elsie whispered. "You can do this."

Since it was first down, Elsie had expected him to do a running play. Something safe. But with only thirty seconds on the clock, 'safe' was no longer an option. She watched as the rookie receiver, Demitri Jameson, went long. He ran down the field almost forty yards and didn't seem to be stopping any time soon. Oliver wound up and then launched the ball toward him. It was a bomber. Elsie clenched her jaw nervously as the football soared through the air.

It was a hard and deep throw.

Oh God, she thought. *Please, please, don't be intercepted.*

Demitri continued to run deep and then turned right as the ball dropped. Elsie winced, afraid to watch, but just as afraid to look away. Ollie's throw was accurate, just like always, and the football landed directly into his receiver's hands.

"No freaking way," Elsie said out loud.

The crowd echoed her sentiment and began to scream so loud that the ground shook. A lineman for The Rockets dove at Demitri, but he spun, avoiding the tackle. He faced the end-zone and sprinted toward it. Each yard that he gained, the crowd got louder. By the time he was at the ten yard line, he couldn't be caught. He stepped into the end-zone and Elsie felt her knees practically buckle beneath her.

"He did it," she said, shaking her head. "Oh my God. He did it!"

A deafening roar filled the stadium. The Bandit's had won the super bowl. Elsie watched as the team rushed the field, jumping and celebrating. The entire place buzzed with an energy she hadn't experienced before. It didn't feel real. She had been sure that The Bandits wouldn't have been able to come back from that. But, just like always, Oliver somehow made it happen. She couldn't hold back her emotion and within seconds, Elsie was crying with joy.

The entire team, from water boys to the other trainers to the entire defensive line, sprinted onto the field in celebration. Oliver saw her immediately and pushed past his teammates in order to get to her. When he did, he lifted her up above his head and spun her in a circle.

The crowd chanted in the back ground, *Ollie Lance! Ollie Lance! Ollie Lance!*

But even though there were forty thousand people calling his name, Oliver didn't seem distracted. His eyes were only on Elsie. She was his focus. He set her back down on the ground and leaned in close.

"I love you, Doc," he said. "This all would mean nothing if you weren't here."

Immediately after, a group of Bandit's players surrounded Oliver and lifted him from the ground. They held him on their shoulders and paraded him around the field, while Elsie watched with a smile. The celebration went on for a while, but when it finally calmed down, it was time for Oliver to accept the trophy. Elsie pressed to the front of the news cameras that surrounded him in order to get a good view.

The team's manager was there, holding the trophy and standing next to Oliver. The crowd went quiet as Ollie took the microphone that was handed to him.

"It's been a long road," he said, his voice booming over the loud speakers. "This was a huge win for The Bandits and I certainly can't take all of the credit. I couldn't have done this without my amazing teammates, my managers, my fans and of course, my beautiful girlfriend."

He looked toward Elsie and the crowd went wild once again.

"Come on up here, Doc," he said, motioning her toward him.

"No, no." Elsie blushed, as she looked at the ground.

"Seriously, Doc," he said. "Someone help her through the crowd."

The news people stepped aside and Elsie walked through the aisle they had created. She went up to Oliver, her face burning from embarrassment.

"This girl right here," he said, causing the stadium to go quiet again. "She's the reason I'm standing here today. Without her, I would be nobody."

Oliver took the trophy from his manager's hands and then held it in the air.

"Without her, this trophy would not be in possession of The Bandit's," he shouted, and the stadium roared again.

Oliver passed the trophy back to his manager and then brought his attention to Elsie.

"She's the best thing in the world," he said into the microphone. "And I can't ever let her go. That's why there's something I need to ask her."

Ollie dropped to one knee and took Elsie's hand in his. Her eyes widened and her jaw dropped. There, in front of tens of thousands of people, Oliver asked her the question she'd always wanted to hear.

"Elsie, will you marry me?"

She brought her hand over her mouth. The stadium went silent. They were just as curious about her answer as Oliver was. She was so overwhelmed with happiness that she could hardly speak, so she just nodded as tears burst out of her eyes.

"Is that a yes?" he asked, sounding nervous for the first time in his life.

"Yes," she managed to say. "Yes, of course, Ollie. Of course I'll marry you."

As soon as she said the words, Oliver stood back up and pulled her in for a kiss. The stadium roared to life once again, but this time, it wasn't in celebration of the big win. It was because they had just gotten to witness one of the most beautiful things in the world. They'd just seen true love.

Made in the USA
San Bernardino, CA
03 June 2017